THE ENGLISH LADY MURDERERS' SOCIETY

To patricia
with the Author's
best wishes

Dec 2011

Also by JIM WILLIAMS

Writing as Richard Hugo

The Hitler Diaries
Last Judgment
Farewell to Russia
Conspiracy of Mirrors published in USA
    as *The Gorbachev Version*

Writing as Alexander Mollin

Lara's Child

Writing as Jim Williams

Scherzo
Recherché
The Strange Death of a Romantic
The Argentinian Virgin

Non-fiction

A Message to the Children (a guide to writing
    your autobiography)
How to be a Charlatan

The English Lady Murderers' Society

A Novel by

JIM WILLIAMS

QUARTET BOOKS

First published in 2011 by
Quartet Books Limited
A member of the Namara Group
27 Goodge Street, London W1T 2LD

A catalogue record for this book
is available from the British Library

ISBN   978 0 7043 7251 1

Typeset by Antony Gray
Printed and bound in Great Britain by
T J International Ltd, Padstow, Cornwall

TO SHIRLEY

a ruby wedding present

How to Form a Woman's Group

1

The villages of France are full of English murderers. They flee there after killing the past and sometimes slaughtering their inconvenient relatives. The weather is better than England, though there's a worry over the exchange rate. Unfortunately no crime is perfect.

Janet found herself on a sunny June morning breasting a hill on the road from Lavelanet to Quillan in the wooded foothills of the Pyrenees. In front of her was the castle of Puybrun and below it the village with its lake and camping site. Wheat fields stretched beyond the village to a rugged limestone escarpment glittering with light, and everything was beautiful.

She arrived after a drive of God knew how many hundreds of miles with umpteen bags and cases crammed in the back of her VW Golf. All the while she told herself, 'I must change this car,' because the journey through France had been slow and tedious. With a right-hand drive, she couldn't see to overtake, and was stuck for miles behind lorries with enormous trailers. Whether she could get rid of a right-hand drive car was another matter. And in any case would she be staying long enough to make a swop worthwhile? She feared she might have to reconcile herself to twelve months of driving along narrow country lanes at the speed of a tractor.

From the main road a narrow lane, the rue du Cimetière, led presumably to a cemetery. A row of three cottages stood on one side and an old barn on the other. Her own house (if that was the right expression for a rented place she'd never seen before) was shuttered and in darkness, and the power was off. The tiled floor was crunchy with dirt and dead insects. If she could find the fuse box, she was capable of switching everything on, but the instructions for finding it needed enough light to see by. And there wasn't of course: not in the absence of electricity.

'I must have a cup of tea,' she said aloud, and worked out a plan for getting one: the old can-you-spare-some-sugar ploy; though did anyone really do that these days: just turn up at a neighbour's door asking for small necessities: tea, sugar, flour? It smacked of running out of housekeeping money until Friday's pay packet; of the War and rationing; of stories in *Woman's Realm*. Of her mother's life in fact.

It seemed implausible in this day and age but it would have to do.

Belle answered the door to a trim attractive woman with auburn hair, who wore a cream blouse and well-cut black slacks; good quality if not absolutely the best; Principles not Jaeger for example (but hadn't Principles gone out of business?); not that Belle shopped there except for accessories. They didn't have clothes in her size. Nowhere had clothes in her size.

The stranger gave a smile and said, 'Hullo, I've just arrived in the village and was wondering if you could tide me over with a cup of sugar?'

Belle stared at her.

'You don't have a cup,' she pointed out.

The stranger looked at her empty hands and after the briefest of hesitations burst into laughter, which she suppressed between cries of, 'I'm sorry!' so that Belle found herself laughing without knowing why.

'Come on in,' she said. 'Let's have some tea; then we'll see what I can do to help you out. My name's Belle by the way.'

'I'm Janet. Belle . . . ?'

'Short for Belinda. I don't know what my mum was thinking of. You can't call a girl Belinda – not in Clitheroe anyway – not without starting a fight in the school yard every playtime.'

'I'm from Oldham,' Janet said.

Belle acknowledged the understanding. 'My mum always did have ideas above herself. She owned a haberdasher's shop. It made her royalty in our street.'

She invited her visitor to sit and went to the kitchen to put on the kettle. When she returned Janet was examining the room.

'Charlie and I have only been here a few months ourselves,' Belle said. 'You'll have to forgive the wallpaper.' It was a dingy brown pattern of acanthus leaves. 'It's weird, isn't it, that a country that's the fashion capital of the world and supposed to know everything about good taste should like grotty wallpaper? But it's the same everywhere in France.'

'Like the cheap Indian restaurants we used to go to when we were students?' Janet suggested.

Belle beamed. 'Just like that. Do you take milk? In your tea? Milk? We only have UHT, I'm afraid.'

'Oh.'

'Sorry. I don't like it either, but it's all the local shop stocks. You can get fresh at the supermarket.' Belle launched into a list of local towns and markets, feeling her tongue running away with her, and finishing with: 'and in Mirepoix on Mondays; perhaps we could go one of these days.'

Immediately she thought, 'Me and my big mouth.' But Janet smiled and said, 'I should like that.' Belle noticed the lines around the smile. She decided that Janet, for all her smartness, would never see sixty again, and she flattered herself that her own skin was smoother, a benefit of being – what was the expression? – 'well-covered'.

'Bugger the tea and the rotten UHT milk.' Belle returned to the kitchen and this time produced a chilled bottle and a couple of glasses. 'We should celebrate your arrival. This is Blanquette de Limoux, the local tipple.' The wine fizzed as she pulled the stopper and poured. 'Not too early?'

'Provided it's just one glass.'

'Why did you come here – I mean to my house?'

'The others were all closed up – because of the heat I suppose. I saw your shutters were open and the car was a Jaguar, and really I was too tired to start practising my French on strangers.'

'Well, you've come to the right place. Where are you staying?'

Janet waved vaguely, 'One of the houses down the lane. It's called La Maison des Moines, which sounds grander than it is.'

'Oh, I know it. In fact there's a story that links it with this place.'

'A story?'

'A murder story – or, at any rate, a sort of a murder story. Apparently about ten years ago an Englishman was living here – I mean in my house – with his girlfriend. She went missing and everyone supposed and still supposes she was murdered, because she was never found.'

'And what's the connection with La Maison des Moines?'

'Well, *your* place was the home of a very sinister old Hungarian called Harry Haze, and he and the English couple were very thick until this Haze also upped sticks and vanished. So the thought is that Haze may have killed the girl, or maybe the Englishman killed the pair of them. No one really knows.'*

Belle thought it was a good story, and possibly even true. It didn't trouble her; after all it wasn't as if there'd been body parts scattered through her house and blood sprayed up the bedroom walls. It might have been better if there had been. Someone would have got rid of that damned wallpaper for one thing. Janet seemed interested rather than concerned.

Belle thought her visitor looked tired, but she liked her not least because of the winning laugh when she was caught out without a cup for the sugar. She was reluctant to let her go, and Janet looked as if she was happy to rest for the moment.

'Are there many English in the village?' she asked.

'A few. I haven't counted. I know half a dozen or so – women, I mean; obviously there are men as well.'

'What are they like?'

But Belle had thought of something else and answered, 'Have

* For the full story see *Recherché*.

you bought your house?' The rapid change of subject threw her visitor.

'Oh, do you mean: am I settling here? I don't know. I've taken it furnished for a year while I decide. It'll depend . . . And the other English women?'

'They're OK, the ones I've met. All sorts – no, that's not true: there are no gangsters' molls or footballers' wives; I think they tend to live on the Riviera. In fact, now I think of it, I suppose we must be a fairly select bunch: people who want to live here and can actually afford to. It isn't everybody, is it?'

'No,' Janet agreed.

Belle nodded. It wasn't something she'd thought of before: that she and the other women had an unspoken quality in common that had brought them from England to a corner of France that wasn't especially fashionable even though it was lovely. She gave thumbnail sketches of those she knew, beginning with Earthy.

'Eartha? As in Eartha Kitt?'

'I don't think so.' Belle supposed it *might* be 'Eartha', but Earthy herself had a ragged-edged, home-made look as if you could unravel her and knit her into something else, so that her name seemed somehow quite appropriate. 'I'm sure she pronounces it "Earthy", but it doesn't seem likely, does it? Then again, neither does "Eartha"; what "Earthas" do you know apart from Eartha Kitt?'

Just as quickly as before, Belle changed the subject and began to talk about her husband, Charlie, and how they'd abandoned England and intended to retire permanently to France. The explanation involved a complicated excursion into Charlie's career and the story of her children and their current partners, which Janet was quite unable to follow.

Then they returned to the subject of the other women, and Belle rattled on until Janet was dizzy from the detail. 'What on earth am I doing?' Belle wondered, but she couldn't stop. 'She probably thinks I'm a drunk; swigging bottles of blanquette in the middle of the day on any excuse. What a dismal start to a friendship, assuming it's going to be one.'

Until the end the visitor said nothing about her own life or circumstances, but now she came out with a strange remark as a sort of comment on Belle's account of the English women of Puybrun.

She said, 'You know, as you were telling me about them, I was thinking that they sound like the inhabitants of one of those preposterous English villages where people are always getting murdered, with bodies turning up in the library or the vicarage: I mean like St Mary Mead or that place in the silly television series *Midsomer Murders.*'

Belle was quite taken by the idea.

Then Janet said, 'But Puybrun isn't really like that, is it? Or not quite. It's a village of exiles. Our murders are somewhere in the past, somewhere in England, in the lives we've put behind us. And maybe there are no bodies, just . . . I don't know . . . *situations* that we've buried somewhere in the shrubbery.'

'I can think of some murders I'd like to have done,' Belle said; then on reflection added, 'But I suppose murder is just another of those things I meant to get round to in life but never managed. Like learning to tango properly.'

'I learned to tango,' Janet said. She spoke as if it were a fond but sad memory.

Janet returned to La Maison des Moines and this time had no difficulty finding the fuse box and switching on the power, after which she could see enough to open the shutters and let daylight in. For the lair of a possible killer (the vanished Mr Haze, or whatever you were supposed to call him in Hungarian) it was really quite pleasant in an understated style, with some nice pieces of country furniture. Not that Janet was much concerned with interior decorating other than the thankful absence of grisly French wallpaper, about which Belle had been right. She unloaded the car and set about opening windows to air the place, dusting and sweeping it through. She suspected there was a wasps' nest in the chimney and there were definitely field mice in the basement. The latter opened on to the road through a double door, but at the rear it was buried in the earth among old masonry that gave a hint of the origin of the house's name: traces of a bricked-up mediaeval arch.

Janet was an observant person. She didn't think Belle was a drunk. She'd noticed that the bottle of blanquette was half-full and closed with a stopper. Belle might drink more than Janet did, but serious topers always finished the bottle. No, Belle was obviously just sociable and didn't find enough opportunities to express her good nature. Was Charlie entertaining company? He hadn't showed his face and so Janet didn't know.

The biggest shock was Belle's size. She was what Janet's mother would have called 'a *big* woman'. It was that as much as the failure to take a cup for the sugar that had caused Janet to burst into nervous laughter on the doorstep. She was fat and had an enormous bosom (again Janet could hear her mother tutting, 'That poor woman must have backache something awful!'). Yet the effect was oddly graceful in its generosity like the fat mamas working the markets of West Africa. She was 'as stately as a galleon', Janet decided from a phrase she'd read, though she had no knowledge of galleons. Why not a galleass, sloop, pinnace or corvette? Or 'as graceful as a dhow'? Dhows truly were graceful. Belle made a success of her size because she had the wit and confidence to wear bright loose clothing and had a good feel for pattern and colour and no fear of being gaudy. Evidently she made her clothes herself and was good at it. Janet had spotted a sewing machine, and Belle had said her mother was once a haberdasher.

When the house was tolerably straight (at least she wouldn't find herself treading on insects in the dark), Janet decided she'd better get some food. The afternoon and evening had faded.

Her cottage was blessed with a view up the hill to the castle and she paused to take in its silhouette against a limpid sky where swifts were still screeching after insects. She recalled that a hundred yards or so along the road towards Lavelanet was a place that advertised itself as a Kazakh restaurant and pizzeria; she thought it was called the Altay. Janet was prepared to give it a try, even if it meant dining on goat pizza.

Disappointingly, the pizzas were the usual kind. The décor was oriental and might mean something to a Kazakh but otherwise looked like the stuff one found from Turkey to China with a lot of hammered brass. The other customers were a Dutch family of six from the campsite by the lake. The father had a blond chin beard without a moustache so that he resembled a mad American prophet from the nineteenth century, Brigham Young perhaps. His family was scrubbed clean and all of them wore startling white socks with sandals.

These days Janet found eating on her own in restaurants fascinating and lonely in equal parts. With David she'd been able to share deliciously malicious comments about the other guests; but that was gone and all her sharply-observed quips that had caused David to collapse in laughter remained stuck in her head or twisted silently round her tongue.

She thought: 'I'm falling out of the habit of speech.' She was aware that she'd left Belle to flounder; that she'd said very little and revealed even less. It wasn't caution or natural reticence: she'd simply got out of the habit of telling the tale of her own life and feelings. *And every time I open my mouth I want to cry.* Which was inexplicable because it had nothing to do with David's death; she'd found herself struggling to hold back tears in all sorts of situations long before he died. What was *that* all about?

She returned to the cottage with its strange name: La Maison des Moines, 'the Monks' House'. It made her think of Munchhausen – a name that seemed to have the same origin, though that was no doubt coincidental and there was no reason to suppose the house was named after the Baron. Interesting though. The Baron was famous for his fantastic stories, and the house apparently had its own story: a tale of disappearance and possible homicide. She wondered if she could make something of it? Probably not.

And now she remembered: Munchausen Syndrome was a term used to describe mad women.

She went inside and everything was in order and there was nothing too horrible scuttling across the floor. She made herself some coffee, having decided against taking it at the Altay, and she set out her laptop on the lounge table and started it up, watching it go through its comforting routines with their 'pings' and short phrases of music. Then she opened a new document in Word and after much consideration began to write:

'What I most regret in life is murdering my husband . . . '

She began to cry.

2

Credit for organising the Englishwomen of Puybrun really went to Belle. Janet guessed correctly that her neighbour had a sociable nature not satisfied by bumping into people for a chance five-minute gossip. Belle was now convinced that in some sense the women already formed a group and her job was simply to breathe life into it. Or to put it another way . . .

'I need a stage!' Belle announced in her best Miss Piggy voice as she examined her face in the bathroom mirror. Fat but attractive, she decided; not exactly beautiful but pert and bright-eyed. And she'd been right to go for a shortish hairstyle that harmonised with her face, not like poor Earthy whose long grey tresses flew off in wiry strands or hung down her back like ropes of old scouring pads. Belle wondered if Earthy still inhabited a Woodstock of the mind, in which she danced like a Pre-Raphaelite maiden with flaming hair. It wouldn't be surprising.

Belle blamed her mother for her desire for attention. Alice had always pushed her forward from being a small child playing the kazoo in a marching band. She remembered the high-stepping march and a chestful of dancing medals and a shako trimmed with braid as they followed the parade of fire engines and coal lorries decked out for the day in crêpe paper and bunting. It had been wormwood and gall to Alice because Belle was too tall and hefty to be a Rose Queen. On the other hand Alice could cut and sew, so that Belle had shone in Nativity plays in well made clothes instead of the usual tea towels and dressing gowns (though more wormwood and gall because simpering Jean Maddox was always the Virgin while Belle lurked as a shepherd with the boys). And in ballet . . . No, forget about ballet. It hadn't been a success.

Behind all this was Alice's desire for her proper station in life to be recognised. As she was forever telling people after Joe got his promotion: 'My husband manages the Biggest Co-op East of Preston.'

But now Joe was dead and Alice couldn't remember him. Instead she passed her days slumped in a chair in a care home lounge, waking only to run her fingers through a box of sparkling buttons whose use she once knew.

Belle sailed down the hill to La Maison des Moines, where Janet, looking elegant in an ivory-coloured blouse and cotton print skirt, was taking breakfast on the small veranda with its view of the castle.

Belle told her, 'You'll want to do some shopping – groceries, cleaning stuff, that sort of thing. I've come to take you to Quillan.'

'You don't have to put yourself to trouble on my account,' said Janet, but she was pleased.

'It's no trouble. I have to stock up as well. We'll take the Jag for the space.'

'Won't Charlie need it?'

'No. Charlie doesn't care for driving in France. Narrow winding roads and a bloody big car. Me, I just charge on and terrify the rest of 'em.'

In fact Belle was a perfectly sensible driver. She kept her eyes on the road even when she was speaking at her usual excitable rate, punctuated with the occasional laugh or shriek as something funny struck her. Today she was interested in Janet's affairs, and Janet saw no reason not to answer. For the moment she didn't feel like crying.

Belle asked, 'What made you decide to take a house in Puybrun? Been here before?'

'Yes – briefly. David and I were touring and we spotted the village and thought it looked pretty; so we stopped for a couple of days. We stayed in a *chambre d'hôte* somewhere on the hill behind the castle.'

'David?'

'My husband.'

'Oh – is he coming then?'

'No,' said Janet. 'He's dead.'

Belle let out a squeak. 'Oh, God! I've put my foot in it. *Again*.'

'It's all right.'

'You poor thing.'

'It was three months ago. He had a massive stroke out of the blue. He didn't suffer, but I was unprepared, of course. I can't say if that made it harder or easier. Life doesn't allow us to judge the alternatives, does it? I get only one version of David's death. I don't know if I'm over the shock or not. I still don't know what life as a widow really looks like, so I can't tell. I . . .'

'Yes?'

'I find myself crying at unexpected moments. It could be grief, I suppose – you'd think it would be, wouldn't you? – but it started while David was still alive. Perhaps a part of it *is* grief, but the rest? A hangover from the dreaded menopause? I mean it's possible, but I hope not. The hot flushes were bad enough and they seemed to go on for years. I shan't be very good company if I'm blubbing all the time.'

I don't cry, Belle thought. Not much anyway. I'm not emotional in that way. But the confession made her warm to Janet even more, though for the moment a pause in conversation seemed the right thing. Outside the car window the wheat fields bordered by a blaze of poppies and broom rolled past in sunshine, and the woods and cliffs bounding the high plateau of the Pays de Sault rose into wisps of white cloud.

Beyond Vieux Moulin the road plummeted to Quillan. The supermarket was on the outskirts; so there was nothing much to do beyond make their purchases and leave. In England shopping had become a leisure activity, but it was less true of the utilitarian sheds outside the towns of France. Belle missed that.

'I wonder sometimes if we're the same species – us and the

French,' she said. 'Where are all the cheap shoe shops? Why are there so many chemists? What's with all the wrapping things up like Christmas presents, with ribbons and fancy paper? I just don't get it. A few years ago they were dyeing their hair a bright copper red. My mum would have thought they were prostitutes. Now everyone's doing it!' Belle hooted and Janet found herself laughing.

On the return journey Belle said, 'I was thinking: we should have a little "do"; I mean invite Earthy and the others so you can meet them. What do you think?'

'I should like that,' Janet said and wondered if she would.

'No crying, mind you.' Belle risked a glance. 'Just kidding.'

'Oh, damn, I'm doing it now.' Janet reached into her bag for a tissue and dabbed her eyes. She noted the concern on Belle's face. Was that the explanation of the tears: that she was simply overwhelmed by the least glimpse of another person's humanity? She hoped she wasn't becoming sentimental.

Back home it seemed the least she could do to invite Belle for a cup of tea or a drink. She'd bought a case of blanquette, though the wine would still be warm.

'Are you sure? Oh, go on then, I love a good nosey in other people's houses.'

'I can rustle up a salad or something?'

Belle made a tour of the cottage, handling objects as though they had no value, like junk in a clearance following a death. And that wasn't so far from the truth, Janet imagined. It was a rented house, no doubt filled with things the owner didn't want: second-best crockery and tin-openers that didn't quite work. Yet the cottage had charm and comfort and the fittings were really much better than she expected; in fact rather good.

'Have you sold up in England?' Belle asked.

'Not yet.'

'We have. Burned our bridges. God help us if it's a mistake.'

'Has it been so far?'

'Give it time.'

'Is your husband happy with the arrangement?'

'Charlie? Oh, he's getting by.'

'And do you see yourself growing old here?'

'That *is* a good question . . . I suppose I don't see myself growing old at all.'

Belle took after Joe not Alice, and Joe keeled over with a heart attack before he made sixty. 'I'd be bloody crying all the time if I thought about things like that,' she told herself; so she didn't.

Belle went home and Janet was left to get on with cleaning the house. There was a wood-burning stove; did she have any logs? She must check. They'd be in the cellar with its ancient masonry, stacked against the wall as if for burning heretics. Puybrun was a place where heretics had lived – and died for that matter. She made a mental note to make sure she had enough logs before winter and also to read something about the Cathars, who had thrived hereabouts until rooted out by crusaders and murdered.

It was odd how the subject of murder kept crossing her mind. Many people would consider it morbid that she dwelt upon it. But Janet didn't. It was too much a part of her life.

In the evening Belle returned.

'There's no getting rid of me, is there? Have you eaten? I forgot to tell you there's a sort of market here every Wednesday evening in summer. It's mostly tat and fast food but it's not bad. Do you fancy something?'

Janet had been dozing – one more habit she'd recently acquired like the crying. 'Yes, OK,' she said sleepily. 'What about your husband?'

'Oh, Charlie can make do with a boiled egg. Let's go, or do you need to change?'

Janet washed her face. She put on lipstick and a cotton jacket in case it was cold. It was nine o'clock and the sky was at that peak of intense colour before it faded to night. She could see down the narrow street almost to the centre of the village. There was a show of lights like a fairground and she caught the strains of an accordion and a hubbub of people.

In the open-sided market hall with its concrete floor and dais for the visiting rock bands of summer, trestle tables had been set out and villagers ate their food from cardboard trays after buying it at one of the vans. Children and dogs ran about and the man with the accordion played for tips. Staff scurried in and out of the adjoining Bar des Sports bringing mugs of beer or Coca-Cola. A bat fluttered by.

Belle proposed, 'We'll have a look round then decide what to eat. We may see some of the others.'

She took Janet by the arm and guided her through the village's two small squares. The Place de la Halle housed the bar, the market hall and the P.T.T. A narrow bridge led over a deep cleft formed by a stream; and on the further side was the Place de l'Eglise with the church, the war memorial and the mairie. Vans were parked and stalls set out in both places. The centre of the bridge was occupied by two primitive toilets that emptied into the waters below. The arrangement struck Janet as a parody of the Rialto, with loos instead of jewellers' shops. She and David had visited the Rialto.

Her eye was attracted by the stalls. One offered sheep's milk ice cream. It looked delicious. The others sold craft items: gim-crack stuff imported from Nepal, jewellery made out of drink cans, pottery with a crackled smoky glaze that had a Japanese name Janet couldn't remember (*reiki* came to mind, but she thought that was a form of therapy). Belle approached the potter, a thin woman of fifty or so with a lined face and hair the colour of wet straw that had been used for bedding. She was smoking cigarettes made of *tabac brun*; Janet recognised the scent. It had once been so typically French but now seemed to have gone out of fashion.

'Carol!' exclaimed Belle.

The potter looked up and smiled narrowly before she was overwhelmed by Belle's bosom and a shower of *bises*.

'I've got a new friend. Carol, this is Janet. Janet – Carol.'

They exchanged murmured greetings and appraised each other while trying not to be obvious. Janet saw in Carol one of those once pretty women whose skin had been ruined by sun and smoking, an effect that made them look peevish, though they were as good-natured as anyone else. In fact, when Carol smiled her prettiness and good-nature shone, only to vanish immediately when the smile was turned off. How sad, Janet thought and – oh, God, she was going to cry again!

'Something in your eye?' asked Carol.

Belle waved a hand, 'Oh, don't worry about her. She thinks she's a film star or summat – anyway she weeps buckets at the drop of a hat, don't you? She's in training for the Oscars, aren't you, love?'

Janet laughed through the tears. Belle had found a way of putting the matter into perspective, and nobody spoke any more of it. Carol issued an invitation to visit her studio, and Belle mentioned the idea of a get-together to welcome Janet properly.

'Next, we'll find Earthy while we're here,' Belle proposed. And there she was, coming out of the toilet by the mairie, looking like a Romanian bag lady in a shapeless mix of printed and embroidered clothes. She went to her stall, where she sold herbs, incense and charms. Belle called out, 'Earthy!' meanwhile whispering to Janet: 'She's a nice old thing, but God knows how she gets by, selling bits of rubbish for pennies. I say "old", but *is* sixty old? They say not – "sixty is the new forty" and all that – still, there are days when it feels like it.' It was the first time she'd hinted at her own age.

Again Janet gained only fleeting impressions while Belle prattled on. Earthy's skin was slack and smooth, sallow, with a skein of broken veins over her cheeks, the effect of living an open air life at some time, Janet suspected. Yet her face gave an impression of kindliness and she had gentle grey eyes. Not a self-confident woman. She had little to say but agreed with Belle that 'a do with a few bits and some plonk' would be a good idea.

'And now for a touch of Mexican!' Belle announced. '*Arriba!*'

They bought food and took it to the *halle*, where they were made welcome at one of the tables. The accordion player was squeezing out a jaunty waltz meant to be danced with small bouncing steps; Janet recognised it from country fêtes she and David had visited on their tours. Among her most treasured memories were recollections of village dances on summer nights by the light of stars and the glare of travelling shooting galleries. She turned away from the image or she would be crying again.

Meantime Belle chatted as she ate. She volunteered more of her own life as well as short biographies of everyone she'd ever met, or so it seemed. Charlie, she said, had been a partner in a successful quantity surveying practice until he made his pile and wanted to retire. Belle herself had taught Year Eight – 'a horror story – don't ask!' They had a daughter married to an estate agent and a son in New Zealand.

'And you?'

'I was a civil servant – a planner,' said Janet, hoping it would sound dull enough to stop any further enquiry. 'David was an accountant.' They had a single daughter, Helen, and a grand-child.

And Helen must be at her wits' end because I haven't phoned her to tell her where I am, thought Janet. It was something she would have to do, but she didn't know how to explain it: the need to get away; the feeling of panic.

Belle looked away. She may have sensed her new friend's distraction. She said, 'Hey, look at those two!' – pointing down the nearest lane to where a pair of young men were lounging outside a house that advertised itself as a gallery of some sort. One of them was tall and shaven headed and wore a saffron *kurta pajama*. The other was small-made, dark, and wore a T-shirt, jeans and western boots decorated with chains.

'The one in the jim-jams calls himself Ravi and I think the other's called Léon.'

'Ravi doesn't look very Indian,' Janet said.

'No, of course not. His real name is Colin or Graham or something ordinary. Don't look! Don't look! God, don't they fancy themselves!'

Janet smiled. Belle was right, of course. Men in their twenties always did 'fancy themselves', and some of them never grew out of it. Ravi was undeniably handsome in the fair, vaguely public school way that Janet had never found especially appealing. Léon, she couldn't tell at this distance. But later he crossed the floor of the *halle* on his way to the bar and passed within a few feet of her, and she saw that he was one of the skinny, not quite ugly men who unaccountably starred in French films and whom French women seemed to find irresistible. His movements were easy and lithe, his teeth were uneven, his nose was slightly bent, and his hair was in black ringlets that stopped short of his collar.

In itself all of this was nothing. Yet Janet felt a sudden rush of sexual warmth that was as inexplicable as it was unexpected.

3

Janet knew that at some point she'd have to phone home to explain herself. Before quitting England, she'd left a letter for Helen but it said little beyond assuring her daughter that she was well and would get in touch. She didn't say where she was going, and there wasn't a word about her motives. As to her destination, she simply wanted a place where she would be left in peace until she felt ready to face others. And as to motives? What were her motives? Janet wasn't sure she could describe them. She didn't doubt that Helen would think she was clinically depressed; people made these facile judgments based on pop psychology. But was she?

'You'd think I'd know,' she murmured, but the complexity of her feelings defied description. At all events she didn't want to kill herself; so if suicidal feelings were a mark of depression, she wasn't depressed.

'Hullo?'

'Hullo, darling.'

'Mum?'

'Yes.'

'Mum! Where on earth are you?'

'I'm in France.'

'Where in France?'

'I'd rather not say. Look, I don't want to make this a long conversation. I just wanted to tell you . . . I wanted to tell you . . . Please, darling, I'm fine. I'll contact you again, maybe in a few days. Give my love to Henry and Chloë.'

She pressed the button to end the call, but before she remembered to turn her mobile off, Helen had called back.

'I ought to be furious but I'm not,' she said furiously.

Janet terminated the call again. A moment later the mobile rang once more.

'All right, point taken. I'll try to control myself, but have you *any* idea what it's like having to field questions without a clue what to say to people? Jeremy Whatshisface has been on the phone every single day, wanting to speak to you about Dad.'

Jeremy Vavasour was David's partner.

'Did he say why?'

'No. Only that he's trying to unscramble the company's affairs and there are things he doesn't understand.'

'And he expects me to understand them? I wasn't involved in your father's business.'

'And other people too. Most of them angry. God knows where they got my number from. But the fact is that I can't tell them anything, and you can imagine how Henry feels about this.'

'I'm sorry. I don't see how I can help. Even if I were there, I don't see what I could do. If there are any papers, they'll be at the house; I haven't thrown any away. Hullo, Helen?'

The phone went dead for a moment except for a faint sound of noises off: someone in the same room pretending not to be there.

'And the police would like to speak to you as well,' said Helen.

'I'm going into Chalabre to pick up some bits and pieces,' said Belle. 'Since you haven't been there before, you can come along. And then we'll make . . . oh, I don't know . . . vol au vents, things with anchovies, and stuff on sticks, all in time for the girls this afternoon.'

Janet told her, 'Dear Belle, you're being very nice to me, but you don't need to be my social secretary.' In an echo of her earlier thoughts she added, 'I'm not about to top myself out of grief.'

'It's not for you, it's for me. I like the company. Come on; get your glad rags on.'

Janet nodded, while her mind went over her various predicaments: I'm going shopping for anchovies and stuff to put on sticks; I need something to get rid of mice; my husband is dead; and on top of everything else the police are looking for me.

Also her daughter was furious and no doubt Henry too – she'd hinted as much. Henry was a super-competent man with a job in finance that Janet didn't understand. He had considerable talent as an organiser which he also put to use in his private life. He provided Helen with lists.

If David had been like that, I'd have killed him.

In fact it was some such occasion, when David had annoyed her by fussing about over-elaborate arrangements for a holiday, that Janet first started planning how to bump him off.

'I'll be glad to come,' Janet said.

It was a ten minute journey through a rolling countryside of woods and small fields. Janet remembered why she liked it: the banks dense with hedgerow flowers; and more butterflies than one ever saw in England. Chalabre was dozing in mid-morning, so quiet that if a dog had crossed the road the town band would have played. They parked and went to a grocer's shop in a narrow street leading to the small central square; and in a few minutes Belle had bought whatever they had to sell and they were on their way back to Puybrun.

The expedition reminded Janet how much she and David had enjoyed this aspect of France: the mornings spent in small towns with their vegetable markets from which one came away as often as not with little more than a bunch of fresh asparagus. It was one of his endearing qualities that on holiday, if not at home, he'd been content to follow her around, taking pleasure in the scent of fruit and cheeses and asking only that they find time to pop into a bookshop where he could browse. On reflection Janet realised it was something they'd done literally for decades, just the two of them since Helen had grown up enough to be embarrassed by her parents. And now it was over – absolutely and completely over. Janet could visit the markets and enjoy those same scents, and she could buy asparagus in season and the small yellow fungi they called *girolles*, and sheep's cheese and dried sausage with hazelnuts in it and . . . But the tenderness would be gone from the experience. Yes, the *tenderness*.

Belle was a good cook and her 'bits' were colourful, inventive and delicious. Janet felt out of place in her kitchen but her new friend was avid for company.

'Where's Charlie?' Janet asked.

'Oh, he's got a workshop out the back.' She put a knife down and sighed, 'I don't get it with men. Have you ever thought how lonely they must be compared with us? They spend so much time on their own at their hobbies or watching football, and even when they talk with each other they're not really listening and it's all rubbish about referees and who was offside, as if any of it mattered. What's that? Someone at the door. Will you answer?'

Janet did and found two women there.

'Hullo, I'm Veronica,' said the older one.

'And I'm Poppy,' said the younger.

And you're the lesbians, Janet remembered because Belle had told her so. They lived together in a luxuriously converted house tucked away somewhere, and Veronica had been . . . a banker, was it?

'I'm Janet,'

'We guessed,' said Poppy in a strong cockney accent; though Janet couldn't tell if it was real or faked as so often the case. It was disconcerting because Belle had said nothing of appearances and Janet had been half-expecting, if not exactly a dyke in a boiler suit, at least someone less *feminine*. Poppy was strikingly beautiful with immaculately cut blond hair and a willowy figure in a full-skirted summer dress with something of the fifties and Grace Kelly about her. Though with the voice of a crow, admittedly.

Veronica, too, was a very good-looking woman with wonderful facial bones and a riveting smile: not a grin but a subtle lively movement as if she saw the funny side of each moment. Like her partner she was turned out in clothes that contrived to look both careless and expensive. *Versace*, Janet thought, though frankly she had no idea; sometimes one simply seized on words to fix a general impression. Veronica had to be forty-five, even if she gave the impression of being younger; and Poppy was no more than twenty-five.

Belle bustled in from the kitchen, enveloped her guests in her fleshy arms and gave the air-kisses everyone gave these days since England to its surprise discovered it was a Mediterranean country. 'Come on, come on, let's get some fizz inside us. Janet, be a love and pour the plonk. God, there's someone else at the door. Earthy! Come in and give us a kiss – don't let my boobs get in the way – there! Mmmm! Carol! I didn't see you behind Earthy. Thanks for the bottle – Janet, can you shove it in the fridge? Are we all here? Yes? No?'

'Where's Joy?' asked Veronica.

Belle confessed later as she and Janet were washing glasses, 'Joy's one of those people – how do they put it? When she comes into a room it feels as though someone interesting has left. I almost forgot to invite her.'

'Who is she?'

'She and her husband live in a big place with a garden out at Campmaurice – that's one of the hamlets: "camp" means "field" or summat. I can never remember his name: it's Arnold or Stanley: something out of the Ark. He's older than her. I think he made his money in second-hand cars; still dabbles in it and goes home to England every summer.'

It was Veronica who reminded Belle that she should invite Joy, suggesting it would be a kindness. It wasn't obvious why Veronica should take an interest. Joy wasn't sparkling company or in the least glamorous; just someone in her forties who wore neat practical polo shirts and shorts as she bounced about the village looking disconcertingly sprightly and doing nothing very interesting. It took Janet, observant as usual, to point out a general physical resemblance between the two women; and yet one was attractive and the other wasn't. Joy lacked style and animation and her hair was wrong for her facial shape. Attractiveness lay in such fine differences.

And here we all are, Janet thought as they sat in Belle's lounge chatting amiably: Earthy, Carol, Veronica, Poppy, Joy, and Belle herself. As different or as alike as women can be who've decided to exile themselves to a small village in south-west France. *These are the people who are going to be my new friends, assuming I decide to settle here – which means assuming I'm also an exile.* Janet wasn't sure she was; and that feeling – the feeling of being on the brink of making a mistake – woke again the sense of panic that afflicted her like the tears and the sleepiness. Maybe she had a reason to panic, if only because for some reason or other the police wanted to speak to her.

'I've had a thought,' Belle announced at last. 'Which is partly why I've asked you here – as well as for a chance to meet Janet, of course. I think we should form a women's group.'

She was disappointed that nobody said immediately what a good idea it was.

'I've been in women's groups before,' Earthy said. Her voice was high-pitched and to Janet's ear upper class in an old-fashioned way. It was like listening to the Queen in an ancient newsreel.

'And? What sort?'

'We used to form a circle and discuss spiritual things. We tried to combine our female energy.'

'Christ,' said Carol. 'Belle, d'you mind if I smoke?' She was already on her feet and went to the door. She opened it and stood directly outside. 'Go on. I'm listening.'

'What did you have in mind?' Veronica asked.

'Something a bit more practical.'

'Swapping recipes?' said Carol. She might have said 'Drinking cyanide by the pint' for all the enthusiasm in her voice.

'It could be that – I mean that could be part of it. I was thinking that all of us have skills and other things that we know about that we could teach the others.'

'You mean like pottery?' said Poppy.

'I heard that,' said Carol. 'Don't start volunteering me for anything.'

'I read a book recently,' said Joy. 'It was about some women who formed a reading club to talk about Jane Austen.'

'We could do that too-' said Belle, adding, ' – but not ruddy Jane Austen if you don't mind. I did her for Eng Lit at A Level and all I can remember is that Emma was a right cow and Fanny Price was a po-faced prig. As for Darcy, don't get me started. A woman would have to be off her head to fall for him.'

'How can you say that?' Carol asked with surprising warmth.

Belle laughed. 'Imagine sleeping with him? I'd be too frightened to fart in bed!'

In those first moments it seemed to Belle that the idea was going to misfire. Earthy was in favour – no surprise there – but she seemed to have a daft notion of them all sitting barefoot and chanting God-knew-what. It would make a cat laugh and was enough to kill the idea stone dead if they hadn't had a couple of glasses of blanquette inside them. However the discussion switched to the skills they possessed. Did they really have anything to teach each other? They'd never thought in terms of 'skills', just of things they did or stuff they knew as part of ordinary life. It was the discovery that the others did *not* do these things and did *not* know this stuff that started interest. And at that point Veronica agreed that, when all was said and done, it wasn't a bad idea and what was to be lost if they tried it out, they could always stop if it was boring? And Carol too said she didn't mind giving it a go. And finally Joy said rather excitedly that she was happy to take part if Arnold didn't mind.

'Did you catch that?' said Belle afterwards. ' "If Arnold doesn't mind". What's it to do with him? I'd murder the sod if he tried to stop me.'

Veronica asked, 'Don't we need a name?'

That's the banker in you, thought Belle. Janet had a similar feeling: that everyone had an inner Henry. Another minute and they'd be making lists. But that was unfair.

'I suppose it'll have to be something dull like "The Puybrun Women's Group",' said Veronica.

' "The Women's Circle",' suggested Earthy.

'It sounds like we're casting spells,' said Belle.

' "The Women's Forum"?' said Carol.

'Pompous.'

Poppy (giggling): "Women R Us"?'

'Save it till we open our world headquarters on a trading estate in Sheffield. As it happens, I do have an idea for a name, but I don't suppose any of you will like it.'

'What is it?' asked Joy, who had no suggestions of her own.

' "The English Lady Murderers' Society".'

'Blame Janet,' Belle told the others.

'It wasn't my idea,' Janet protested.

'I'll grant that you didn't invent the name. But it was something you said that got me wondering. Janet thinks we're all a bunch of murderers.'

'Really?' said Veronica.

'I didn't mean it literally. I was simply curious.'

'About what?'

'About why we're here – here in France. Not on holiday but apparently for ever. Why have we left England? Why have we become exiles?'

'The weather,' said Carol.

'The food,' said Joy.

'It's just so lovely – I mean all of it,' said Earthy.

'Yes,' said Janet. 'I understand. I understand all of those things. Yet, at the end of the day, everybody likes those things but only a few of us are here.'

'Hundreds of thousand when you count them up,' said Carol.

'I suppose so, but a small minority all the same – only a fraction of those who *could* retire abroad if they wanted to. Do you see? There's nothing obvious, nothing self-evident about our being here. We come and settle and we make a new future, abandoning the past.'

'Is that so bad?'

'No, I don't mean to suggest that at all. I don't know. I don't have an opinion. I'm simply curious.'

'And why are we murderers?' asked Veronica, pouring herself another glass of wine.

'It's just a figure of speech. I'm guessing that in some way or other each of us wants to forget something in our past: wants to "kill" it in a sense. I . . . It's just something I said to Belle: an attempt to capture what we're doing. I wasn't trying to be witty or profound and I don't say it's definitely true. The words simply popped into my head.'

Like the idea of starting a women's group, Belle's suggestion for the name seemed at first as if it would fail for lack of interest. But in fact it had simply taken the others by surprise. As Belle reminded herself afterwards: it wasn't exactly *obvious*.

Carol said, 'If anyone gets wind of it, they'll start calling us "The Murdering Bitches".'

Poppy spluttered wine over her dress as she tried to choke a laugh. 'Oh fuck,' she said in her cockney drawl.

'But no one else is likely to find out, are they?' said Belle. 'I don't think we'll be posting notices on the board outside the mairie.'

'The English Lady Murderers invite the villagers of Puybrun to their annual bring and buy sale? No, I suppose not.'

'Why "murderers", why not "murderesses"?' asked Veronica.

'I think it's one of those words like "actress",' said Belle. 'Do you remember how we used to have "actresses"? Nowadays they're all "actors", though I've no idea why it's thought to be feminist to adopt a word that used to apply only to men. If that makes sense we may as well have kept "chairman" instead of changing to "chair" as if we were a piece of furniture. Sorry, don't get me going: I did English language at Uni. How about a vote?' she proposed.

They held a show of hands and the motion was passed unanimously. Which is how they came to be called The English Lady Murderers' Society; though, as Carol suspected would happen, they often referred to themselves as The Murdering Bitches, or the 'MBs' for short.

How to do Tatting

4

'Tattin'?' said Poppy. 'Never heard of it.'

'It's a kind of lace-making,' Belle said. 'My Mum showed me how to do it.'

Most of Alice's friends learned how to knit. Alice learned how to tat. The difference was that knitting produced useful things such as cardigans, scarves and gloves, but tatting resulted in table cloths with fancy edging, coasters, and baby bootees. Woollen garments, even the most hideous ones, wore out. Tatted objects didn't – not so as you'd notice.

'I like to have something to show for my efforts,' Alice explained. In her heart she wanted to take up the fancier forms of lace-making such as bobbin or needlepoint but they required time and dexterity beyond her capacity and she confined herself to collecting a few small pieces of Honiton which she kept in a drawer of the sideboard wrapped in tissue paper and brought out only on special occasions.

At home the front room – or 'parlour' as Alice called it – was kept for best. It was used only for visitors or family occasions and at Christmas when the men drank whisky and the women port and lemon . After Joe became manager of the Biggest Co-op East of Preston it slowly filled with tatted decoration: mats and coasters under every photograph and ornament, and anti-macassars on the backs of chairs. Tucked in the drawer with the Honiton lace were half a dozen table cloths embroidered with pansies, pierced in elaborate patterns of broderie anglaise, and edged in tatting, all of it Alice's work in preparation for the day when someone worthy enough – someone capable of understanding the spirituality of Alice's devotion to 'having things nice' – would stop by to take tea. Ordinary visitors were now received in the living room (also decorated with lacy bits) and family parties crowded into the same space, though people might get a peep into the shrine of the parlour to admire its glory.

'You do keep your house lovely, Alice,' said her friends, and she glowed in their approval. It would have to do until Jesus came again, or whoever it was for whom the room was prepared, a question to which Belle never learned the answer.

Joe was indulgent towards Alice's obsession and even proud of her in a general way. Belle too had loved the tatting when she was a little girl and her notion of Heaven was somewhere painted pink and trimmed with taffeta and lace. But that take on the world was designed for dainty girls and didn't fit the hulking reality.

'I weigh the same as I did when I was twenty,' Alice still repeated in her lucid moments. She'd always been flat-chested, stick-thin and shapeless, but these were details she overlooked. She'd read in a magazine that the Duchess of Windsor had once said, 'You can never be too thin or too rich,' and Wallace Simpson had also been flat-chested, stick-thin and shapeless.

Belle, on the other hand, took after her father's side of the family: in particular after his mother, Grandma Threddle, a giantess who drank stout and smoked a pipe. And as she grew older and was cast out of ballet classes for making the whole performance look ridiculous, she knew she would have to create another Belle: one who was attractive on quite different terms.

By then she'd come to loathe the whole process of tatting. Its prettiness and delicacy were evidence of the fraud that Nature had perpetrated on her body. It was the distraction that stopped Alice from loving her. It was, in a sense, the outward raiment of another, invisible daughter whom Alice was trying to bring into existence, and a standing reproach to the one who was really there.

On the other hand, like riding a bicycle, tatting was a skill you never forgot once you'd mastered it.

'Why did you choose to teach it then?' asked Janet. She understood why Belle had volunteered to give the first class to The English Lady Murderers' Society: the business had been her idea after all. But why tatting?

'Because it's something I can do. And I don't really *hate* it. It's just that my Mum went daft about it, though I suppose if it hadn't have been tatting it'd have been something else. And I have one or two things that Alice did that are really nice.'

She showed Janet a lace edged collar of a kind she'd seen on simple day dresses of the 1930s and thought rather attractive.

'And here are some bootees she made for our Catherine.'

Janet nodded. Bootees were irresistible. They just were.

'Does Catherine tat?'

'No, she never had the slightest interest. I'd have liked her to. I know that sounds silly, given what I've just told you about me and my Mum, but there we are; you can't always be consistent.'

After Joe's death, Alice had lived on in the same house and continued running the small haberdasher's shop even though it scarcely saw a customer from one week to the next and hadn't for years. The shop, like the parlour and perhaps much else in Alice's life, was kept in waiting for someone indefinable, someone who would explain everything. And given that Alice was in any case inclined to brood, it gave her a purpose and a place to go, and the perpetual reorganisation of her tired stock was an absorbing activity.

'How long has she been in care?' asked Janet.

'Four years. She kept falling down and her mind's gone, but otherwise she's as strong as a horse.'

The haberdasher's shop had been converted into an unattractive house with bright new brickwork and a small PVC window filling what had once been the display window. The other house, where they actually lived, was sold to a teacher with a young family and these days the garden was full of bicycles.

Most of the tatting had gone to charity, but Belle had kept her mother's workbox with its shuttles, threads, crochet hooks and scissors. It stood on folding legs and was made of pale varnished wood trimmed with a darker stain. Italian prisoners of war in Wales had made it – Belle had no idea why she should remember that.

Belle didn't mention it, but the fact that Alice was still alive and likely to go on for a while yet had been the subject of arguments with Charlie when the topic of moving to France had first been raised. They compromised that Belle would return home every month or two. But once the concession had been made by Charlie, Belle hadn't bothered. Alice had no idea who she was. Her visits had no more significance than one of the care assistants bringing a cup of tea and a biscuit. Once a month or once a year, it was all the same.

Then events overtook Belle and Charlie, and now she couldn't return to England whether she wanted to or not.

'Shall I give the police your mobile number?' Helen asked when they next spoke.

'Wasn't that the police with you when I called last time?'

'What a suspicious thing you are; anyone would think you had a guilty conscience. No, it was Henry. He wanted to speak to you; give you a piece of his mind. He's in one of his noisy moods.'

'Yes, you can give them this number,' Janet said. She didn't care. She intended to keep her phone switched off most of the time, so it wouldn't much matter.

It was Sunday. Belle proposed they go to the market at Espéraza, half an hour away by a hilly road along the side of a secluded valley dense with trees, where little stirred except a black kite circling in a clear sky.

'I love the place,' Belle confided. 'It's full of hippy types: awful posers and as daft as a brush, but they give it a bit of colour.'

The river Aude flowed through the town under an ancient

stone bridge. The market was held on a large square by the river bank.

Belle said, 'My Mum was a hoarder and her box has got most of the stuff we need to get half a dozen of us started, but I could do with picking up some extras. I think I know of a shop.'

'I'd like an English newspaper.'

'Shall we do separate errands and meet up, or stick together?'

'Stick together,' said Janet. This morning she was feeling a little anxious. But she was also curious as to how Belle was going to manage 'size 10 mercerised tatting thread' in French.

They found a newsagent where Janet bought a *Guardian*, then a shop that seemed to sell goods for a variety of handicrafts, where Belle translated her needs by the usual expedient of shouting and gesticulating. Janet could do simple sewing but had never acquired any other skills of that kind. It was one reason why learning the basics of tatting appealed to her. However, once she saw the range of hobbies some women took up and the bizarre productions they considered desirable, the whole business, rather like the name of their group, seemed faintly mad.

'I know,' said Belle. 'It's like a horror film, isn't it? *Vampire Soft Toy Makers from Hell.* '

In the market they bought fresh vegetables and *pain de campagne*. Janet gave thought to picking up some plants: she had several pots on her veranda and a small bed along the wall and by the gate, but she would probably need a bag of compost before considering planting; it was something for another day. A jewellers shop offered a number of attractive items, so that Janet wished she had someone to give them to. Half the fun of shopping was buying things for other people. It allowed you look seriously at things you wouldn't dream of keeping for yourself.

'Didn't I tell you?' Belle pointed at a figure by one of the stalls. It wore a huge purple felt hat and a flowing garment Janet couldn't put a name to, made of unbleached cloth with a crotch somewhere near the ankles. Apparently the owner was a man and his smile of self-satisfaction was delightful.

They continued their turn around the stalls. As Belle had promised, among the displays of cheese and charcuterie were others of handmade soaps, incense, crystals and other things Janet thought of as rubbish. They caught up with the young man in the purple hat and found he'd paused by someone they knew: Ravi alias Colin or Graham. He was sitting cross-legged, plucking notes from an instrument that looked almost but not quite like something one could put a name to. The thin music sounded Indian in the same generic way that Ravi himself looked Indian: namely unconvincingly in Janet's opinion. Behind him was a table with a collection of books for sale and a cardboard sign that read in English and French: *The Holy Brotherhood of OM*. The books purported to explain the teachings of the Brotherhood.

'Flogging Wisdom today, are you, Ravi?' asked Belle.

'Wisdom is Beauty: and Beauty is Wisdom – so I've got nothing to sell to you, have I?' said Ravi with a disarming smile.

'Oh, you *are* full of it!' said Belle, and both she and Ravi laughed.

'He could charm his way into Mother Teresa's knickers, that one,' Belle said to Janet. 'Let's have some coffee, shall we? I need to get out of the sun.'

A café looked across the narrow end of the square to the bridge. On market days tourists gathered there: large-boned Dutch girls blazing with health, and Englishmen in Panama hats and strange shorts. To Janet the French seemed to play bit parts in this world: selling vegetables and bringing coffee; but no doubt it was only a matter of perspective. She ordered an *allongé* and began to read her paper.

Meanwhile Belle watched the throng. Tourists passed by carrying cameras and groceries. She noted the clothes the younger French women were wearing. Not that Belle could see herself in them: they were dull browns and greens with large, simple geometric patterns; not her style at all. And those who were wearing them had nose studs and tattoos.

With Janet buried in her newspaper the world seemed to have gone silent despite the white noise of the crowd about its business. Belle fretted for conversation; for someone to pay her attention. How pathetic, she thought. It was one of those aspects of decamping to France to which she hadn't given enough thought. A lack of self-knowledge, she supposed: a lack that life had revealed to her after a week or two, when she realised that the only person to whom she spoke on a daily basis was the baker. She'd met the other women, of course, but only casually, for example on Wednesday evenings in the market place. No doubt things would get better as the circle of her acquaintances grew, but these initial months had made her feel a terrible vulnerability.

She glanced at Janet. Still preoccupied. A more self-contained person, Belle suspected. Watchful. Sad. Which was under-standable enough, given the death of her husband. Insightful too: she had, after all, understood that they were all of them on the run from nameless crimes, of some of which they might even be innocent or quite possibly framed by Life or God according to your point of view.

And there was Earthy coming over the bridge from the other bank of the river where, if Belle rightly remembered, old women rummaged through stalls of second-hand clothes. Just her style.

And there too was Ravi, smiling at Earthy and joking with her.

What a tart he is, Belle thought. Her curiosity got the better of her desire for company, and she watched them amble towards the further end of the square deep in conversation.

Janet's habit was to read the newspaper from the back to the front, so she took in the style and opinion pages before the main stories. She also cast an eye over the business news, not that she made a habit of reading it closely unless a headline grabbed her.

Today one did. There was a small item on a page that otherwise dealt with latest developments in the mobile phone industry. It read simply:

VAVASOUR & BRETHERTON
CALL IN THE RECEIVERS

Manchester-based investment managers, Vavasour & Bretherton have called in the receivers. The future of the company has been uncertain since the death of founder-member David Bretherton in March. Fellow director, Jeremy Vavasour said, 'David was the heart and soul of the company and his skills have proved irreplaceable.' He added that he remained hopeful investors would be able to recover their money in full. Vavasour & Bretherton was set up five years ago and its client base is principally local authorities and charities.

Janet stared at the article.

David was the heart and soul of the company.

She knew what that meant. For all the reassurances the story was signalling that the investors would lose money. And in ordinary language, Jeremy was setting David up to take the blame. Janet felt angry. With Jeremy Vavasour (not a name she believed genuine for a second) for trying to escape the consequences of the affair. And with David because he was such a fool for involving himself in it. He was an accountant trained in local government work. What had he been doing in an investment management company?

In retrospect she realised she'd been waiting for a moment like this: sensing its inevitability, though she couldn't say exactly why, beyond having noticed a dimming in David's sunny nature in the weeks before his death. She'd sensed it and yet had never raised her concerns because . . . well, because one didn't. And now the disaster had happened.

At least the newspaper story had clarified the truth behind her fears. And, too, it gave her some sort of insight into her emotional difficulties of the last three months. She'd thought that the distress of grieving was the feeling of loss, and probably to a large degree it was. But there was more to it.

One got so furious with dead people. For some reason they couldn't just go quietly without leaving everything screwed up behind them.

5

In basic tatting, two threads are used. The anchor is drawn from a shuttle small enough to be held in the fingers of the right hand. The working thread is taken from a ball, twisted round the little finger of the left hand and manipulated by the other fingers. The fundamental element of the art is the double stitch, in which the working thread is tied round the anchor thread in two operations known as half stitches, so that two 'halves' make a 'double'. Because the stitches formed by the working thread remain free to be moved along the anchor thread, it's inaccurate to describe the result as a knot. If you do create a knot, you have to unpick it using a crochet hook.

A series of double stitches forms a chain, and by pulling on the anchor thread it's possible to form the chain into a ring. Tatting is essentially a pattern of chains and rings.

The first lesson in tatting was a success. Everyone came and everyone enjoyed it, and it was agreed that The English Lady Murderers' Society had got off to a good start.

Belle refused Janet's offer to help with the clearing. For once the company had been enough; in fact she felt quite dizzy with the need for concentration while listening to others.

In one respect, however, she took herself by surprise. She told them the story of Alice and the shrine she made in the parlour and sanctified with lace. It was the same tale she'd told to Janet, disclosing a confidence and not expecting to repeat it. Yet there was no reason why it shouldn't be repeated; after all there was nothing shameful in it. And wasn't it natural that, as she introduced them to tatting, she should explain how the skill had come down to her?

All the same she felt as if she'd exposed herself: let the others into the secret places of her life. Of course she said nothing of the blazing rows she and Alice had had, such as the time when, after an argument about what good girls did and didn't do with boys, she'd run out of the room screaming, 'Fucking, *fucking* tatting!' to her mother's complete incomprehension. But this further story had been implicit in what she *had* said. She was sure Janet understood as much.

The problem was that no matter that Belle had made the picture of her mother as funny as possible, the role of Alice wasn't a comic part: it was deadly serious. All the others had mothers. All of them *knew*.

'I like Belle, but she's a silly woman, isn't she?' said Poppy as she and Veronica walked home. 'Did you see how Earthy was all thumbs? She couldn't tie a half stitch to save her life. Carol was good though. I suppose making pots means you're clever with your hands. She can probably play the piano.'

'I think it helps to be musical if you want to play the piano,' Veronica said. Sometimes Poppy's triviality would try the patience of a saint.

They all told their own stories about lace. It was inevitable if they were to show they were interested. Belle's was funny – hilarious really – though with an edge to it, all that stuff about her mother. Janet's was vivid: quite moving at times. Veronica threw in something about buying a couple of pieces at antique fairs: one of them a christening robe, though God knew why she bought it, given she hadn't and never would have kids. Carol was actually familiar with the technical side and could tell at a glance the difference between needlepoint and bobbin lace and hinted, without actually saying so, that she thought tatting was pretty inferior stuff. Earthy simply prattled on with a smile on her face; really one wondered if she was all there. And Joy told a story that seemed to be about curtains insofar as it was about anything.

As for tatting itself, Veronica couldn't get excited. The examples of her mother's work that Belle showed were quite attractive, but they seemed pointless in this day and age. Her own mother had some good Victorian lace, but Veronica had no interest and told her sister-in-law she was welcome to it. And then she bought the christening robe. Possibly not the world's greatest mystery after all.

Poppy went to the bedroom and changed into a swimming costume over which she slipped a loose dress.

'I'm going to the lake,' she said.

'Be careful of the sun – your skin. I'll join you in an hour or so for a drink at the *buvette*.'

Poppy went out of the door and down the lane. Her flat pumps lent a lightness to her step and didn't distract from her perfect ankles and calves. Veronica watched her and felt a pang at the completeness of her beauty. It seemed beyond the powers of anyone to try to hold onto it. It was ridiculous really that she should even want to.

She was glad that the women's group had formed. She loved Poppy passionately, but she would go insane if they stayed trapped, each of them with only the other.

For Janet, lace meant Burano. She remembered it because the island was so different from Venice despite being only forty minutes away by vaporetto across the lagoon. She and David had made the crossing during a New Year break: a dismal season, very cold, with the sky and water grey, the lagoon partly covered by a sheet of ice, with more ice around the base of the *pozzi* in every square they visited.

In short it was wonderful.

The vaporetto called first at Murano. Young touts met visitors, took them on a tour of the glassworks, and persuaded them to buy flashily gilded goblets in the Venetian style. The memory came back because the young man who attached himself to her had the same attractive loucheness she detected in Léon, and on that occasion too she felt the same flush of sexual warmth.

In contrast Burano was a sleepy village of small houses painted in bright pastels, and had a museum celebrating its history of making fabulously expensive needlepoint lace.

A year or two later she and David went to Madeira and stayed at the Savoy and dined and danced at Reids. In a shop they came across one of the specialities of the island: fine pierced cottons worked with flower patterns of coloured thread. Strictly speaking it wasn't lacework but a sort of broderie anglaise, but someone who wasn't familiar with the difference would recognise the general similarity and lump them together, as Janet had.

Belle's lesson in tatting brought the memories back to her. She and David had been middle-aged already; yet age didn't figure in how she re-imagined the scenes. Huddled in thick coats they'd walked hand in hand through winter-chilled squares and over bleak canals. In a black cocktail dress she'd gone with him to the lounge-bar at Reids, and they'd danced closely to witty Cole Porter numbers and the accompaniment of a pianist and singer, while through the window was a vista of lights along the shore of Funchal and up the hill to Monte. And in each case the feeling of the memory was the same.

For her, lace was associated with recollections of love.

Janet listened again to Belle's story and was touched by it, which was why she volunteered her own. She didn't disclose that her scenes of Venice and Madeira were chapters in a love story. The others would see that, or perhaps they wouldn't. Janet didn't care.

When Belle refused her offer of help she understood. A temperament as exuberant as her friend's was bound to give occasional cause for embarrassment and Belle was neither so stupid nor so insensitive as not to recognise it. Her tales about Alice had been genuinely funny, but there was no escaping the undertones of pain and conflict. Probably Belle was having second thoughts about telling them, but in the end she'd be glad she did, because there's a catharsis in story-telling. It was why people did it.

What did strike Janet about tatting was its role as metaphor. Perhaps that wasn't surprising, because metaphor seemed to be a part of the way she thought. For example she'd seen murder as a symbol of whatever motives had brought the women to Puybrun. And now the first chain of double stitches produced by Belle reminded her of something she used to do as a child. She'd cut figures from a concertina of paper that, when it was opened, formed a chain of little people linked hand to hand. And, so it seemed to her, the Englishwomen of Puybrun had linked themselves to each other, able to move and to form chains or rings, but always tied by the anchor thread of the group. Not a particularly insightful metaphor, admittedly, but very few of them were. They just helped to clarify things that would otherwise remain only as vague feelings.

Enough! She needed to find out what was behind the story in the *Guardian*. There was no point in calling Helen and a good chance she'd be forced to speak to Henry if she tried. The article hadn't named the liquidators; so there seemed no option but to get an explanation from Jeremy. His number was in her address book.

'Hullo, Jeremy?'

'Ye–es?' Cautious. A click.

'It's Janet. Are you recording this?'

'What? Oh – yes. Sorry. Nothing personal. I'm recording everything. My solicitor says I have to.'

'Your solicitor?'

'Par for the course. These days, if an investment management company goes to the wall, the first thing you have to do is get lawyered up. As a friend, I'd suggest you do the same.'

As a friend. It wasn't a term Janet would have used. She hadn't disguised – leastways from David – her distrust of Jeremy Vavasour. She didn't find his over-groomed looks and upper-class manner either appealing or convincing, and the association between the two men had never seemed to her to have a natural basis in mutual liking or respect. The fact was that David's previous experience in local government had involved close relations with a number of charities, which fit the profile of the new company's target market. As far as Janet was concerned, Jeremy had head-hunted her husband for his contacts and bagged him.

She asked, 'It's true then? The company has gone to the wall? I read about it in the *Guardian*.'

'You read it in the *Guardian*? You mean David didn't tell you we were in deep trouble? No – forget that – he didn't tell me either.'

He didn't tell me either. Janet detected a remark made for the record. Jeremy probably assumed the police were listening in.

'How much has gone?'

A pause.

'Who knows? A couple of million for certain, but I'd bet on it being a hell of lot more. The investments are all over the place and it takes time to check them out, and some you don't know if they're good until they mature and you discover whether the debtor pays up.'

'And you didn't know what was going on?'

'Is there an implication behind that question?'

'You were the senior partner.'

'In name . . . just in bloody name!'

'Are you saying that David was running the company? That's convenient, isn't it? A dead man!'

If Jeremy wasn't frightened, he put on a good imitation – though, of course, a guilty man would also have good reason to be frightened. He said, 'Ask yourself: who was the accountant? Who was in the best position to know about banks, bonds, credit swaps and god-knows-what?'

'He worked for a local authority, Jeremy. He drew up the housing department budget and paid out grants to charities to build sheltered accommodation. It's not exactly the City of London, is it?'

'And the Icelanders used to flog fish until they discovered the charms of banking. I worked in advertising and IT. Between the pair of us, who do you think was best qualified to run the show?'

Neither of you, apparently.

'I'm going to end this call now,' Janet said. She was finding herself unaccountably sympathetic to Jeremy and that wouldn't do at all. She thought she'd handled the call well – very coolly in fact – but she couldn't count on keeping it up. And she knew there'd be a price to pay.

'Goodbye, Jeremy.'

'What? Oh, yes, goodbye.'

Janet felt tears running down her cheeks once again. *At least I'm not having a fit of hysterics.* And then, of all things, she couldn't find where, in the unfamiliar kitchen, she'd put the biscuits to have with a cup of tea. She stood by the kitchen sink with both hands clutched over the lip until her fingers were white. She shook with sobs.

Probably I *am* suffering from depression, Janet told herself, though between the crying jags she felt remarkably cheerful. She wasn't sure how far grief and depression were different or the same thing. She supposed that, when one was depressed, one felt . . . well, *depressed.* Instead of which she felt a sort of philosophical sadness that was only intermittent and seemed perfectly rational. Wasn't it after all appropriate to feel sad at growing older (not that sixty was old) and the loss of a man she loved? The crying might have nothing to do with it. Just the fading memory of the bloody menopause as she'd suggested to Belle.

Well sod the menopause and Jeremy Vavasour with it. And sod David, too, if he was going to interfere with the business of getting on with the rest of her life. His memory would have to learn to mind its manners and speak only when it was spoken to. That was how her dead parents behaved, and these days the three of them got on very well together, and they occasionally gave her useful advice.

She found the biscuits and made another cup of tea, and when she was finished she decided she ought to call Helen again. But before she did that she remembered that in their last conversation Helen had been emphatic that Jeremy had wanted to speak to her; it was partly why Janet had phoned him. So what was odd about the call?

Jeremy hadn't asked her about anything. That was it. According to Helen he wanted to talk to her, supposedly about the company, but when it came down to it he hadn't actually pressed her with any real questions. It was as though he was just going through the motions: doing those things that an innocent man would do and using the opportunity to get his protestations of ignorance onto tape.

Or was she simply biased against him? Perhaps he hadn't put his questions because it was she who'd called him and he'd been taken by surprise and the call was over before he collected his thoughts? Or perhaps he was indeed a slippery piece of work and trying to manipulate appearances exactly as she suspected, yet wholly uninvolved in the deals that had brought the company down? The confusing and not very helpful truth was that it was difficult to read other people.

Almost as difficult as reading one's own character – a matter about which people are such dreadful liars to themselves.

'What I most regret in life is murdering my husband . . . '

Why on earth did I write that? Even if I thought it, why write it?

'Helen.'

'Mum.'

'Is Henry there?'

'No. He's having a bore-fest with his pals at the golf club.'

'You sound cross with me.'

'I think I'm keeping my temper very well in the circumstances. You've still not told me where you are exactly, and you have your mobile switched off all the time. Which means I'm the one still fielding the calls from the police, not to mention Jeremy-bloody-Thingummy.'

'I've spoken to Jeremy.'

'Hurrah.'

'He blames your father for the company going under. He doesn't come out with it but he implies that some of what was going on was fraudulent.'

That put an end to the flat tone in Helen's voice.

'Not Dad! No way! He was too . . . too . . . Well, for one thing he was too big an idiot. Lovely with it, of course,' she added.

'Of course.'

'If he was involved in something – and there's no way he would be – there'd have to be someone with far more brains and *commonsense* behind him.'

'Yes, I think you're right.'

'*You've* got more brains and commonsense than Dad ever had.'

'You're starting to make him sound like a moron, and he was certainly never that.'

'No, no, I didn't mean that!'

There followed a pause; then gradually a chuckle; and finally they were both laughing at the memory of David Bretherton. In life he'd always disarmed them like that, and now he was doing it in death too.

Then Helen was back to business.

'The bank has been on the phone to you. I've been to the house to sort the mail, throw away the junk and . . . '

'I should have redirected the post.'

'There were half a dozen calls from the bank on the answering machine.'

'I'm not overdrawn,' Janet said, which sounded feeble, even bizarre, but she couldn't think why the bank would want to speak with her.

'And then they wrote,' said Helen. 'I opened the letter. I didn't know what else to do, given they seemed to be making such a fuss and they wouldn't speak to me and I couldn't forward anything to you.'

'I understand. Really I do.'

'I hope so. Because the letter was a bit of surprise.'

'Oh? I . . . Do I need to prepare myself for a shock?' Janet wondered if she was about to be told that the matters Jeremy had hinted at were all true and David had cleaned out their savings, mortgaged the house and done God knew what else. Why did she think it was even vaguely plausible, other than that, in the end, almost anything was credible about men?

'It's something to do with money-laundering regulations, apparently,' said Helen. 'It seems that someone has paid a hundred thousand pounds into your account – *your* account, not the one you and Dad share. The money just turned up. Paid in with no explanation. From some place abroad.'

Janet had no answer.

Helen said sceptically, 'It's a bit of a puzzle – isn't it?'

6

Make two double stitches. Leave a space of a centimetre or so along the threads; then tie a further double stitch. Close the space by sliding this third stitch along the anchor thread so that it sits alongside the other two. You will remember that stitches slide only along the anchor thread, and so the effect of closing the gap is to leave the working thread at its original length, causing it to slacken and form a loop. In tatting this is called a 'picot'.

Picots can be used to decorate either loops or chains, so that they form a pattern of stitches and picots; or they can be used to join two sections of a design by drawing a thread through the picot and in effect tying the parts together.

Joy hadn't expected to join The English Lady Murderers' Society. Quite the contrary: in the shop, when she overheard Earthy saying something or other to Carol about it, she felt a pang of disappointment that she would of course be excluded. It was a reaction so automatic it never occurred to her even to question the assumption. In any case she knew the explanation. She was boring and pathetic.

'I'll never know how I came to marry such a dull woman,' Arnold told her all the time in his ungracious way.

Possibly because I was twenty-five years younger than you, Joy thought.

And possibly because I was quite pretty – though she was less sure on this point since, unlike age, prettiness was something about which one could be mistaken, and the memory played tricks.

To be fair to Arnold, fifteen years ago he'd been an attractive man: well made, with large forceful features and a voice like the voice of God, always assuming God had come from Dudley and prided himself on being, as Arnold said of himself, 'the largest independent dealer in pre-owned mid-range cars in the West Midlands'.

Joy had been thirty and Arnold fifty-five. As far as she could gather, his first wife, the sainted Kathleen, suffered from depression and finally killed herself quietly and without fuss – possibly fearing that Arnold would criticise her even in the afterlife if she did otherwise. She took a mess of tablets and Arnold found her. Now, when he was feeling maudlin after a Masonic dinner, he would describe the event, making it sound like the discovery of Ophelia's drowned corpse: Kathleen all pale, beautiful and covered with flowers; though, as Joy understood these matters, it was more likely she was soaked in vomit and wearing an expression suggestive of second thoughts. Joy sometimes found herself in her low moments addressing prayers to her deceased predecessor, hoping for a revelation or at least a few tips on handling Arnold. Perhaps suicide was one.

Then Veronica had approached her – again it was in the shop – mentioning the inaugural meeting of the women's group, which at that time didn't have a name, and treating it as understood that Joy would be attending. She'd been so surprised and flustered she thought she must have seemed like an idiot.

'But I haven't been asked,' she stammered.

'I'm asking you,' said Veronica.

'I . . . Do I have to bring anything?'

'I shouldn't think so. I don't intend to.'

Joy didn't know what to say. It was absurd really, but she felt as if Veronica had done her a great kindness: as if they'd been close friends for a long time and Joy had inexplicably forgotten the fact. She was so excited she even told Arnold, but he said only, 'Isn't she a lezzie? You're not turning that way, are you?'

'No, Arnold,' Joy said. In fact it hadn't crossed her mind that Veronica had asked her out of anything other than friendship.

Arnold didn't go on about it. He never needed to. His put-downs were always economical, relying on force of character.

But they were effective. Joy enjoyed the first meeting of The English Lady Murderers' Society; yet she thought how much more fun it would have been if only Arnold had sensed her delight and been happy she was doing something that gave her pleasure. Instead he spoiled the experience with his suggestion of ulterior motives. On the day, as with everything she did, she found herself asking, 'What would Arnold think?' And the thought impoverished her.

Joy had never heard of tatting. She had a notion of lace but couldn't tell the different kinds apart. It was fortunate she had no great interest in the subject because ('What would Arnold think?') her husband disliked anything he considered 'fussy', whether it was furnishings, food or suicides, and wouldn't have tolerated anything in the least lacy. She didn't know any stories involving lace and didn't expect to tell any. In fact she hadn't expect to say anything very much, since for the last few years she'd been hardly anywhere without Arnold; and he spoke enough for both of them – if not for several more.

And then, at Belle's, she found herself in the company of the other women, who all chatted away warmly and paid attention as Belle showed them how to tie double stitches and picots, and laughed at each other as they fumbled in their attempts to reproduce her deftness. She gave it a go and was pleased to discover she could manage as well as the others (and better than Earthy whose fingers were hampered by the chunky New Age rings she wore). It was difficult not to enjoy herself despite the scornful shadow of Arnold.

She particularly liked the stories. Belle, all large gestures, arms flailing, gurning and pouting, was wonderfully funny as she told how she'd acquired the skill of tatting from her dreadful mother. Janet's account of holidays in Venice and Madeira was a tender one: Joy was surprised at its intimacy, at Janet's lack of concern in making her revelation. She thought with a twinge of jealousy how naturally elegant the other woman was, and what confidence it must take to run such risk of self-disclosure. Then Veronica joined in with a simple story about buying a christening robe at an antiques fair. She told it in her cool, mildly amused way, as though it had no particular meaning, even though it seemed obvious to Joy that it had something to do with not having children, since lesbians clearly couldn't have children and it was natural they would have regrets about the matter as Joy, who had no children, also had regrets. Arnold had two: Spencer and Alan, both of them surly and frankly not very nice.

Then, to her own surprise, she found herself talking – perhaps with the same surprise that people at religious revivals find themselves 'speaking in tongues', somehow overcome by the Spirit, or at all events moved to an enthusiasm out of the ordinary. It felt as if she'd been visited with an insight into something profound, something the other women would understand and thank her for because until now no one had ever expressed it so clearly. Which admittedly was a lot to expect of a few remarks about curtains.

And what was it she'd actually said? She couldn't remember. It was something about the way that lace curtains screen off the interior from the exterior of life. Nowadays people pursued their lives in public as if everything needed a poll of readers of *Hello* magazine. But in the past the private sphere was exactly that: *private*. What Joy wanted to know – dearly wanted to know – was whether there was a place somewhere between the secrecy of the private and the vulgarity of the public world: a space where women could talk to each other with confidence. She supposed there was because the others seemed to belong to it. And Joy wanted it so desperately.

Instead she was trapped in the big house at Campmaurice, alone for the most part while Arnold spent hours in his own room hammering away at his computer. He was running the business remotely, he said. That was the way things were done nowadays in the new electronic age.

She was left to pass her days at make-work in a house that was already too clean for comfort; or to stomp up and down the road to Puybrun on her sturdy legs, occupying herself with unimportant errands; or to stare through the windows and catch the excitement of a tractor in the lane, or an escaped hen, or a holidaymaker who'd lost his way on a walk. The truth was that she felt at times as if she were viewing life through a lace curtain, trapped in a world of respectability and unspoken secrets.

Carol didn't tell any stories about lace. Tatting held an interest for her as an artist, but – face it – the results, all those dainty and useless bits of lace-edged cloth, were total crap. And the thing was, everyone *knew* they were, even Belle whose interest was obviously no more than sentimental, a part of the fraught relationship she had with her bloody mother.

Yet . . . yet . . . In a corner of her mind Carol could imagine subverting the form: making something different out of tatting: a work that would expose its pretence. How about a pair of baby bootees? Stuffed full of rotten meat, humming with flies and oozing blood? Yesss!

The trouble was you couldn't sell that in the market at Espéraza or to browsing English tourists fingering the goods in her studio with half a mind on whether to buy a cottage in Puybrun because it was cheaper than the Dordogne.

Carol tied a few stitches, made a chain and a ring with a handful of picots to decorate them, and fastened several pieces together. Easy-peasy. She went outside for a smoke. Poppy was there, watching swallows circle and dragging on an American cigarette. She glanced at Carol.

'It's a bit poxy – tattin' – innit?' she drawled. 'Still, it's sumfink to do.'

'Yeah,' Carol agreed, but wondered if Poppy were having her on. Surely that accent couldn't be real? Estuary English was one thing, but Poppy spoke like a costermonger's daughter in an amateur play. She could be Eliza Dolittle: her beauty was just as luminous as Audrey Hepburn's in *My Fair Lady*. Any moment now and she'd cry out, 'I'm a good girl, I am, 'Enery 'Iggins!'

And I'm an ugly bitch with a face like a crumpled paper bag, though I used to be beautiful once. That's cigarettes and sunshine for you. Sod them.

Carol burned with dissatisfaction and knew it. Every few years she upped sticks entirely, abandoned the old life and took on a new one. Where had she lived in her time and for how long? Paris (expensive and overrated). Seville (beautiful but provincial). Naples (she'd rather not think about it). The Greek Islands (a succession of villages boring enough to drive you to despair after a few weeks, though Mnemonikos wasn't bad). Were any of them an improvement on her tentative beginnings in the roving life: a tinker's camp near Luton, not long after leaving art school?

And the men!

A few weeks ago, she and Belle had spent an evening introducing themselves. They put away a couple of bottles of wine and Carol found herself talking about her past while incidentally picking up another version of Belle's life with Ma.

A few glasses into the session Carol was in tears of laughter and confessed, 'I've slept with enough guys called Dave to earn points and a discount from the next one I shag!'

'I don't remember any Daves. A Derek once.'

'I've also done a Colin, a Paul, a Ned (posh, that one), a Damian (ten years younger than me but ugly with it) – and even a Barry, God help me!'

There were also the anonymous gropers met at parties and in pubs when she was feeling low. And foreigners: the Pierres and Pedros and the Greeks with unpronounceable names. She'd even slept with women once or twice and didn't mind, but saw nothing in it to make it a habit – though admittedly none of them had been as transcendently lovely as Poppy (shame about the voice).

'And what's it about, eh' she wondered, leaning to fix Belle with an earnest though out of focus gaze. 'All the moving around and screwing? What's it all for? I suppose some cod psychologist could give me an explanation. But is there any point in finding out?'

'Why am I always going on about my Mum?' Belle asked.

'Exactly! You know in your heart that any explanation will be dreary and the knowledge won't be any damned use. In my experience any improvement that depends on changing the real you – the one that's been getting you into trouble and making bad decisions all your life – is doomed to failure.' Carol waved her arms dismissively. 'A few weeks of enthusiasm and then back to the same old ways.'

The memory of that conversation – and the hangover next day – faded.

'I'm going back in,' said Poppy, stubbing her cigarette in a patch of stonecrop.

'I'll join you,' said Carol and followed.

What a beautiful bum, she thought.

Earthy was still struggling with her tatting when Carol and Poppy came back into the house. Her various productions were scattered on a coffee table in front of her, all of them flawed with knots or rips or coffee stains. She smiled at them; they might have been naughty children who had somehow got away from her. She looked at her fingers.

I should take off my rings, she thought. Each finger held several: a Celtic design in pewter; a silver one with an enormous cairngorm; an Italian poisoner's ring that probably wasn't; a moonstone set in a band with Fëanorian lettering; and so on. At a guess she had a hundred rings and probably the same number of necklaces and bracelets. Each of them had its particular energy, and studying the combinations in which they should be worn in order to harness and balance the celestial and tellurian forces within them was an art in itself. Sometimes on certain days she would know what jewellery to wear; she would just *know*. It was a gift, but she would experience the most dreadful panic if she couldn't find the pieces she needed. Then on other days she'd have no sense at all of what was necessary; and on those occasions she could find herself paralysed into inaction. The jewellery was a comfort because it empowered her. But at times it was such a burden.

How beautiful the lace was that Belle's mother had made. Earthy examined it intently and saw what apparently Belle and all the others had missed: the way that Alice had worked magick into her designs. It was cunningly done, nothing too obvious; but if you had an eye, you could see the pentacles and signs for earth, fire, air and water, and read the symbolism of the flowers embroidered here and there in coloured silks. Belle's description of Alice didn't strike Earthy as in the least funny. Alice had known the importance of her work and her care in disposing it around the house had been no more than that which any Wise Woman would take to protect her family against the evil and chaos around them.

Alice had been misunderstood. Earthy too was misunderstood, but she accepted her fate and tried to smile benignly at it.

'Shall I make tea?' she offered.

Janet was ambling down the lane to her house after the second tatting session when her mobile rang. When she answered it an unfamiliar English voice spoke, she thought: Damn it, I meant to switch the thing off.

'Hullo, Mrs Bretherton?' said the voice.

'Possibly.'

'Only "possibly"?'

'Very well, Janet Bretherton speaking.'

'That's better,' said the voice. It was deep and engagingly cheerful. Janet was attracted by voices. It was why she liked listening to the radio. The men were so good looking.

'Who am I speaking to?'

'Stephen Gregg.'

'I've never heard of you.' Janet thought she could afford to be rude, but most likely only because she was cross with herself for leaving the phone on.

'*Inspector* Stephen Gregg. Police? You must have heard of us. We dress in blue and wear pointy hats. If we're good, they let us direct traffic.'

Janet laughed. 'You've been talking to Helen, haven't you?'

'She said you have a sense of humour. "Quirky" – I'm quoting her.'

'Children can be quite cruel in their observations.'

'Don't tell me. I have two.'

'Oh, what ages?'

'Fifteen and eighteen.'

'Boys? Girls? In between?'

The caller chuckled. 'Do you mind if we change the subject? I think I've used up the department budget for flirtation; so I'd better get back to the day job. Do you mind telling me where you are?'

'France.'

'Where in France?'

'You know, I'd rather not say. Not now. Not just at the moment. I know you'll be able to trace me by the mobile phone signal or somehow, but it may take a day or two, and I'm weary, and time is rather precious to me.'

'Yes,' said Stephen Gregg. He didn't try to pressure her nor mutter any sympathies. Janet read into that simple 'yes' a plain unvarnished understanding, and liked him for it.

But, of course, one could be mistaken about people – and so often was.

'I'll tell you what,' said Inspector Gregg. 'Would you mind answering a question or two until I find time to hunt you down and sling you in prison for being annoying?'

'I suppose so.'

'I shan't bother to ask whether you knew that Vavasour & Bretherton was robbing its clients blind.'

'That's kind of you.'

'It doesn't mean you can't tell me.'

'I didn't know.'

'Ah well, there goes my hope of a confession. I suppose I'll have to do some detecting. What can you tell me about the hundred thousand pounds paid into your bank account only two weeks ago?'

'Nothing. I'd never heard about it until Helen mentioned it.'

'Did anyone owe you a hundred thousand pounds?'

'No.'

'Did anyone owe your late husband such a sum? They may have paid it into your account by mistake or because you're his widow.'

'David and I aren't the sort of people that anyone owes a hundred thousand pounds to. The idea's ridiculous.'

'Specifically: Zarathustra Fidei-Anstalt.'

'I can't even pronounce it,' Janet said. Yet there was something in the name she recognised. Zarathustra was a character in a book by the philosopher Nietzschze, and Nietzsche had died of syphilis. It was one of those trivial facts that David was always parading – as a sort of substitute for real knowledge or insight, or so it seemed. No doubt it was supposed to mean something, but Janet could never pay attention long enough to find out what.

Gregg anticipated her question. 'It's sort of trust based in Luxembourg.'

'What is it for? Who's behind it?'

'Wouldn't we all like to know? I've spent a year trying to discover the answers.'

Janet caught the implication: that Gregg's investigations dated from before David's death; from before the collapse of the company.

'So far I've managed only one nugget of information,' Gregg went on. 'And I've got to say it puzzles me. You see, the only person with authorised access to the ZFA bank account is called David Bretherton.'

'David? My David?'

'Yes. And you do understand what that signifies? The fact that the transfer to your account was authorised only two weeks ago?'

'You're suggesting that David is still alive?'

It was a question that didn't really invite an answer, for the facts spoke for themselves.

'I don't know about that, but I *should* like to talk to you, Mrs Bretherton,' said the Inspector in the same relaxed tone. 'I'm sure there's an explanation for everything, but at the moment we don't know what it is. You see: the money transfer indicates that your husband is still alive. And in that case we have a mysterious body on our hands, don't we? The one that was found in his car three months ago.'

'I identified David,' Janet said.

'I'm aware of that,' said Gregg.

'And the body wasn't injured or burned and I didn't have to identify it by the teeth or the jewellery or in some other silly way. I saw him as plain as day and knew him straight away.'

'I know,' said Gregg. He waited for her to speak further, and when she didn't, he said, 'And that's our problem, isn't it? You identified the body.'

LESSON THREE

How to Dance the Tango

7

Tango is a dance of the slums and brothels of Buenos Aires. Its origins lie in the *milonga* and the *candombe*, partly as a parody of black dance by the city's swaggering underclass of *compadritos*. The characteristic instrument of tango music is the *bandoneon*, a formidable development of the piano accordion that gives the music its force and sonority.

The dance crossed the Atlantic in the first decade of the twentieth century and caused a sensation in 1913, 'the year of the tango'. The notably married and clean living dancers, Irene and Vernon Castle, adapted the steps to European bourgeois morals and made it respectable. When Irene wrote: 'If Vernon had ever looked into my eyes with smouldering passion during the tango, we would have both burst out laughing,' the dance died.

The tango was at one time the most popular dance in Finland.

Janet knew she was mad to offer to teach the tango. For one thing, she didn't really know how to do it.

She'd danced from being a child. Her uncles were dancing men: tall and graceful; and her father had supplemented his earnings as a coal heaver by playing the piano in working men's clubs. At home at Christmas and birthdays he would beat out a tune and they would pull up the carpet and dance. And at weddings the uncles would sweep every woman in sight off her feet and quickstep or foxtrot across the floor of the local Co-op ballroom. Even the disreputable Catholic side of the family did Irish jigs.

David knew only a basic waltz step learned in the school gym at the age of ten. His efforts at anything modern were embarrassing and rarely attempted while sober. Like most men (if one excluded blacks, foreigners and homosexuals, of course) he assumed that this was the natural condition of the male sex.

He even used the same language they all used. He'd say, 'I've got two left feet,' as if there were only one pair of feet in the world, which men passed between them as part of a conspiracy.

Then one year, with a Christmas dance in the offing, he pulled a small ad from the local evening paper that advertised a dance school, and proposed that they go there. This was twenty years ago, when he was about forty years old, and possibly it was a last effort at adventure or sheer recklessness – Janet never really understood but was grateful. And to universal astonishment he found he liked it. Even more, he was actually quite good in a flashy, undisciplined way. Since then they'd danced at every possible opportunity. In Barcelona they hunted down a sleazy salsa club where elderly men took their mistresses. In France, they danced to the music of the show bands who toured through the summer bringing a parody of Las Vegas cabaret to quiet villages and provincial towns. And in general they made a fool of themselves in public places out of love and lust for life.

Once the children had grown up, Janet wondered how she and David would have continued if they hadn't danced. Would they have been able to go on if he'd simply grown florid, seedy and boring, and she'd become . . . what? She wondered sometimes at such unknowable lives in other universes: the lives that might have happened but didn't.

Still the fact was that they didn't tango. Not in a way that would pass muster. They'd learned a little at dance school, but afterwards there'd been no opportunity to practise at the sort of event they normally went to. It was a dance that had dropped out of fashion in England sometime between the Wars. It survived only as a set sequence, 'the square tango' that elderly ladies with large bosoms did, trundling each other round the floor as if pushing a pram with a stuck wheel.

It didn't mean they never tried. Both of them were up for it if occasion arose. And sometimes it did. The French included different dances in their repertoire, and the tango was one. Perfectly respectable elderly people, attending an equally respectable *bal musette* held in a covered market on a balmy evening, would rise to the clarion call of a fiddle or piano accordion, grasp their partners in a close embrace, and fling them about the floor as if suddenly remembering some very disreputable sexual encounters – not necessarily with each other. On such occasions Janet and her husband would join in, and David would exercise his talent for improvisation and Janet hers for being led into any step he cared to invent, and at the end they would hoot with laughter and clap with the other dancers and collapse exhausted onto the nearest chair.

But none of it amounted to knowing how to dance the tango.

After the success of tatting, Janet volunteered to lead the next session. She felt that, after Belle, she was responsible for starting the group and that some of the others still needed time to gain confidence or simply come up with ideas.

God alone knew why she chose to teach the tango. She supposed that, in a subconscious way, she wanted to talk about David and this was as close as she could come. Certainly she wasn't going to open up her marriage in front of all the others; she'd hardly discussed it even with Belle. At most she'd let slip some bits and pieces as they exchanged small talk over tea while the invisible Charlie beavered away in his workshop.

'He's building a scale model of the *Sir Nigel Gresley*,' Belle said. 'I think it's a train. Don't say anything. Leave me to my private grief.'

It was in a general conversation about Men, that Janet mentioned Jeremy Vavasour.

'He's one of those people you can't believe are entirely real,' she said. 'I don't know whether it's because they adopt an image of themselves from something they've seen or read, and think that's how they're supposed to behave. It's particularly noticeable

73

with him because there's something old-fashioned in the idea of upper class types, driving around in sports cars and pinching the bums of any girls they fancy – not that I know if Jeremy has a sports car or pinches bums.'

'I know what you mean,' said Belle. 'He sounds like one of those posh spivs the writers of *The Archers* come up with when they want to give one of their female characters an Unfortunate Romance.'

'Exactly!'

Belle pooh-poohed Janet's reservations about the tango.

'It doesn't matter. You don't suppose any of us is actually going to take up doing it afterwards, do you? Everyone seems to have enjoyed my lessons in tatting, but I think the World's safe from a plague of frilly wotsits. And who would we dance with? I can't see Charlie taking to it, nor Arnold from what I've heard. Veronica and Poppy, just maybe . . . '

Yes, it was possible to imagine Veronica in a beautifully cut tuxedo leading out Poppy in a fabulous frock by Balenciaga. Though not in the *halle* in Puybrun, obviously.

'If we'd wanted to learn something practical, we could have taken up computing,' said Belle.

Computing was Joy's idea. With Arnold locked in his room working, or back in England keeping tabs on the business even though he was retired, Joy was lonely in the house at Camp-maurice, living in a hamlet where scarcely a soul passed all day and no one visited. She'd heard of e-mail and vaguely about social networking sites and she thought that, if she had a computer of her own, she could keep in touch with friends at home (not that there were any really) or with Arnold when he was away, or she could make new friends through Facepage or whatever it was called. But evidently, if it were to happen at all, she would have to arrange it for herself: Arnold would have nothing to do with it.

'It's too complicated for you, and at your age you're too stuck in your ways to learn anything new,' he said.

I'm not an idiot, she wanted to tell him. And when did you learn? Not till you were well into your sixties and had retired and were looking for something to do. And now I can't get you off your machine.

But she said nothing. Instead she raised the subject with the others only to find that all of them – even Earthy – had access to PCs and knew enough to manage their daily lives: certainly more than could be taught in a few afternoon lessons punctuated with gossip. Carol and Veronica, indeed, were quite expert for professional reasons: Carol used photographic software in some of her complicated art productions; and Veronica because of her high-powered job in banking that required spreadsheets and data bases and risk-analysis models (whatever any of that meant).

Joy thought it would be one more thing to add to her heap of failures. Then Veronica, who seemed to have noticed her look of disappointment, said in a surprisingly sympathetic way, 'Look, if you want to, I can get you started. A few hours training will set you up with basic e-mail and how to use the internet and from there you can probably find everything else you need on your own.'

Joy was grateful beyond words, just to know that someone else didn't think she was a complete moron.

Inspector Gregg called again.

'Have you found out where I am?' Janet asked.

'Oh yes, that was easy. You're in a village called Puybrun, in the Aude. I can't say I know it, though my wife and I once visited Carcassonne.'

'Carcassonne's about an hour away. These days you can get cheap flights from Liverpool.'

'I must remember that.'

'Does it mean I'll be seeing you?' Oddly enough Janet thought she wouldn't in the least have minded seeing him face to face; his voice was so attractive.

'I don't know. You didn't murder your husband did you? If you did, I could probably persuade my boss to chip in for an air fare.'

'No, I didn't. In any case I got the impression you thought he was alive. Wasn't he responsible for paying a hundred thousand pounds into my bank account?'

'It looks that way. We've been doing further checks and it seems certain that the Zarathustra Fidei-Anstalt was controlled by your husband. Which means we still have a problem with the identity of the dead man you identified as David Bretherton.'

'Because he *was* David Bretherton,' said Janet.

There was a pause.

Gregg asked, 'Are you all right?'

'No, I'm crying. It's not your fault. These days it's something I do all the time for no good reason.'

'I really don't want to upset you.'

'I'm sure you don't. You seem to be a nice person.'

'I don't know if I'm nice or not. I'm a copper doing his job. And that brings me to the point of this call. Would you have an objection if we exhumed the body . . . your husband's body? Now you're laughing. Why are you laughing?'

'Because you seem to have made a slip for once. David was cremated.'

'Ah – was that at his request?'

'He never expressed an opinion. He was indifferent to death. It was my decision.'

'I see.'

Janet got the impression Gregg was talking to someone. She thought she heard a muffled 'Fuck!' She remembered Jeremy's assumption that his calls were being tapped (even if he hadn't actually said it). It seemed that these days everyone was spying on everyone else.

Gregg said, 'This is going to sound offensive – in fact I think it *is* offensive, but I have to ask. Did anyone except you see the body after death?'

'Ambulance men, doctors, whoever performed the post mortem.'

'I'm thinking of people who knew David, people who could make a reliable identification and confirm yours. Your daughter or son-in-law for example?'

'No. Helen was too upset, and Henry . . . He isn't a sentimental man.'

'That's a pity.'

'I didn't kill David,' said Janet. 'He died of a stroke. Neither did I kill anyone else.'

Stephen Gregg didn't answer.

It got worse. Janet had committed to teach the tango but given no thought to where it was all supposed to happen. Not in her cottage, where none of the rooms was big enough, nor in Belle's for the same reason. In fact the only suitable spot was the *halle*, with its large smooth floor. Her humiliation, if it came, was likely to be a public one.

She hadn't given thought to music either.

'The *halle*'s easy enough sorted,' said Belle. She accompanied Janet to the mairie, where Monsieur le Maire was delighted to oblige, not least because his wife Sandrine ran the Bar des Sports immediately next to the covered area and the tango class would provide entertainment for her customers.

Oh God! thought Janet when she heard.

'I haven't got any tango CDs with me,' she said. 'And a tinny little player won't be of any use in that space.'

They were taking a coffee at the bar and Sandrine overheard. 'It will not be a problem,' she interrupted. 'I ask Marcel for you – Marcel who play the accordion and know the tango.'

Marcel was sadly obliging. He was happy to play for an hour

in exchange for a glass of red wine and any tips that came his way. After all, it was what he did every Wednesday evening during the *nocturnes d'été*, the only difference being the repertoire. And tango? What accordion player worth his salt couldn't play the tango? *Bof!*

There was nothing for it but to go ahead and pick a time when no one was likely to be watching: the early afternoon, when dogs doze and everyone is at lunch and even the bar closed because Sandrine would be serving *merguez-frites* to campers at the *buvette* by the lake.

And so they assembled, all of them. Belle wore one of her dramatically patterned tent-dresses. Earthy was arrayed in her usual bag lady chic. Joy was in shorts and a polo shirt; Carol in a check shirt and jeans; Veronica in a beautiful but severe blouse and slacks; and Poppy in a stunning black dress, quite perfect for dancing. To which add two pairs of flat pumps, one pair of trainers, Poppy's fabulous handmade dance shoes, Carol's Doc Martens, and Earthy's barely describable footwear, which vaguely resembled something put together by a Native American from road kill.

Contrary to expectation, the bar was open with a fair sized clientele; and a crowd of twenty or so, including some hungry campers denied their lunch at the *buvette*, had gathered in the square to chat and keep an eye on the antics of the English.

If only they knew what we call ourselves, Janet thought. She smiled at the others. Courage, girls! Let's hear it for The English Lady Murderers' Society!

Marcel lounged by one of the columns supporting the roof, a glass of wine beside him and a cigarette glued to his lip, and obliged his employers with *La Cumparsita*. As tangos go, this one was a classic if something of a cliché; but it came to Janet as a relief after fifteen minutes of pairing off the others and drilling them in the basic step without benefit of music. She imagined they must look like conscripts to a shambolic army.

Neither was pairing easy. It seemed natural to put Veronica with Poppy; and Joy and Carol were of similar height and build. But Belle and Earthy? It was impossible to get them into anything even approximating a dance hold: rather they looked like two fairground cars butted nose to nose with the drivers frantically waving at each other to get out of the way.

How to put it tactfully?

'This isn't going to work, is it?' said Belle.

'No,' said Janet.

'Someone ought to tell Earthy about her weight.'

'Possibly.'

'I'll do it. Earthy, you're a fat cow.'

'One of us definitely is,' said Earthy good-naturedly.

They switched and Belle danced with Joy, and Earthy partnered Carol. They took turns as to who led or followed.

'The measure in tango music has eight beats,' Janet began, hoping this might be true. She took them into the basic walk, the promenade and the *corte*. And to her astonishment something – a glimmer of the true dance – began to emerge. She didn't know where it came from: a feel for the music that all of them had to some extent; Belle's natural grace that allowed her to carry her weight with distinction; Earthy's innocent charm; Poppy's beauty; Veronica's intelligence. Only Joy seemed to have difficulty, but she smiled and stuck at it doggedly.

This is going to be a success, Janet thought.

And then she saw Léon and Ravi watching her, and her confidence flowed away.

8

Fred Astaire recommends that in tango the body should be kept tall with the knees slightly flexed. The step is similar to a walk without the rise and fall motion characteristic of the waltz or slow foxtrot. In the alternation of slow and quick steps, the slow should be held to the last moment before the opposite leg is moved. This gives a dramatic, staccato action characteristic of the dance.

Veronica had never lived with another woman until she took Poppy under her wing. She hadn't felt the need and, frankly, sharing a house or apartment was inconvenient: just a source of arguments over money and domestic arrangements. It wasn't that she lacked commitment: on the contrary she'd never cared for one-night-stands. Her affairs had always lasted a year or two and been fun, and they'd ended without recriminations; but she'd never wanted to live with her lovers. The truth was, she thought wryly, that she liked to be in control; she was used to bossing other people about, both at the bank and generally. It was love for Poppy and a desire to give her space that had toned down the former tendency to insist on her own way and made her a nicer person, she hoped. And Poppy had been biddable. She'd had few choices.

For a year or more Veronica been very close to Diana, an insurance broker five years younger than herself and different in temperament: less cool, more outgoing, flirtatious even. Veronica had never tried to join the 'lesbian scene', or indeed any 'scene'. She wanted the life of a cultivated, high-earning professional woman regardless of sexual preference. She enjoyed travel, theatre, ballet and good restaurants, not hanging about clubs, dressing too young and hoping to pull unsuitable girls who were years her junior.

'I think one should take a chance,' was Diana's attitude. She had a mischievous streak, which was probably why Veronica was drawn to her. It marked an attractive degree of difference between lives that were otherwise similar enough for them to feel safe with each other.

Diana picked the club from a lifestyle magazine: a fashionable dump on the south side of the Thames: a warehouse that hadn't yet been converted to studios. The place was stuffy and smelly and the noise was appalling; and everywhere girls were downing alcopops or swigging water to counter the effects of Extasy. Veronica hated it and knew she was at least fifteen years too old to be there.

Still, Diana liked the place and Veronica decided to make the best of the evening. She joined the press of bodies and found herself dancing with a girl scarcely more than twenty, who spoke badly and dressed badly, and had the face of an angel.

And today she was dancing with that same girl, taking her through the steps of the tango, assuming the role of the man and finding it erotic in its arrogance even though the two of them tackled the movements clumsily. Then, in a reversal because Janet wanted them to learn both parts, she was in turn led by Poppy and she let herself fall into the character demanded by the dance. It was a shock. She felt almost painfully feminine and filled with a brutal sadness. The force in Poppy's demeanour was terrifying, perhaps because her expression, which at times could seem vacuous, was for the moment one of . . . passion . . . love . . . uncertainty?

'I'm like the boss now, innit?' Poppy said softly. Her face was radiant, but Veronica found the meaning of that expression as unfathomable as all the others. Who was this person she adored so helplessly?

Four years before, in the club in Bermondsey, Poppy had been a Goth. And her name hadn't been Poppy. Veronica had invented her.

'Those two look as if they're up to no good,' Belle said when she noticed Léon and Ravi.

'As long as they don't throw eggs,' said Janet. Thank God, this was going well. No one had made a fool of herself and one or two of the holidaymakers had even joined in, coming up onto the floor and taking a position shadowing the women so they could follow the same steps.

'And as long as they don't make fun of us,' said Belle.

So far nobody was making fun; there was only some discreet pointing and a few good-natured chuckles. Belle hoped it would stay like that. Although she was thick skinned about her weight there were situations when she felt real hurt. Sometimes people made remarks with quite heartless viciousness. 'Look at you! I'm surprised you dare show yourself in public!' That was a good one, and Belle had heard all its variants. There seemed to be an assumption that with her weight came lumpish stupidity, and that she would feel an insult no more than a cow would feel a whack on the rump with a stick. Yet, ballet apart (for obvious reasons and much to Alice's chagrin), Belle was a graceful person, who loved to dance because she'd seen for herself that even people who were overweight or plain or downright ugly could appear beautiful if they did it well. Beautiful, that is, to everyone except people who had no sense of beauty: people who had to mock others in order to boost their own self esteem: people who themselves possessed a deep inner ugliness.

Fortunately good old Charlie had no trouble in taking her on, weight notwithstanding. Perhaps because he was a fat bugger himself and no picture by any standard. What they must look like in the street! Two characters out of Dickens, Belle suspected.

Charlie was thirty-nine when they met. She was thirty. Like any other female, she told herself, a fat woman can get a free fuck if she wants one. But she didn't want one – not after the first few – and nobody seemed inclined to offer her anything else. She was teaching and still living at home in her mother's hellhole of pristine lace, while Alice became progressively bizarre and Joe was within a year or two of keeling over with his heart. Her university friends had scattered to the four corners and now she was lumped with the other eager or desperate spinsters at school. If she didn't watch it she'd be condemned to a lifetime of Good Works.

She tried amateur dramatics. Pantomime dames are almost invariably men, but they were prepared to make an exception in her case: 'Because you're so outgoing.' *No thank you.* She received no other offers of acting roles and instead found herself plying her skills as a seamstress, making and repairing costumes. Then somebody said of her, 'This is our Belle. What can I say? She's a *treasure.*' Belle quit next day and never went back.

She gravitated to dancing with a fellow school teacher called Brenda, who was forty years old and a divorcee with a taste for drink and men with comb-overs. They attended classes in an upper room: the same that Joe had been to before the War. 'Bloody hell, are they still in business?' he said, when he learned. But this was Clitheroe, so of course they were.

Where on earth do they get them from? she wondered after reviewing the men. Those she didn't suspect of nameless crimes thought it was sophisticated to wear Boots' own-brand aftershave, and several seemed to have lost the power of speech. Still they were polite and one or two of them could dance. And they probably think the same of us, Belle supposed: that there's something *not quite right* about us.

But it was an unfair judgment, of course. One that was born of self doubt. Charlie didn't in the least fit the stereotype: he was well-dressed, witty and attractive in a golf club way – not exactly Belle's style, but something you could get used to. True, he was distinctly stout; and his face could be described as 'homely'. But he was also good tempered and respectable.

What do you *want*, woman? Belle asked herself.

Glamour. Passion. Admiration.

I'd settle for a size sixteen figure or to be able to wear narrow-fitting shoes.

But she settled for Charlie, and learned over the years that sometimes second best is best. And that none of it lasts.

'All change,' said Janet.

'I'll take the man's part,' said Carol, 'If that's all right with you. What do you think those two are up to?' She nodded in the direction of Léon and Ravi. They were lounging against one of the columns, talking to Marcel.

'I don't know. I don't care. This is going well isn't it?'

Two of the holidaymakers, Germans by the sound of them, had decided to throw away caution. One was dancing with Veronica and one with Poppy.

'They'll be out of luck there,' said Carol.

Marcel struck up with *Caminito* and after a few bars broke off while Janet went to sort out Joy, who was having difficulty remembering if she was dancing the man's or the woman's steps or indeed that there was a difference.

Belle said to Carol, 'When Charlie and me learned to dance, we used to do set routines – everybody did – and they started in one corner of the floor. Every time we were interrupted, we had to begin all over again, back in the same corner. You can always tell people who've learned to dance routines. They pile into a corner all on top of each other like hamsters in a cage.'

Janet came back and took up position again. Marcel resumed playing. Carol stepped out in a long fluid stride and took Janet into a couple of figures she didn't know, finishing with some elegant *ochos*.

'You've danced tango before,' said Janet.

Carol grunted.

'You photograph, you paint, you sculpt, you can tat. Is there anything you can't do?'

'Not much. I've had a rackety life.'

They broke off again for instruction. When Janet returned, Carol said, 'I can't pee over walls.'

'What?'

'Something I can't do. I can't pee over walls.'

'Can anybody?'

Carol shrugged. 'Men can. Leatherhead Dave could.'

In memory he became Leatherhead Dave to distinguish him from the other Daves. He was first of his line and named after his home town. Carol hooked up with him when she was twenty three, after her spell with the Luton tinkers, when she learned to trap rabbits – a skill not recently put to use. They met at a pub in London and Dave claimed to be a musician. He was putting together a band, he said, to take English pop music to benighted Argentina. In those days Carol didn't understand that being a musician was like being a Catholic: that music was a broad church welcoming even those who didn't practise.

They flew to Buenos Aires (Carol paying for both of them with borrowed money). The rest of the band would follow, Dave said. But they didn't. A change of plan was in order, which was how Carol discovered that her boyfriend thought he had a natural talent as a pimp.

In one version of this story, Leatherhead Dave gets his come-uppance and is knifed by Carol's jealous protector. But Carol and her listener have to be fairly drunk before she tells it. In reality Dave found that pimping was an overcrowded profession and his Spanish wasn't up to it; and so he cashed the return portion of Carol's airline ticket and went back to Surrey on his own.

Carol haunted the city's tango bars for a while and in the end, for want of choices, shacked with a middle aged bandoneon player called Pedro Something Italian. He was fat and amiable and helped her with accommodation and money in return for the usual services until she could scrape together the cost of a flight. At that point the honourable bargain between them came to an end without regrets either side.

For these reasons, Carol knew that Marcel was rubbish on the accordion and Janet didn't really know how to dance the tango.

The first hour's practice over, they agreed that they'd enjoyed their venture into the tango. Even the Germans.

'*Ausgezeichnet!*'

'Thank you.'

'*Bis nächstes Mal!*'

'Possibly.'

'I'll give you a hand next time, if you like,' said Carol.

'Would you?' said Janet. 'Thank God! I've shown them every tango step I know.'

They took coffee at one of the tables outside the Bar des Sports and chatted a while. Janet explained how she and her husband had learned to dance. Carol gave a sanitised account of her journey to Buenos Aires with Leatherhead Dave and the two months spent living with Pedro Something Italian until she raised her fare home.

'Story of my life,' said Carol. 'You'd think I'd learn, wouldn't you?'

'Perhaps you did,' Janet suggested. 'You're here on your own, aren't you? Not a Leatherhead Dave in sight.'

'Maybe. Yet, take that Ravi. It's obvious he's a complete shit; but if he wanted to give me a good seeing-to, I'd probably say "yes please".'

'Do you really think so?'

'Who the hell knows?'

Janet had no answer. Marital fidelity had been a condition of her existence; she'd never seriously contemplated the alternative. She suspected that what Carol called 'a rackety life' must be wearing on the nerves and couldn't imagine anyone wanting it. Even in her lowest moments, when David had been at his most selfish and stupid, her thoughts (other than plotting his murder) had never gone beyond getting a divorce. She certainly hadn't considered going through the whole business a second time with another husband who all reason told her was likely to be as bad as the first one. In the event, it was something she never had to put to the test; David became wiser or slower (the two can be indistinguishable), and they blundered their way into happiness – astonishing really.

'I'll see you tomorrow then,' Janet said and watched as Carol ambled down the lane to her nearby studio. It occurred to her that the other woman had taken a shine to her, perhaps because Janet represented a contrast: an embodiment of the other life that Carol would now never have: the one that was forever unknowable in the universe of different choices. She'd noticed too that Veronica seemed to have taken up Joy after a fashion, and wondered if something similar were going on.

When they resumed next day, Janet detected an air of real enthusiasm. It didn't surprise her because people whose minds aren't closed against dancing find themselves stimulated by it. The novelty gone, today there were fewer spectators, but a couple more Germans from the campsite had come along and joined their friends as part of the class as if they'd always been invited. Léon and Ravi also turned up.

Carol stubbed out a cigarette. 'How do you want to play this?'

'Be my guest,' said Janet.

Carol gave some instructions in English and repeated them in German.

'You speak German?' said Janet.

'I used to be roadie for a band.'

'I suppose the singer was called Dave, too?'

'No, Gunther actually,' said Carol.

'I was joking.'

'But close – Dave was the bastard who took me to Munich in the first place. Now, are we dancing or what?'

From the accordion came the first bars of *Adios Muchachos*, an old-fashioned, undemanding tune. In her no-nonsense way Carol put everyone through their paces. It seemed she applied a discipline to artistic matters that escaped the rest of her life. Another of those curious points of human nature, Janet thought, and wondered where the inconsistencies were in her own life. She partnered Earthy, who was remarkably light on her feet but floated through the dance without any sense of drama while throwing sidelong glances at Léon and Ravi. Surely . . . ?

Marcel finished his playing and took a mouthful of wine. Carol called five and started explaining some of the points of the steps in English and German. Léon meanwhile went over to the accordion player and had a few words with him.

The old fellow picked up his instrument again. This time he began a Carlos Gardel classic, *Volver*. Carol was taken by surprise and was about to turn on him, when Léon leapt onto the floor of the *halle*, and took Ravi in his arms and they began to dance together. Again Carol was about to speak, but there was nothing to say. The two men ignored her and swept across the floor.

Janet had seen men partner like this before, and it never failed to shock her because, quite contrary to what one might expect, the dance became a perfect fury of masculinity. Marcel seemed to pick up on it. His flaccid playing became sharper. The tempo of the music grew faster. The staccato rhythm became more pronounced, and as it did so the fierceness of the two men became even more marked so that you could almost imagine they hated each other. They grunted and cried between the steps. Fine droplets of sweat were flung off Léon's hair. Ravi's normal calm expression became a painful grimace. And there seemed no end to it for as long as Marcel was prepared to play, which he did, though increasingly chaotically as he lost track of the music and began to throw in phrases and snatches from other tunes he knew.

Across the floor they went, changing from male to female parts every few measures, their legs entwining as they stepped in and out of each other's space in a frantic display of *ganchos*. Marcel was beside himself with effort, now scarcely playing a tune at all, simply squeezing out raucous chords in a tango rhythm. When he slackened people urged him on with cries of *Encore!* or *More!* When he hesitated, the spectators took up the music by clapping in time. It seemed that there could be no end to it.

Then Marcel, in desperation it seemed, squeezed one shattering chord from his accordion and threw it onto the floor.

The clapping stopped, and the two dancers stopped with it. They grinned, wiped the sweat from their faces, and strolled off whistling.

9

In 1910 the Uruguayan singer, Lola Candales, asked the musician, Enrique Saborido, 'Please write a tango that may be sung in the presence of women without making them blush.' He did so, but some tango lovers think it was a mistake.

At breakfast Janet's phone rang.

'Inspector Gregg?'

But it was Helen. She said, 'You sound like you want to hear from him.'

'No need to be bad-tempered. I'm expecting a call. He has my number; and he wants me to help with his enquiries, as the police say.'

'He's short and middle-aged.'

'What does that have to do with anything?'

'I thought you'd appreciate the information. You like poking through the bars of the human zoo, stirring up the monkeys, don't you?'

Janet was puzzled.

'What's this about? Why are you being provocative?'

'Because I have to live with Henry and you don't.'

'I see. And what's happened now?'

Quite unexpectedly Helen began sobbing and Janet found herself saying soothing things as if suddenly her small child had come back.

Helen said, 'They've found parts of Dad – or, at least, someone who's supposed to be Dad.'

'What do you mean? I don't understand. Your father was cremated.'

'Well, was he? Oh, I don't know! The police say they've found some of his organs, kept back at the post mortem for tests that were never carried out.'

Janet felt oddly cool at this news. She'd held one funeral and got over it, and now her immediate thought was that she would have to organise a second and it seemed bizarrely comic. She was sure David would have laughed.

'They want to do tests,' Helen said. 'They want to know if the body we cremated really was Dad. I've had to go to the house with them to hunt for hair brushes and socks and dirty underpants so they can find some of his DNA.'

'I gave everything away to charity – well, not the dirty underpants, obviously.'

'They took a mouth swab from me.'

Janet was shocked. The procedure amounted to nothing, but she could imagine her daughter's sense of violation.

'I'm sorry you're having to go through all this,' she said and, when Helen didn't answer, added, 'Truly I am.' It was a sad coda. She felt she was being forced to sell her sincerity to her daughter as if it were PVC windows or a pension plan; having to make the extra effort because there was no longer the implicit trust. She supposed it was the general experience of parents and children.

'Apparently they think you may have murdered someone,' Helen said.

'So I gather, though I don't think Inspector Gregg really believes that.'

'He thinks you're clever enough to have done it – and to get away with it.'

'Really? I suppose I should be flattered. He's an odd man: he says what he thinks, exactly as your Dad did. Who does he think we cremated?'

'Some tramp or other.'

'A tramp? How old-fashioned, and a bit Agatha Christie. I don't think there are any tramps these days – not in the way there used to be. And in any case, in whodunits the tramp always turns out to be someone's lost business partner or a missing relative or of the opposite sex to what one thinks. I wonder who this one really is?'

'Sometimes you can be so literal.'

'It's just that, if we're going to be silly, at least we should be imaginative. Speaking purely artistically I would have had your father bump off Jeremy, then steal his identity in order to escape from his terrible crimes.'

'I used to hate it when you and Dad played games like this,' said Helen. 'I hope to God you're not giving me a clue.'

'Goodbye, darling,' Janet said gently.

'Goodbye, Mum – I love you.'

After the call Janet felt a need to go for a walk along the path by the lake. She was feeling angry, but didn't know with whom: Helen for her snitty manner; Henry for his insensitivity; Stephen Gregg for the misplaced doggedness of his enquiries and his disconcertingly attractive voice. And David of course for dying so unreasonably and because she knew in her heart that there was an explanation behind it that would be deeply stupid, David being who he was.

She distracted herself by going over the details of how she'd murdered him, and meanwhile wandered back along the path and past the *buvette* where Sandrine was just opening up. On the beach a group of pubescent teenagers were parading their attractive new parts before each other. In the place de l'Eglise she ran into Belle standing by the notice board outside the mairie.

'There's a dance at Le Peyrat on Saturday night,' she said. The poster advertised a *fête des rues* with various attractions including a band with a Spanish name that was probably misleading. The bands on the country circuit tried to cater for all tastes. Janet remembered one that comprised only grubby old rockers playing heavy metal, and a following of scrawny women with bleached hair and piercings.

'We could all go,' Belle suggested.

'It's unlikely they'll play much tango.'

'No, probably not. But we're in the mood for dancing, aren't we? What do you think? While we're about it, we can eat disgusting food and ride dodgem cars.'

Janet thought it was a good idea. They told the others.

Arnold had gone to England for a few weeks to see to his affairs as he did every summer. It was a relief because it meant Joy didn't have to tell him she wanted to go to the dance and bear with his grudging agreement and offensive remarks about her dyke pals (which in Arnold's eyes was all of the women). It also meant she didn't have to mention her plan to take lessons in using a computer.

It was really very good of Veronica. She probably had time on her hands, but even so. Joy cycled from Campmaurice to her friend's house in the village proper. It was one of the larger places that had probably belonged to a professional man such as a doctor. Like many of the village houses, it had fallen into semi-ruin until it was done up again. Veronica had bought it from a divorced English couple; then decorated it according to her impeccably restrained taste. Joy could hear Arnold saying, 'More money than sense,' though he was more than willing to spend money on luxury cars and golf clubs. She wished she could rid herself of his inner voice. It was like being haunted.

'What lovely pictures,' she said by way of an ice-breaker. The walls of the main room were painted a delicate off-white, the floor was of brecciate marble and the few items of furniture were Biedermeier; though Joy recognised none of it.

'Poppy's work,' said Veronica. Joy watched her brush her fingers across one of the watercolours. The other woman smiled. 'Would you like a drink? There's an open bottle of fizz in the fridge.'

'I won't – thanks,' said Joy. She accepted the slightly surprised response. 'I'm cycling,' she said and tried to laugh it off. 'I don't want to come off my bike, do I – not if we're going dancing tonight?'

'I suppose not,' said Veronica.

They sat facing each other. Veronica drank blanquette and Joy a glass of orange juice. Joy felt strangely as if she were on a date. She thought Veronica was very beautiful for her age and responded to her simply because one falls in love with beauty without regard for sex: in fact the sexual aspect never occurred to Joy, who had been substantially neutered by Arnold.

Veronica asked, 'Shall we begin?' and took silence as a 'yes', and led Joy to the smaller room set aside as her office.

They settled, and Veronica showed Joy how to boot up the computer, access the internet and set up an e-mail account.

Afterward Joy decided that it was time she changed appearance. She would have her hair cut, and for this evening she would wear a dress.

Janet called at Earthy's cottage to suggest she come to the fete.

'Oh, what a terrific idea!' said Earthy.

Janet hadn't been to Earthy's house before, and now she saw it she was surprised. It was unexpectedly middle-class with old-fashioned well-made furniture: not antique but the kind someone with a moderate amount of money and taste might have bought at Harrods or Heals forty years ago. Inherited, she supposed. It was too good for junk shops and cheap auctions. There was also a lot of rubbish that might be art, or magical items for use in Earthy's New Age fantasies, or stock for the stall she occupied at the local markets. It was difficult to be sure.

If she was selling the stuff, how could she possibly be making a living from it?

Earthy said, 'Aren't Ravi and Léon wonderful dancers?'

'Did you know that before their little display?'

Earthy didn't answer. She pointed at a group of figurines on a side table. 'Léon made those. Ravi gave them to me.'

They stood with a mirror behind them and a tea light burning in front of each one. Janet thought of votive offerings. They were crude: little more than scraps of wood picked up while walking; each one painted in several primary colours and dressed with pieces of cloth and a bead or feather. Janet had seen peg dolls that were more carefully made, but these had a disconcerting life to them. She could imagine their owners hiding them away in a box or locked drawer because they'd been infused with a piece of the soul and so must be protected.

'There's something about them, isn't there?' said Earthy.

'They feel dangerous,' said Janet without thinking.

'Oh?' Earthy looked worried. 'I thought they were life affirming – that they added to the harmony of the room.'

Janet wasn't certain if they were discussing art, magic, *feng shui* or interior decorating. She said, 'I don't suppose they really are . . . dangerous. What are the tea lights for?'

'I thought they looked pretty.'

Earthy wasn't about to say that Ravi had encouraged her to keep the candles lit. There was an intimacy about certain gifts that was destroyed if revealed. Ravi had suggested that a part of him was there in each of the figures. She didn't know which part or even if it was physical. It might be something small like the thread of twisted hair tied round the waist of some of the pieces. Ravi himself wore a sacred thread.

It might equally be something more intimate.

The seven of them piled into the 4 x 4 Arnold had bought for country motoring. It was called 'the Tank'. Joy volunteered to drive so the others might drink if they wanted to. Belle was particularly elated. Her face was shining and Janet thought she looked very pretty.

'It's like a hen party,' Belle said and nudged Janet in a knowing way. 'I love really bad bands that are full of themselves. You'll have to stop me if I want to throw my knickers at them.'

'Do you think you might?'

'I'll try not to. They'd probably think a marquee had blown over.'

'It's a pity Charlie can't come. He dances, doesn't he?'

'Oh, don't worry about him. He'll be watching telly and dreaming of *Sir Nigel Gresley*.'

Janet wondered if she was ever going to see Charlie or he would remain forever one of those characters who get mentioned but never appear – like Timothy in *The Forsyte Saga*, for example (though she had a feeling he turned up in one scene just to emphasise that something serious had happened). It occurred to her that David had now fallen into that category. He figured in the narrative of her life but no one would ever see him – short of coming back from the dead.

They waited until night was falling. If you went too early to these affairs, there was a good chance you'd find the dance floor occupied by tables and the French wading into dinner. By daylight, too, the villages were often dull to look at: the houses rendered in unpainted cement and the shutters closed; and the carnival rides and sideshows, so full of tawdry glamour at night, would be simply shabby.

They parked by the bridge. On a nearby patch of ground, men were playing pétanque by the light of flares, and children in party dresses were dancing to the music in their heads.

'When I was a child,' said Janet, 'there was a fair held in Oldham every year during Wakes Week.'

She looked at the others. She wanted to tell them more because her memory had been quickened by the faint scent of candy floss and fried onions. An image came to mind: herself as a little girl holding her mother's hand, and her mother wearing a headscarf tied in a mill worker's turban, and a hoopla stall where they lost sixpence. But it was evident most of the others had no notion of what Wakes Week was, and to take the time to explain would cause the fleeting sensation to be lost. I've had a Proustian moment, she thought to herself, but there was no point explaining that either. She smiled, intent on enjoying the evening.

The market hall flanked the main road to Laroque d'Olmes. Stalls had been set up either side and a shooting gallery and some dodgems. There was a stage at one end of the hall and the band, like all bands, was still setting up its gear after the official starting time had passed. Old people sat grumbling on the low stone wall around the perimeter and children dropped ice cream onto the dance floor.

'Hey up, here are the Bad News Boys,' said Belle.

Léon and Ravi were at the shooting gallery taking potshots.

Belle whispered, 'Don't let them know we've seen them.' Her voice had the urgent flirtatiousness Janet remembered from being a girl, when it was important that boys shouldn't know she was paying attention. Coming now from Belle the words said that she still considered herself a sexual, attractive woman, one still filled with hope and lively feelings: in fact not so far removed from the girl she'd once been. And Janet felt tender towards her.

They clustered round a catering van and helped themselves to snacks. They didn't mind the grease flowing on their fingers, not even Veronica whose smartness was usually tinged with a hint of starch. Now she was laughing and chatting. The effect of the evening and the company of friends, Janet supposed; and perhaps, too, she had her own memories.

In the way typical of bands, this one was transformed in an instant from a collection of shambling deadbeats into musicians completely in charge of their music. They struck up suddenly and loudly and the singer, a jowly type in his forties with a pompadour hairstyle, began to belt out a number Janet didn't recognise. Either side of him two young women with pert breasts, glittering smiles and clothes like truck stop whores crooned an accompaniment with bizarre gestures and thin voices. The rest of the band wore shades, chin stubble and biker chic, and clearly regarded the audience as scum.

'Welcome to French country dancing,' murmured Janet and grinned. 'David and I used to love coming to these things.'

Belle glanced at her.

'Oh, don't worry,' said Janet. 'David would want me to enjoy myself.' She wondered if Belle would understand. Her grief at her husband's death was always more likely to express itself in laughter than tears. That was why she thought her crying jags reflected no more than the state of her hormones. She reminded herself: David would be furious if he thought I wasn't trying to be happy. For all he cared I could have kissed every man at his funeral.

The band went through its opening repertoire of waltzes, rumbas and pasadobles for the benefit of the older fans. They brought on a blowsy woman in a tight spangled dress.

Belle said, 'There's someone whose hair has gone prematurely black. I hope to God that frock has reinforced fasteners.'

The band played a tango. The blowsy woman sang.

'On your feet, ladies,' said Carol.

'Must we?' said someone. But they did and made a fair fist of it. It wasn't particularly difficult because the other dancers were doing what, in Janet's experience, people did. They danced the tango as if it were a parody: as if they were in a silent movie and about to launch into a slapstick routine. If it went on long enough, the man would dump the fat lady on the floor, or the woman would sock the man in the 'kisser'. In other words it was ridiculous and good fun.

'You and Ravi didn't dance,' Janet said as she stepped from the floor. Léon was standing as if waiting for her. She'd never spoken to him before and now felt she had to say something.

'People here would not understand,' he said, and extended a hand to help her down to the pavement level. She took it cautiously.

'I don't see why not. I understood well enough.'

'Because you dance the tango – badly, but with feeling. It is simply that you have not been trained.'

'And Ravi?'

'He teach me English and I teach him dance.'

'You know other dances?'

'Yes, I used to be teacher. In a city,' he said without naming it. Janet inferred that it wasn't Paris but somewhere unfashionable, the French equivalent of Leicester; not that she cared to know more. She was about to rejoin the others when the band began again, and this time she felt a cold shock as the male singer began to croon an old Charles Trenet number, *La Mer*.

'Excuse me,' she said and pushed Léon gently away. But he held her hand.

'You will dance with me please?'

'I'd rather not. My husband and I used to dance to this song.'

He held onto her hand, and she thought: *I'm being silly*; and said, 'Oh very well.'

He helped her back onto the floor of the *halle* and sprang onto it himself. The singer was caressing the words and, for all that he looked frankly absurd with his nodding black pompadour, Janet found herself affected just as – now she thought of it – it was possible still to be moved by Elvis in his final tragic period when he looked equally absurd but could still sing like an angel. At all events it no longer seemed odd or inappropriate when Léon put his arm around her waist and led her off into the delicate glide of a foxtrot. He danced very simply, using few variations, but with exquisite care so that they swept round the floor as if she were bodiless. But at the end of a couple of circuits, before the music had even finished, he stopped and thanked her, and walked away.

The spectators clapped enthusiastically. And Janet found herself wondering if she'd insulted him.

They drove back to Puybrun by a shorter route that was little more than a country lane. All of them tired and, except for Joy, a little drunk and elated. They'd seen Janet dance with Léon. She waited for them to say, 'I think he fancies you,' in the same knowing way that her girlfriends would have said it forty-odd years before, which was stupid beyond belief; and in any case it wasn't *that*: it was something else that for the moment she couldn't fathom.

Finally Carol said, 'That Léon is an ugly, sexy little beggar, isn't he?'

No one spoke for a moment; then Belle said, 'Come off it, Carol: he isn't *really* called Dave.' And all the others laughed, even if they'd never heard of Leatherhead or thought it was just a town in Surrey.

Outside the windows of Arnold's car the margins of the road were a waxy green in the headlights. Stoats and rabbits dashed into the ditches and an owl floated by. On one side the world was black and starlit, and on the other billows of dark woods stood in silhouette against a moonlit sky. And Joy began to sing.

'*Ten green bottles, standing on a wall. Ten green bottles . . .*'

How perfect, Janet thought. She joined in, as did the others. Ten, then nine, then eight, and so on. And when that was finished, Poppy of all people, in a sweet though untrained voice, sang, '*Ten men went to mow – went to mow a meadow . . .*' And they joined in that song too, by now half in tears through drink and tiredness and the pleasure of friends and the recollection of days when those same songs had been sung to while away the boredom of long journeys. Childhood was gone, but the ten men like the rest of us would always step forth to mow the meadow. And like the rest of us their number would be cut down until finally there were none.

Janet gave Belle a kiss to say good-night and watched her until she was safe inside her house. The moon was shining on the further side of the hill, throwing the castle into relief. It was so enchanting she couldn't bear simply to go inside and to bed; and so, once she'd opened the house and checked that everything was all right, she stepped out again to breathe in the magic of the night – the magic of the whole evening.

One of the village girls, a teenager, was leaving Belle's house, closing the door behind her. Janet hadn't seen her arrive; yet there had hardly been time to miss her, and how was it possible for her to have come on an errand no matter how small and concluded it so quickly, and why so late?

It was a mystery, but apparently a trivial one that was quickly forgotten by morning as if it were something Janet had merely dreamt.

How to go Country-Walking

10

From the gentle terrain of the piedmont to the towering heights of the Pyrenees, the Aude and Ariège offer to the wanderer all the pleasures of hiking. Caught between Atlantic and Mediterranean influences, the Departments provide geographic, cultural and climate diversity. They contain many places redolent of history, among which are caves dating from the upper paleolithic period, the Gallo-Roman city of Saint-Lizier, and the great fortresses defended by the Cathars such as Puybrun and Montségur.

Joy knew in her heart that she was powerless to save herself. The insight had been forced on her when she lost her teaching job and life was collapsing around her, back then, all those years ago, when she was thirty.

Arnold with his confident bullying manner had been an attractive man but never a nice one – the suicide of the sainted Kathleen was a hint that Joy had chosen to ignore. She accepted him because the powerless have no choice except to deliver themselves into the hands of the powerful, however they may care to disguise their decision. And there's always the hope – never a strong one in Joy's particular case – that somehow it's possible to change a partner's fundamental nature.

Arnold had 'saved' her, no doubt about it. He'd sorted out the disastrous and disorganised state of her life and given it shape. But he'd also crushed her. She knew it. She could feel it. Fifteen years on, even his limited attractions had disappeared. His physical presence, in truth, disgusted her, though not because it was especially repulsive or worse than that of other men nearing seventy, who nevertheless remain attractive because they are loveable. She bore with him only because she felt the deep humility of the powerless that even the anger of oppression couldn't displace.

And then came the women's group: The English Lady Murderers' Society – the Murdering Bitches, as they sometimes called themselves. Joy was intoxicated by their confidence, their liveliness, their sense of their own power, and their friendship. She felt she'd never in her life met such wonderful women. She was dizzy with gratitude. Although she didn't know how, she was sure they offered her an exit from the thraldom of Arnold and a blessed end to the voice that haunted her, reminding her of her inadequacy.

As a mark of her gratitude, while Arnold was unable to inter-fere, she volunteered to lead their next project: How to Go Country-Walking.

'Is that mad cow trying to kill me?' Belle asked as she took coffee at Janet's house. 'Does she think for a second that I'm built for hiking?'

Janet tried to be sympathetic. 'Have you spoken to Earthy? Between you, you might persuade her to come up with another idea.'

'Earthy's a daft as Joy,' Belle grumbled. Then, contradicting her refusal to have anything to do with an idea as insane or potentially fatal as this one, she asked pitifully, 'What the hell am I to do for *shoes*?'

When Belle had gone, Janet spent half an hour mulling over the business of murdering her husband, which caused her to remember a chore she'd been meaning to clear ever since he died. When she packed to leave England, she'd heaped a pile of David's loose papers into a carrier bag, intending to go through them. They were bills, notes and private correspondence. Any-thing to do with business she'd left to Jeremy – which in retro-spect may have been a mistake.

It was a tedious job, and on the first pass she simply sorted the material by topic such as pension, investments and various subscriptions. It left a miscellany of scraps: petrol receipts, ticket stubs and bits and pieces of notes. None of it appeared important but a couple of items made her mildly curious.

The first was a credit card slip for a roadhouse she knew on the A34. It was dated the day that David died. It wasn't detailed, but she surmised he'd picked up the tab for the dinner he and Jeremy had eaten together; not in itself a mystery. She'd always known of this rendezvous; Jeremy had made no secret of it and in fact David had mentioned that morning that he and his partner would be dining together.

Yet, something about the receipt struck her as odd. She looked for the actual restaurant bill, but evidently David hadn't kept it.

The second item was more obscure: a single word written in pencil on a page from a loose note block. When David was dealing with unfamiliar names or words, his habit was to write them in capital letters. He'd done so on this occasion: 'L-A-N-O-C-K-S-Y-N (sp?)'. The note in brackets meant he wasn't sure about the spelling.

LANOCKSYN.

It sounded like a place in Wales or Cornwall, or it might be a surname, though Janet couldn't think which country it came from. Bearing in mind the international character of the business he'd become involved in, Janet wondered if there might be a connection with the Zarathustra Fidei-Anstalt. Perhaps it was a company name? A computer password? An ethnic restaurant where David had an appointment.

The problem was that the possibilities were endless.

Google failed to turn up a match.

They gathered at Joy's house in Campmaurice for the first walk. None of them had been there before for fear of the awful Arnold. Belle said afterwards, 'It was like one of those places you imagine a football player living in, wasn't it? I mean First Division not Premier League. Or the setting for a tacky Australian soap opera.'

It was new and built on a large plan, and looked vaguely as if it belonged in California. There was a garden with palm trees of some kind, an outdoor hot tub, a swimming pool and a garage big enough to hold the Tank as well as a couple of other cars. Nothing about it was actively ugly: rather the place had a dreary ordinariness: a collection of objects chosen because they fell within a certain price range and would 'do'. Arnold's personal taste ran to a large photograph of the sainted Kathleen in a faux-Victorian frame from Past Times, golf trophies and motoring magazines. The only book was a biography of Jeremy Clarkson.

Janet wondered where Joy figured in this scheme. Her presence in the house seemed to make no more impact than that of the cleaning lady. She glanced at Veronica, curious how she would react, given that she and Joy had become friends. Carol wondered the same. Later, while they were out walking, she said, 'Did you see the look on Veronica's face? It was like someone trying to be polite while ignoring the dog mess on the carpet.' She laughed until she coughed, then lit another cigarette.

Janet had read Veronica's expression differently. She'd looked distressed, as one does at the fate of someone one cares for, if only a little.

'We're going to walk to the Maquis de Puybrun,' said Joy brightly. 'I've done it lots of times. It's a bit of climb,' she added.

'Christ on a bike, it's a ruddy mountain,' Belle muttered.

Certainly it looked challenging. Beyond Campmaurice the plateau butted up against an escarpment a couple of thousand feet high. It was formed of sheer cliffs and rocky pinnacles breaking out of steep slopes dense with trees.

They set off along paths between fields of wheat and alfalfa, crossed a stream and entered the outskirts of a wood. Janet hung at the rear to encourage Belle. Ahead of her a line of middle-aged backsides waddled like ducks on the way to a pond. She felt a prickle of tears in her eyes, but on this occasion it was definitely not grief or the result of the Bloody Menopause. She was simply happy to be among friends who were so kind to each other and so ready for anything. And if their emblem was to be a fat bum striding along the road ahead, she didn't care, as long as it was a good road that good women could tread together.

The sunlight gave way to the shade of trees and undergrowth. The base of the climb was covered in thickets of box broken by clearings where wild strawberries grew. They stopped to collect some, but for all their profusion, a hundred of them amounted to nothing. Still, what mattered would be the memory not the fruit itself. They would recall a sweet taste and a sunlit day spent with friends in a wood. It was a recollection that would remain when the exact day and year were forgotten; and the key to unlock it would be something slight and accidental, perhaps a punnet of Spanish hot house strawberries bought in a supermarket on a rainy day in December.

As they walked, Veronica pointed out flowers – hellebores and wood vetch and others Janet hadn't heard of, and a wild plum that was shedding fruit – she was surprisingly knowledgeable. The path continued to be well marked, but it rose steeply as it wound through oak and beech wood.

'I wish you'd go ahead of me,' Belle complained. 'I'm fed up of you shoving me up the arse every time I pause for breath.'

'How else are you going to get to the top?' Janet asked.

'I think I'd rather die first.'

'No, don't do that. Have pity on the stretcher bearers.'

'Bugger the stretcher bearers: it serves them right. Oh God, does it never end?'

'There's a viewpoint, near here,' Joy called out, which meant that everyone stopped for ten minutes and the rearguard was able to catch up.

'I'll strangle her if she gets any more jolly,' said Belle.

A buttress of rock jutted out from the main climb forming a turret, from which they could see the whole plateau.

'Now, isn't it worth it?' Janet asked.

Below them lay Puybrun with its lake and castle, the scattering of hamlets, the patchwork of fields, and a ribbon of road that sparkled now and again as sunlight reflected on the windscreen of a passing car. Woods covered the further hills: a soft grey-violet in the midday sunshine. Two black kites were patrolling the sky in circles, their notched tails clearly visible.

Finally they reached the top where the path came out in an abandoned meadow scattered with conifer saplings. A cabin stood nearby. Inside was a memorial to the Resistance. Panels of text and photographs explained that in August 1944 the local maquis had attacked the Germans and in reprisal the Nazis burned Campmaurice to the ground. Janet felt she should be shocked, but at such distance of time it was difficult to believe that war had once touched this lovely countryside. When she tried to evoke some feeling about the event, it wasn't possible, no more than she could cry over the battle of Hastings. David would have felt more. He was always moved by war cemeteries and Remembrance Day, while the tragedies of everyday life – children knocked down by motor cars, whose deaths were marked by rain-soaked teddy bears and dead flowers tied to lampposts – left him unaffected. How could one ever understand these things? How could she hope to fathom her own grief?

They ate a late lunch sitting in a circle in the long grass between the saplings, chatting and whiling away the time plaiting stalks of grass or making flower chains or stretching out a hand to catch a passing butterfly. After half an hour of this they got to their feet and slowly made the return journey. Among the trees they heard a blackcap singing.

It was Wednesday again. Belle proposed they should round off the day by eating together. They snagged a table in the *halle* and took turns to get food from the catering vans.

'What shall I have? Mexican? Curry? *Both*?' asked Belle.

They bought everything and shared it.

'I'm not convinced that chicken madras goes with pizza,' said Carol, but she was prepared to give it a try.

Without Arnold, Joy was chatty. She said, 'Speaking of curries, I like a good *balti*. I think I read somewhere that it's the national dish of Birmingham. Can a city have a national dish? Anyway Birmingham does.'

It was disconcerting to see her so animated and looking less bedraggled since she'd restyled her hair – in imitation of Veronica, though no one said it out loud. Before she could say much more Ravi and Léon emerged from the lane where Léon had his studio.

'Hang on to your handbags, girls,' said Belle. 'Tweedle Dum and Tweedle Dee are here again.'

They were speaking with Marcel. The old man picked up his accordion and squeezed out a slow number Janet didn't recognise. Léon came over and asked her, 'Would you like to dance with me again, Mrs Bretherton?'

'I . . . ' Janet was astonished. In the sharp contrasts thrown by artificial light ,Léon's face was gaunt and it was impossible to read his expression. She looked round and saw there was a small space where a couple might dance well enough. But the idea was preposterous. 'Don't be silly,' she said, hoping her voice didn't sound too sharp. From the corner of her eye she saw Belle grinning and nudging Carol.

Léon smiled. 'You have not seen my gallery. Miss Earthy says me you like my art very much, when you see at her house. Tonight and every Wednesday night it is open, my gallery. Would you like to visit it?'

Janet felt she couldn't refuse. She was carrying a shawl against the coolness of the evening. Léon picked it up and offered her a hand and they walked the few yards down the lane to where a door was open throwing a patch of light into the darkness and the air smelled of sandalwood incense.

The gallery amounted to a single long room and to Janet's relief it wasn't empty; a pair of Dutch campers were going over the exhibits with bemused concentration. By the door a beautiful girl with a shaven head and the profile of an Egyptian queen was sitting on a stool, breast-feeding a baby.

Janet noticed a small table. On it were various books and pamphlets about the Brotherhood of Om.

She asked, 'Are you a follower?'

Léon shrugged. He halted, forcing Janet to halt too so that she found herself taking in the whole length of the room at a glance. It was lit only by candles, one in front of each of the figurines. There were fifty or more of them. The unevenness of the fugitive light made Janet think of a cave and she had again the feeling that the wooden manikins were cult objects.

She asked, 'What do they mean?'

'What do you want them to mean?'

'They look like primitive fetishes.'

He considered this but gave no sign of an opinion.

'Do you sell many?'

'The tourists like them.'

'Do they say why?'

'There is no sense to what they say. Some think like you that they are magical. But others think they are dolls and give them to their children. I do not know.'

'But surely you must? You must have had some intention?'

'I intended to make objects that look exactly as these objects do.'

Janet could make nothing of this answer. It might have been simplicity or pretentious nonsense. She was riveted by the power of the crude carvings. Some of them, she saw, were in groups like hierarchies of gods. Others were single as if symbolising specific forces: the moon or storms or death. Nothing in the pieces themselves explained this arrangement. They were horrible. Janet found it unsettling that people would buy them and take them into their homes, where they would find their way into dark corners to work whatever spell was in them.

'Miss Earthy was mistaken,' said Léon. 'You do not like them, do you, Janet?'

'Please call me Mrs Bretherton,' Janet said quietly. 'I'm old enough to be your mother.'

'You do not like them?'

A tinkle of music came from the doorway. Ravi was squatting there. He had small bells on each of his fingers. The shaven headed girl was smoking a cigarette and winding the baby, which regurgitated a trickle of milk down her back.

'I think they're very effective,' Janet said. 'I understand why people buy them. But they're not meant to be liked, are they?'

'No.'

'I thought not.'

Léon grinned. He might be odd-looking, but his snaggle-toothed smile was enchanting. It was ridiculous but Janet found him deeply alluring, though she would never do anything about it, of course. He was as dangerous as his dolls, and she told herself she really didn't want to have anything to do with him.

'I must go back to my friends.'

'Of course.'

She wondered if he expected her to buy one of his pieces. Or perhaps he would make her a present of one – a notion she found vaguely frightening, as if by her accepting it the figure, like a vampire, would become more potent because it had been invited over the threshold.

Instead he said nothing but came with her only as far as the door where he watched while she returned to the *halle*. Janet felt that she was pinned between gazes: Léon staring at her back and the other women watching her expectantly.

'Look who's too sexy for her bra!' said Belle, giving her a spontaneous kiss.

'Now what the hell was all *that* about?' said Carol.

11

The name Ax may derive from the Latin *'aquae'*, meaning 'waters' or from the Basque *'ats'* meaning 'stench' because of the sulphurous smell of its thermal springs. In the year 1260, the Count of Foix, Roger IV Trancavel had a leprosarium constructed at Ax in order to take advantage of the healing powers of its waters. In this he was continuing a tradition extending from before the Romans.

Earthy knew she was a disappointment to her parents; not that they ever said so because they were good people. They just sighed and looked at her in a certain way: the way that good people do.

Her grandfather had been a boot maker, who worked hard to educate his children. Her father was a consultant oncologist, and her younger siblings, Donald and Margaret, both became general practitioners. Earthy was just herself. Her family referred to her as 'our Valerie, bless her' so often that the two word addition seemed to be her surname as if she'd been raised in a fanatical puritan sect. It was never difficult to say nice things about her – bless her – because she was a nice child who'd grown to be a nice person. But always people said them with a shake of the head. No one expected her to come to anything much, and she was an obliging child and didn't.

At school she obtained no qualifications worth a mention. Afterwards she took various jobs above her abilities because she was polite and well spoken. She even entered medicine as a doctor's receptionist, but was fired because they said she was stupid and disorganised. It wasn't true that she was stupid. She simply thought differently.

Her parents wondered what was going to happen to our Valerie, bless her. The answer was that she would be seduced by Flower Power and the Summer of Love and fall into the company of hippies who were even more disorganised than she was. She drifted from festival to festival and finally to Wales, where she holed up in a tented camp in a damp valley until one day some thirty-odd years later she found that the fey pretty girl she'd once been was gone, to be replaced by a distracted but amiable elderly lady with long grey tresses and a profound ignorance of anything very much.

Earthy never married, unless she counted a pagan wedding to a boy called Sir Gawain Warlock of the Shire – which may not have been his real name. She carried two baby girls to four months and finally gave birth to a son. She put him up for adoption after Sir Gawain picked up two years for dealing in drugs and Earthy fell into a long depression. Otherwise her health was good, except for a hysterectomy at the age of thirty-five when she almost died and was rushed through a rainy Welsh night in a converted ice cream van, chimes ringing, to the hospital in Llandrindod Wells.

In the course of all this she was re-christened 'Earth Child', and learned to settle for 'Earthy'.

Carol was her best friend in the village. They attended the same markets: Carol to sell her pots and paintings; Earthy her herbs and trinkets. To save cost and for company they often shared transport. That was how Earthy learned the other woman's history. Carol had called her life 'adventures in Dave World', making it sound like a visit to an exciting theme park. Yet Earthy saw a similarity. It seemed to her that they'd both spent their lives in exile: Carol in Dave World and Earthy in Wales; and both had only recently emerged. Earthy thought Janet was mistaken in regarding Puybrun as a place of exile. She always felt she'd finally come home.

Earthy suggested to Joy that for the second walk they should go to Ax-les-Thermes. It was put to the vote.

'As long as it's not another ruddy Death March,' said Belle.

'We can call at Montaillou,' said Janet. Which was what Earthy had in mind.

The proposal was carried.

Janet had got used to receiving phone calls and no longer switched her mobile off. Was it a sign of something? That morning she received another call from Helen sounding bad tempered and at her wits' end, which seemed to be the case all the time since David's death.

But if there's a connection with David, why aren't I bad tempered and at my wits' end? Janet wondered. After all, I'm the one suspected of fraud and murder.

'How are you? How's Henry?' she asked.

'Don't talk to me about Henry. He's taking medication. His nerves are shot to pieces. He thinks the bank will take a dim view of him if it learns his father-in-law is a fraudster and his mother-in-law a murderess – his words, not mine.'

'He thinks I murdered your dad – or are we talking about the mysterious Unknown Corpse?'

'Everyone who knows you thinks you could have killed some-body and got away with it, even the ones who don't think you actually did. I'm one of the latter, by the way.'

'Thank you. And Henry?'

'Oh, I don't suppose he thinks you really did kill anybody, or steal the money for that matter. But he's concerned for his job.'

Janet changed the subject: asked about children and holidays and then for more general news.

'The police have done the DNA test. The organs they found are Dad's, so they're finally convinced you cremated the right chap.'

'Yes, well I did think I'd recognised him after so many years of marriage. Still it's a shame about the tramp.'

'Which tramp?'

'The mystery man: the one your dad and I killed in order to switch bodies. Dad's missing partner? The long-lost heir to the family fortune? I was getting attached to him.'

'It still leaves unexplained the matter of who accessed the bank account of that trust with the funny name and transferred a hundred thousand pounds to you.'

'Does it? I always thought that was obvious. Jeremy did it. He has the IT skills and could probably find your dad's password. No doubt he wanted to throw suspicion away from himself. Of course proving it is a different matter.'

'You don't seem bothered.'

'No. It's no crime to receive the money as long as I'm willing to return it. And no one can show that I did the transfer, because I didn't.'

'I don't know how you can take these things so calmly,' said Helen half admiring and half exasperated.

'It comes from years of living with your father,' said Janet.

They all piled into the Tank again and Joy drove. They took the narrow road that wound past Campmaurice through forest to the plateau of Sabarthès. There was no traffic except the occasional lorry and trailer loaded with timber. Overnight it had rained and water lay on the road surface in the shadow of the trees, but the open ground was sun baked.

Montaillou was in the high country, little more than a hamlet off the main road in a broad expanse of meadows in flower, though in winter it would be snowbound and remote. The Holy Inquisition had visited it in the early years of the fourteenth century to hunt out the remains of the Cathar heresy among the villagers and shepherds. By chance the record of their inter-rogations survived to give a human voice to these poor people; and for no other reason Montaillou had become famous.

They parked the car and for the space of quarter of an hour walked the lanes and stared at the land around them. In mediaeval times it was likely the village had a greater population that at present; there were suggestive traces of stonework and terraces, but the reality was hard to imagine. There'd been a castle: a small affair on a hill that left a negligible ruin on which a pair of honey buzzards perched. The building figured only slightly in the story of Montaillou but the record left a lively picture of its chatelaine, Béatrice de Planisoles. She was a passionate woman from an old Cathar family, who was caught up by the Inquisition and forced to wear the yellow cross of a heretic for the rest of her life.

'She was a bit of a goer, eh?' said Belle.

Janet smiled. 'You might say so.' She recalled a scene disclosed to the interrogators. Béatrice and her lover, Pierre Clergue, had one day sat in the sunshine here in the lane, somewhere not far from where the women were now, and, while they chatted as friends and lovers do, Béatrice had picked fleas from the priest. Janet found the warmth and sensuality of this image impossible to ignore. It seemed more intimate and expressive that the sexual act itself. She could think of moments with David that were just as intimate, and she remembered them vividly because they marked their marriage in its uniqueness; though she imagined that in truth all couples must have similar experiences except those whose life of the senses had died.

'She was a Wise Woman,' said Earthy, speaking of Béatrice. Her tone was serious. 'When they looked in her bag they found umbilical cords from two babies – as well as other things I've forgotten: magical things.'

Earthy remembered the two cords because of the two babies she miscarried. She believed in resonances and connections across time and space and that this coincidence was not an accident but had a meaning for her. Once, when she'd under-gone some past life regression, the hypnotist had hinted that . . . But it was only a hint.

Earthy came to Montaillou whenever she could in case some day, by dint of her efforts, a revelation would be granted to her and she would understand why her life had been as it was. So far the revelation hadn't come.

At Ax-les-Thermes they parked by the main church near the

casino. They decided to eat lunch and found a restaurant, where they sat in the shade of an awning and talked over a dish of cassoulet. Janet shared a table with Belle, Earthy and Carol.

Carol drank a couple of glasses of red wine and told her tale of adventures in Dave World. Then Earthy gave her account of life as a hippie, though it wasn't a term she used because she thought it was frivolous. Earthy had been deeply serious through those long years of hard living. What had sustained her was a belief that it represented spirituality, community and self-sufficiency, even if these things for the most part amounted to dope, petty wrangling and state benefits. It was only after she left that she realised her commitment had faded years, even decades, before. She'd continued from absence of choices and, even more, failure of imagination, much in the way that people thoughtlessly suppose they believe in religion out of nothing more than habit, not seeing that their lukewarm practice is the result of a lack of faith and that they are for all practical purposes atheists.

'Then my parents died,' Earthy said.

'And?'

'It turned out my father was quite well off – by my standards anyway. He left me enough to buy my cottage in Puybrun and a bit more, and with that and my work, I get by.'

Janet wasn't sure what to make of this story. It seemed like a confession of a wasted life, though it was difficult to think what else Earthy might have done: what 'contribution' she might have made that had been wasted. Perhaps it was in her nature or perhaps her experiences had taught her a kind of wisdom: at all events there was something sublime about her: something that Janet found admirable. However, to the eye she was a plump elderly woman with frizzy braids of grey hair, who spoke in a piping voice and the polite accents of fifty years ago like Her Majesty gone to seed.

Earthy explained that she'd left Wales as if leaving a prison.

Carol said, 'I didn't exactly *leave* Dave World. I just grew older, and as soon as my boobs began to fall they threw me out. That's what men are like – blokes called Dave I mean. I suppose they did me a favour. I discovered I really *was* an artist.' She shrugged, evidently puzzled at the way her life had turned out.

'I always used to say I was, but I thought I was just talking bollocks.'

There was no more time for revelations if they were to walk as planned; so they paid the bill and set off, leaving the town by a stony lane that rose through trees towards the village of Ascou. They strung out in a line of couples, chatting as they went along. Janet found herself still with Earthy.

Earthy asked, 'Do you have children?'

'Yes,' said Janet. She found herself confiding about Helen and confessing that she'd never liked Henry from the moment he first appeared on her doorstep wearing a suit and tie. 'I know he was trying to make a good impression, but young men didn't wear suits in those days. He looked like a City wide boy or a convicted burglar hoping to get a suspended sentence.' It remained a mystery to her what held that marriage together. Perhaps it was Helen's version of living in a tent in Wales and she would emerge without faith in a decade or two, wondering what she'd done with her life. Janet was determined not to interfere. 'And you?' she asked of Earthy.

Earthy told of her two miscarriages. 'Girls – I sometimes wonder if they'd have lived if I'd had better care – if I hadn't been living the way I did.'

She seemed to think it was likely and Janet suspected she might be right. But you never knew, and you were forced to make choices for good or ill. Earthy's choice hadn't been an ignoble one. David would have understood perhaps more than Janet herself because of his pronounced sense of the ridiculous. He expected people to make bad decisions – including himself.

'And I had a son,' Earthy went on. Before Janet could congratulate her she added, 'I had to have him adopted. We called him Moonstone.'

She explained about the father's imprisonment and her depression.

'What happened to him afterwards – I mean the father?'

Earthy shook her head. 'Prison changed him. He became a fascist. These days he's something high up in the British National Party. I think he's changed his name.'

'He probably has,' Janet agreed. She thought she would have remembered if a Mr Warlock of the Shire had appeared in the news for winning a council seat in Burnley.

At a drinking trough the path turned right. It rose steeply and came out at a viewpoint overlooking a village, a river, and a tree-clad slope on the further side, all lying quiet in the balmy sunlight of late afternoon. They sat there a while, smiling at each other, and passed round fruit, chocolate and water bottles. They rubbed insect repellent on the tops of each other's shoulders and muttered about bites to their ankles. Poppy sat apart on a rock, seeming to dream in the sunlight. Seeing her with her immaculate blond hair and the trees and sky beyond her, Janet was reminded of old railway posters in which clean-limbed youth advertises the delights of seaside resorts that no one any longer visits. Was that what Veronica saw in her? A kind of frozen perfection?

They descended by a precipitate rocky path in a series of bends to the valley floor and through the village of Orgeix. The return followed the edge of the trees with the river to their right, past a charming church and a small chateau by a lake where the river was dammed.

'Have you enjoyed yourself?' Janet asked Belle.

'What? Oh, yes, it's been OK, but I'll be glad to put my feet up. Still, I feel better for it.'

'You should go walking with Charlie. I'm sure it'd be good for you both.'

Belle looked at her sharply.

They took coffee in the town. They were tired and contented and thanked Joy for coming up with the idea of walking and providing the transport. Joy beamed but said nothing. She was frightened that she might spoil the moment with her gaucheness.

During the walk she'd partnered Belle. In the past she'd been a little intimidated by the loudness of the other woman, her brash self-confidence; but in conversation she discovered how much they had in common. Because Belle always noisily acknowledged and laughed at her weight, Joy had supposed she was at ease with it. And perhaps she was – now. But in her teens and twenties, when she had to live under the regime of her mother, and with a slender string of boyfriends so pathetic they made Joy's look like film stars, she'd suffered the same crises of confidence Joy had gone through, though Joy had tried to solve hers differently. In the end, too, they'd both settled for older men: good men in their way, but not quite perfect, like Marks & Spencer's seconds. Charlie was nine years older than Belle and Arnold was twenty-five years older than Joy. The difference was starting to tell.

Driving home, they sang *Frère Jacques* for a change. They were tired and fired off unconnected squibs of conversation.

Carol asked Janet, 'So what's all that with Léon about? Do you fancy him?'

'I've no idea what it's about and don't be silly: I'm at least thirty years older than he is.'

'You're still a very beautiful woman,' Earthy said from some-where at the back. In her peculiar way she spoke sincerely and not out of politeness or kindness, and Janet was shocked. Of course David had always told her she was beautiful and she loved him for it: it was one of his virtues that he could make her feel good about herself. But she was a woman of sixty with no expectation of being beautiful and she quite reasonably supposed he was lying. To hear it said by another woman seemed some-how more truthful and it was disconcerting because she knew she still found some men very attractive, without thinking for a moment she would do anything about it.

They were elated from the day and so, once they arrived at Puybrun, they went to the Bar des Sports for a nightcap. They sat outside watching bats flutter past and cats slink across the place de la Halle, while inside the bar a muted television was tuned to a football match. Poppy was exhausted and dozed with her arms crossed on the table and her head lying on them. Janet noticed how they were all drawn to watch her: her astonishing beauty, the smile on her lips, the sheer mystery of her, though like as not it would amount to nothing at all.

'It's magical, isn't it?' said Earthy.

Janet nodded. It seemed that they had created something magical out of their ordinariness. – or was Earthy simply referring to the evening light or the events of the day?

'We are magical – *us!*' said Earthy.

Yes, *us*, thought Janet. Earthy was smiling at her. She had lost two babies and had her son adopted and spent thirty years pursuing an illusion of 'peace and love, man', and yet she was still alive to give and receive love and willing to take risks to do both. What was Janet to make of it? What was she to make of Carol? After her rackety life she'd succeeded in her art, and yet, despite all experience, seemed to wait like a Christian for the Second Coming of the Blessed Dave? It was astonishing: the persistence of love.

David wouldn't have been in the least surprised. He always thought that love was like a weed. It would spring up unless you rooted it out. And, of course, some people did.

Janet was musing over this when her mobile beeped and a message from Helen turned up.

It said: DAD HAD A TWIN.

12

Through millennia of patience and perseverance the Douctouyre has worn a passage through the hills of the Plantaurel, scouring out deep gorges that provide a playground for today's rock climbers. They are also home to many raptors, including vultures, eagles and falcons, as well as smaller birds such as rock swallows and martins. Humans are present only in small settlements and as a bauxite quarry that is no longer used.

For their third expedition they chose the gorges of Péreille.

'It's not as adventurous as it sounds,' said Joy.

Belle was sceptical. 'I should ruddy well hope not. I've enjoyed the last two walks, but my legs are killing me.'

Janet suggested they combine events and do some shopping in Lavelanet.

'Shopping!,' sighed Belle. 'My feet have spread with all this traipsing around. I wonder if I can persuade Charlie to let me change all my shoes?'

Belle liked to buy shoes. Given that circumstances had forced her to make her own clothes using the skills she learned from Alice – not a subject she cared to remember – shoes were both compensation and a mark of rebellion.

Alice used to say loftily, 'If you have well made dresses with a good cut in a classic style, they'll never be out of date;' though in fact she ran up most of her own on a second hand Singer from material bought at the Biggest Co-op East of Preston, and trimmed them with bits and pieces from her haberdashers' stock. She collected patterns over thirty years from women's magazines and dusty little shops that sold corsets and support stockings so that she always looked as if she clothed herself using ration coupons. As for her store-bought outfits, they came from the Manchester sales. Alice liked to say pointedly of some dowdy frock or other: 'This isn't from just any old place.

It's Kendals. They didn't make many of them. It's almost *bespoke*.'

'She used to pick up odds and sods of fur from auctions,' Belle said. 'Stuff you find in wardrobes when old relatives have died. She must have had half a dozen jackets and more moth-eaten stoles than you could shake a stick at: horrible things with a fox's head at one end and tatty feet at the other, and the fox would have only one glass eye. She had this long coat: "faux chinchilla" she'd say – rabbit more like it. She couldn't go anywhere in it: it smelled too much of mothballs. She'd just take it out every now and again and parade round the bedroom like Lady Muck; I could always tell because the bedroom would stink of camphor. But – ' Belle's eyes glinted.

'But what?' asked Janet.

'She couldn't wear nice shoes because of her bunions!'

'So you buy nice shoes.'

'Whenever I can. It's a way of getting my own back.'

Belle's story made Janet wonder how different the women were from their mothers. And, if they were different, was it because of personality or circumstances: affluence for example, which had given them a broader perspective? Carol's rackety life in Dave World was a tale of travelling round the globe like a character in a picaresque novel. If her mother had wanted to take up the same career she'd have been confined to picking up 'chaps' in the pubs of Nottingham or wherever it was Carol said she came from, and having a quick knee-trembler in an alleyway for want of anywhere to take them to. None of that generation could have abandoned the past and its murders to live in Puybrun. They didn't have the money.

'What did your mother think of them – all the "Daves"?' Janet asked Carol as they sat over lunch before the walk. 'Did she understand what was going on?'

'Not really,' said Carol. She stubbed out her cigarette and stared at the coil of smoke, thinking the matter over. 'If the latest one was good-looking or flush with money I'd take him home and show him off. Of course she knew nothing of the fights or being dumped in places that, believe me, you don't want to be dumped in. She used to love them: think they were so handsome. She'd bring out the best china and look at them starry-eyed. Then she'd say to me afterwards, "I hope you can settle down with this one." And I'd say "yes" like an idiot because I really thought I might – with some of them, not all of them obviously.'

Janet was struck by the picture of tea served in the best china cups, no doubt with biscuits, and could imagine Carol's mother and the expression in her eyes. Carol said her parents were teachers: very respectable and chapel-going, who stayed married all their years without a breath of scandal.

As for her own mother, it was impossible to say if she were like Janet herself. A life spent working in cotton mills and bringing up five children was simply too remote to afford comparison. Janet had imagination – everyone said so – and the talent to express it. Did her mother have the same? Perhaps she did but had lacked experiences that would provide material to work on, so that it had died for want of nourishment or at best expended itself on small things. Perhaps, if Janet were to search her memory, she would find signs of her mother's imagination. Perhaps the shell work box that held buttons and safety pins was a thwarted attempt to find beauty and not just a souvenir of Blackpool. *The past is a foreign country: they do things differently there.*

The Ariège has unreliable weather despite its closeness to the Mediterranean. Today was rainy: not a downpour but an intermittent drizzle with a mist that hid the tops of the steep wooded slopes. The women wore light waterproofs but otherwise did as before, walking in pairs and chatting as they went.

A few miles along the road to Foix a lane on the right led to a horse riding centre, before winding through a narrow gap in the hills. It ended at a hamlet, where they parked the car and set off.

Joy walked ahead jauntily, guidebook in hand. Janet found herself partnered with Veronica.

Wondering how she would react, Janet said, 'Don't you think Joy is someone who makes other people uncomfortable without one ever really knowing why? I've met a number of people who are like that. When they talk, you want the conversation to end. When they come into a room, you want to leave. I don't mean that you actually dislike them – in fact you may even like them or at least feel sorry for them. They're simply odd.'

'Why do you suppose that is?' Veronica asked, without saying she agreed.

'Poor social skills? An uncertain control over their own bodies? Their voices are always a shade too loud or too soft. They hold your gaze too long or else avoid it. They go on about something or other when they ought to see that you aren't listening any more. I don't mean to be cruel: on the contrary, if you recognise the clumsiness for what it is, you can make allowances.'

Veronica didn't answer.

They followed a muddy path along the line of a stream. It took them uphill through beech and oak woods. At a small cluster of buildings, Joy gave a cheery cry, waved her stick and indicated they should take the path to the right.

Janet asked, 'How long have you known her?'

'Two years or thereabouts. I understand she and Arnold retired ten years ago; at all events they were already here when Poppy and I arrived. It's stretching a point to say I "knew" her until you and Belle organised the Group. She was just a face one saw about the place. Campmaurice is a fair distance, so dropping in on each other for coffee was never really on the cards – not that it was ever something I felt inclined to do.'

'But you seem to have taken her under your wing, now,' said Janet.

They came across a memorial, where the path divided. Joy waited for the others with her stick pointed to the right hand fork.

Janet asked, 'How are her lessons on the computer coming along? You are teaching her, aren't you?'

'Enough to send e-mails and shop on line. And she has a rather touching desire to join one of the social networking sites. She seems to be lonely.' Veronica glanced at Janet. 'For the reasons you mentioned, I imagine.'

At a crossroads they took a path along the forested crest of a ridge, keeping to the edge of the trees. They paused at the high point to munch apples and sit for a while, listening to the tap of rain on the leaf canopy and looking over the valley, which was partly veiled by cloud. Veronica took out binoculars and swept the sky for birds.

'A peregrine falcon,' she said, but no one else could see it.

Janet switched on her mobile and searched for a signal. She was surprised to find one. Since receiving Helen's text message she'd kept the phone switched off: dealing with other people's frustrations was too annoying. But now and again she checked for missed calls in case there were some she should return, and once in a while she looked at her messages.

There was one from Helen. It said: IDENTICAL TWINS HAVE THE SAME DNA.

Possibly, thought Janet. But what does it have to do with anything?

'Time to go, ladies!' Joy chirruped.

'If somebody kills her, I'll give them an alibi,' Belle said but got to her feet nonetheless. Veronica put away her binoculars and took up her position alongside Janet. She seemed thoughtful, and Janet wondered if she'd gone too far. If Joy were indeed Veronica's friend, it wasn't exactly tactful to point out her oddness. There are times when I'm not a nice woman, Janet thought, examining her own behaviour as coolly as she did that of others.

'We're not friends,' Veronica said quite suddenly. 'At least not as you'd ordinarily understand things.' Seeing that Janet wasn't inclined to answer she went on, 'I don't think I'm a naturally sympathetic person.' She laughed. 'I held a top job in banking, for God's sake! It doesn't exactly evoke images of being warm and cuddly, does it? I lived on my own for twenty years, working at my career and unable to form relationships that amounted to anything much.' She stopped there, knowing she was being unfair to herself and to Diana, whom she'd loved in her way. She said slowly and quietly, 'Yet all along I wanted to fall head over heels in love.'

Janet nodded, wondering to what degree the other woman was speaking of Joy or Poppy; one could interpret the words as comments about both. So often words were a mosaic out of which one tried to piece together a pattern: incoherent because one didn't understand things; not true explanations but merely steps on the road to understanding. Sometimes Janet tried to describe and explain her relationship with David. She could come up with something, but the picture seemed lifeless or ridiculous or conventional, whereas the reality had been vibrant and intense.

'Are you all right?' asked Veronica. 'You just went all quiet on me.'

'What? Oh, I was just thinking. You're right of course: one does want to rush headlong into love. Not at first sight – that's foolish, though I suppose it happens. But I think it's possible, even in a long-lasting marriage, for a moment to arise when you see into the heart of things and . . . simply fall in love. We've rather got off the subject, haven't we?'

'Yes,' said Veronica and smiled. 'Still, I did fall head over heels in love with Poppy, and it was love at first sight, and I do agree with you that it was foolish. But so far I seem to have been lucky.'

Nothing else was said about Joy's strange appeal, and Janet put the subject into the box labelled 'Life's Mysteries'.

Away from the trees the path wound downwards between meadows to the hamlet of Péreille d'en Bas; then made a hairpin turn at a wayside cross before dropping into the gorge. The rain was now more intense, and the women trudged silent and bedraggled. The limestone dust had turned slippery underfoot and they supported each other in order not to stumble.

Fortunately the path wasn't too steep and the trees gave some shelter. Then, a little way into the gorge, they heard a high, hollow sound of voices and laughter. They stopped and peered; yet there was no one to see and, echoing off the limestone walls, the voices seemed all around them, spirited and playful, and ignorant of their presence.

'Kids,' said Belle. Earthy looked uncertain. 'Oh, come on!' said Belle. 'It's not the Wee Folk.'

Poppy pointed. 'It's from over there, innit?'

The ground sloped away from the path to a dip. It was hard to be certain among the spindly trees and undergrowth but it seemed that Poppy was right and the sing-song voices of invisible children were coming out of a cave. The women stopped a while and nibbled chocolate and dried fruit to restore their energy. At the end of five minutes the cave children were still playing and laughing, but none of them had appeared, and so there was nothing to do but continue the walk with the voices fading behind them until they vanished entirely at a turn in the path.

Beyond an abandoned quarry the women emerged from the gorge and returned to the car, and the walk was over.

They stopped for coffee in Lavelanet, sitting outside a café in the rain with the waiter loitering in the doorway, staring up and down the street with unfocused eyes. On a whim Janet decided to phone Helen and took herself aside to one of the empty tables.

After the preliminaries – Chloë fine, Henry dreadful – Janet asked, 'So what's this about identical twins having the same DNA?'

'Well, they do,' said Helen.

'So what if they do – why do I care?'

'It means one can't be absolutely certain that the remains tested by the police were in fact Dad's, and so we can't be sure that the body we cremated was his either.'

For a moment Janet was stunned and all she could say was, 'Has the world gone mad?'

'*Uncle Patrick*,' said Helen.

'Who on earth . . . ?' Then Janet remembered David's brother, Patrick. But he had disappeared too long ago to be called 'Uncle' by anybody. 'Patrick?'

'Yes! He was Dad's twin brother.'

'I know that, but they weren't identical twins.'

'Are you sure?'

'I'm sure your father would have said so if they were, but he never did. Identical twins are like each other in character and very close. David and Patrick weren't. After school your father went to university and studied to become an accountant. Patrick – I've never even met him – he had itchy feet and took himself off on foreign travels. He hasn't been seen in forty years. Last heard of he was milking kangaroos in Australia or doing something equally silly. For all I know he may be dead.'

'For all you know, he may be Dad's identical twin and he may have come back to England.'

'And what? Not a soul knew he'd returned and your father lured him to a dark and secluded place and bumped him off to cover his tracks after robbing his investors? We're back to the mysterious tramp who suddenly throws off his disguise and reveals himself as the Black Sheep Of the Family In Search Of A Fortune. It's ridiculous! Even the Great Agatha herself wouldn't use such a silly plot – apart from the fact she probably did. Try to get a grip on reality. Your father was a middle-aged accountant who died of a stroke in a lay-by on the A34. I wish . . . ' Janet found herself on the cusp between crying and breaking into a temper. 'Darling, I wish it could have been otherwise, God knows, but it was the most ordinary death in the world. Forget about Patrick. There is no mysterious identical twin. He's dead – David is dead – and there's nothing we can do about it.'

Helen didn't answer and after a minute of silence Janet switched her mobile off and sat for a while with her back to the others, dry eyed and shuddering. She felt a hand on her shoulder.

'Are you all right?' asked Veronica.

The rain depressed their spirits and they were wet and dirty with mud splatters. Back at the village they separated and returned to their homes. Veronica fixed herself a brandy and soda while Poppy luxuriated in the bath. She put some Delius on the CD player and curled up in a chair, nursing the glass and trying to make sense of the day.

Janet, in her astute way, was right about Joy. She was a strange, sad, friendless woman who'd probably been a strange, sad, friendless child. Veronica was astonished at herself for having any interest in her. We sympathise more readily with people we identify with, and someone – probably Janet – had commented on the slight physical resemblance they shared. Veronica wondered if that was it. Did she see herself in this plain, clumsy person, and was that faintly narcissistic inclination the reason? It seemed too frail an explanation.

Poppy came out of the bathroom wearing a white terry robe and smelling of lily of the valley. 'I'm bushed,' she said. She picked up a magazine, and gave Veronica a kiss before going to their bedroom. Half an hour later, Veronica opened the door and found her asleep with her blond hair fanned across the pillow. She sat for a moment, wanting to do no more than take in the picture: to enjoy her love silently in the way that one loved cats and children while they were asleep, without the messy reality of their behaviour. She returned to the lounge, poured another brandy and changed the music to Tchaikovsky. She continued to let her thoughts stray over the day's events, while outside the rain was blown like rice grains against the window pane and night fell.

Towards ten a knock came at the door. Veronica opened it.

Joy fell into the room. She was distraught, drunk and in tears.

How to Break the Bank at Monte Carlo

13

In roulette a 'voisin' or 'neighbour bet' is an 'en plein' bet on each of five adjacent numbers on the wheel (not consecutive numbers or adjacent in the standard layout of the table). The gambler calls his number 'and the neighbours' and passes five chips to the dealer to place. A professional gambler will use a neighbour bet if he has reason to believe that for technical reasons the behaviour of the wheel or the dealer means that a certain segment of the wheel is favoured above chance.

For twenty years Carol was a Queen in Dave World.

The disastrous expedition to Rio might have dismayed a lesser woman; but once it was over and she was back in England she realised she'd survived by her own intelligence and courage and that life held few terrors. The question was simply what she was to do with the lesson.

She had no money and returned to Nottingham. Her parents welcomed her kindly. They urged her to do teacher training: it was a steady job. They gave her a bed, food, and money for cigarettes, all doled out sparingly like Red Cross parcels, so that her home began to resemble a prisoner of war camp from black and white films of the 1950s, and her mother the civilised German commandant saying, 'I hope you are going to settle here without causing trouble. For you, Englander, life is over.'

Carol agreed to conform, and meanwhile began digging a tunnel.

Unsurprisingly no one was interested in her art college qualifications, and anyone who claimed to like her paintings simply wanted sex. To get by she defrauded social security and took bar work in the evenings; then three months later graduated to a casino where the tips were better.

She explained this to Belle at one of their tête-à-têtes over a wine bottle. Belle, ever curious, wanted to know more.

'What were they like, the gamblers?'

'Car salesmen, jobbing builders and journalists called Geoff. It was the eighties, and they all fancied themselves as J. R. Ewing and thought Nottingham was Dallas. I had big hair and wore shoulder pads.'

'I understand,' said Belle, 'though the eighties is a bit after my time. The blokes I knew wanted to be Steve McQueen. Except Charlie, obviously. He was too fat for it.'

'And where is Charlie?' Carol asked.

'Oh, you know *him*,' Belle said airily. 'He's in his workshop making something or playing with his train set. Go on, tell me what happened next.'

Next was a croupier by the name of Nick, who told Carol about life on board cruise ships. There was a demand for casino staff: eight months on and two months off, and a chance to see the world. Carol ran off with him to join a boat at Southampton.

'But he turned out to be mostly gay,' she said. 'Not that I cared. It wasn't love, just a chance to escape from Stalag Nottingham.'

'And your parents?'

'I think my mum pitied me. She could never really believe that someone mightn't want to have a career, babies and a settled life. That's probably why she used to get so excited whenever I took one of the Daves home. She could see grandchildren and me in a nice semi. The funny thing is that it was the gay fellas she liked best; not that she ever knew.'

'You took gay men to see your mother?' Belle tried to imagine introducing them to Alice, and to her surprise found the picture worked very well: her mother laying out her tatting for the admiration of her guest, and the latter cooing over it and asking for lessons so that he could while away the weary hours at sea.

Carol lit another cigarette. When she was thoughtful she would stretch her neck with her head back and her eyes closed and blow smoke lazily at the ceiling. She said, 'On and off I did nearly twenty years on the boats. Most of the staff were kids who'd put in a couple of seasons and move on. Those of us who stayed in the game were either like me or gay. That's just how it was. All my long-standing men friends are poofs.'

'And you never married?'

'No,' said Carol. 'Well . . . probably not.' Her friends told her that she'd gone through a ceremony of sorts in Bali, but her own memory was hazy and she'd forgotten the name of whomever it was she might have married, except that he was a fellow croupier and was Chinese. She learned that Cantonese was a language in which the meaning of words was determined by the exact tone in which they were pronounced. She never got the hang of it, and whenever she attempted her putative husband's name his friends fell into hysterics and told her she mustn't repeat it in polite company. She was left to wonder if she called him 'Fuck Off' or 'No Trespassers' but no one would ever say. She had the vaguest idea he called himself Quentin or Peregrine to his European friends. Apparently the Chinese had no feeling for Western names either.

The wedding was held on a beach after a party and the celebrant was an Australian backpacker with a pony tail, who wore an orange T shirt and jeans. Everyone was drunk and Carol was pregnant.

'She wants to teach us what?' said Janet, thinking she'd misheard.

'How to gamble,' said Belle, who'd got over the initial shock and become matter of fact about it. 'Apparently she used to work as a croupier on one of those cruise liners – well, more than one, to be exact; which is why she's been everywhere. By the way, once upon a time she was married. To a Chinaman – she says – except that after the ceremony she shagged a Hindu priest from Brisbane called Alan, so she's not certain it was ever valid.' With her habit of changing the subject Belle added, 'Are we going swimming or what?'

Belle liked to swim and was a powerful swimmer when young.

But as she grew older and became fatter, and the friends to whom she looked for moral support or simply to have fun with found other things to do, the swimming stopped. It was something Janet recognised: how with age and for no particular reason one got out of the habit even of things one enjoyed. When she and David fell in love for the second time – the time they liked to think of as the *real* time even though they already had a child and a mortgage and all the rest – it came with a feeling that they must try to live intensely: that they must revive the things that gave joy to life.

They stripped off on the stretch of sand by the lake among the Dutch matrons and teenagers. Belle ballooned out of her costume like pink bubble gum and attracted stares. Janet was trim and elegant but she assumed no one paid her attention.

Belle said, 'Hold my hand.'

Janet gave it an affectionate squeeze. She was proud of her friend and her bravery in taking to the water again. It seemed that in small ways the women's group had made all of them brave, giving them confidence to think they had something worthwhile to teach to each other and the opportunity to try. How else could Joy have come out of her shell and led their walking party?

Belle swam up and down the length of the small lake. She'd lost none of her strength, and those who stared grew bored, and in any case Belle no longer cared, absorbed in the long leisurely strokes of her swimming and the flicker of sunlight through the trees along the margin. Janet swam a little and dived from the raft unaware that Léon was watching her; and it never occurred to her that he might think that at sixty she was beautiful.

Belle came out of the water and ran to the toilet. 'I don't know why I always rush to the loo,' she said afterwards as she flopped on her towel, 'except that my mum always thought weeing in the pool wasn't nice, and if I did it now, people might think I was a whale.' She paused. 'Thanks for coming with me.'

'I like swimming.'

Belle grinned. 'Yeah – right – whatever.' She caught herself and hooted, 'Bloody hell, I'm turning into Poppy!'

They swam a little more, then changed and ambled through the village to have a drink outside the Bar des Sports. They heard the roar of a motorbike and a large fancy machine came from the lane to the left and swept past them on its way to the highway. Ravi was riding it and on the pillion was the hauntingly lovely young woman whose resemblance to an Egyptian queen Janet had noticed once before. On that first occasion she'd been nursing a baby. Now she was carrying it in a sling on her back and there was a suitcase strapped to the bike rack.

'Somebody's coming up in the world,' said Belle. 'That bike looks brand new. Do you suppose the baby is Ravi's?'

Janet was only half-listening. Earthy had just entered the square from the lane and seeing her friends came to join them at their table.

Belle repeated, 'Somebody's coming up in the world. I don't know the price of motorbikes but that one didn't look cheap. Earthy, you've lived here longer than either of us. Do you know who the girl is?'

'Hatshepsut,' said Earthy. 'She's Ravi's muse.' She spoke the words almost dreamily, which disconcerted Belle.

'Hatshepsut? There's posh! And a "muse" as well. I don't remember anything like that being advertised at Clitheroe Job Centre.'

'She was a pharaoh,' said Janet, 'I mean the original Hatshepsut.'

'Was she now? Oh, well. Then this one was probably christened Tracey.'

A thought came to Janet. 'Have you noticed how Carol plays with names? Leatherhead Dave. Pedro Something Italian . . . '

'Quentin the Chinese croupier!'

'Names are magical,' said Earthy. 'They contain energy.'

'Maybe,' said Belle. 'But a lot of the time they're just plain funny.'

Janet glanced at Earthy. 'They do seem to define who we are, which I suppose is why actors, writers and popes change theirs. Who knows? Perhaps they do have a kind of magic. I wonder if Ravi would keep his mystique if the rumour that his real name is Graham happened to be true?' She looked back to Belle and asked, 'Would you join the Brotherhood of Om if it was led by the Prophet Graham?'

Janet wasn't certain but she thought Earthy blushed.

'We're going to start with roulette,' Carol announced. 'Which is a game of pure chance as you all know, with a built-in margin of odds in favour of the house. Using the French wheel that amounts to 2.7%.'

'How is that?' asked Earthy.

'Because, my chuck, there are thirty-seven numbers on the wheel, counting the zero, but the bank pays out as though there are only thirty-six.'

'Wossa French wheel?' asked Poppy.

'A single zero. The American wheel has two zeros, which increases the house take to 5.6%. To make things fair, we'll rotate the bank so that everyone gets the same advantage, except that I won't take the bank – so you all get the chance to skin me. Minimum stake one Euro: maximum stake eight. That way no one ends up in queer street. All understood? Then place your bets!'

Janet had never been to Carol's home. She lived in a small house in the row on the north side of the lane leading from the Place de la Halle. Downstairs was her studio where she kept her painting kit, modelling materials and kiln. Upstairs was a flat of two rooms with a bathroom and galley kitchen. Janet had expected everything to be in a mess, with a scattering of trophies from the famous 'rackety life' and a stink of cigarettes. Instead the rooms were very spare and tidy and smelled of . . . Janet thought it was hyacinths. She didn't think Carol had especially cleaned for the occasion; there were no giveaway signs. Instead it was an unexpected insight into another side of her friend's character, though she didn't know what it meant.

They laughed when Carol laid out the equipment. It came in a cardboard box with a picture of children on it.

'It's a toy,' said Veronica.

'You don't think I'm going to shell out a fortune for casino quality stuff, do you?' said Carol.

The roulette wheel was the size of a medium plate and came with plastic chips and a green baize cloth printed with the layout for the French version of the game. Carol explained it: how the cloth was segmented for the different types of bet; and how to place chips correctly so the intention was clear and the stakes were kept separate from those of other players. She told them the odds on the various wagers. They amounted to gambling on numbers individually or in groups of various sizes, and a series of even money bets on red or black, odd or even, high or low. To Janet it sounded frankly boring.

After the first few spins she said, 'It's like bingo, isn't it? But without the drawn out tension. In fact not half as exciting.'

'Can you imagine James Bond playing bingo?' Belle asked.

'His game is *chemin de fer*,' said Carol. 'Which also isn't as much fun as bingo in my opinion. But I was never interested in gambling; it was just a job.'

'I'm still trying to get my head around James Bond in a tuxedo shouting "House!" at the top of his voice,' Belle said. 'Ooh, yes! Can't you hear Sean Connery in that lovely Scottish accent, telling some Russian spy that he'll kill him if he touches his lucky pen?'

'Stop it!' Carol complained. 'We'll never get on if we can't place bets for laughing.'

They concentrated on the game, but they all agreed that roulette wasn't as good as bingo. And Janet was secretly pleased that for once the rich had been fobbed off with something second rate, and that poor people had the best of it.

To be truthful the game did become more interesting as it went on and the women saw their little piles of chips growing or diminishing. Janet decided on a strategy of betting only on red, reasoning that every time she lost, she need only double her stake in order to recover her previous bets and come out with a profit equal to her original stake.

Carol smiled. She said, 'I thought someone would try that. It's called a "martingale".'

'Oh, and does it work?' Janet asked. 'I don't see why it shouldn't. A long run of black is very unlikely and that's the only way I can lose.'

'You'll see.'

'Yes, I shall.' Janet was five euros up and felt she had reason to be satisfied.

Then she faced a run of four blacks, which didn't seem so many now she thought of it. For the next play she would have to stake sixteen Euros, which was twice the house limit of eight Euros and in any case quite a lot of money in her opinion.

'I can't double because of the limit,' she said.

Carol looked her with a glimmer of sympathy. 'Do you really think it makes a difference? If I let you bet, you'd have only a fifty-fifty chance of winning, and if you lost you'd have to stake thirty-two Euros on the next turn. Look at your pot. You don't have that much money.'

'But there've been four blacks on the run! Five of them is just not likely.'

Veronica answered before Carol had a chance. She put her hand on Janet's and said quietly, 'It's time to quit. You're wrong. The wheel doesn't remember the previous spins: it doesn't know there have been four blacks. Carol's right: next time black is still as likely to turn up as red – believe me.'

Janet stared at her and believed her. She felt a flush of humiliation because she prided herself on her intelligence and it was so unexpected that others should in this case understand things better than she did; and truthfully she wasn't certain she understood even now. If the odds of black and red were the same, then five blacks on the trot *was* wildly unlikely. Surely red was more probable this time?

Except that apparently it wasn't.

Earthy supported her. She said, 'Of course red is more likely to turn up than black.' But Janet found her conviction unconvincing. On a matter of numbers, who was more likely to be right, Earthy or Veronica?

She smiled. She said, 'Never mind. I've reached the house limit so it doesn't matter.' On the next turn she placed a single chip and didn't care about the colour.

After her earlier small wins, Janet was ten Euros down and she didn't recover them during the rest of the session even though she had a spell as the bank. The others ended a few Euros either side of where they started. The clear winner was Carol with a gain of twenty Euros even though she never had the advantage of the bank.

'How did you do that?' asked Poppy. 'It's like *incredible!*'

'It's just luck,' said Veronica, slightly annoyed at Poppy's admiration for someone else.

'Possibly,' said Carol.

'What do you mean: *possibly*? It's a game of pure chance.'

'Yes and no.'

'You're being mischievous.'

'Possibly. Let's have a drink, shall we?'

Carol produced a couple of bottles of blanquette from the fridge and filled a half dozen glasses. She ushered the others to their seats and once they were sitting she gave grin of satisfaction.

'Out with it,' said Veronica. Her voice was somewhere between amusement and annoyance.

'All right. I'll tell you a few secrets about roulette and how to win – which is quite a trick because, as Veronica pointed out and Janet discovered, it's a game of chance with a built-in advantage to the house. Believe me because I've seen the lot: no system of picking numbers can win in the long run. Except . . . '

'Oh go on, you cow,' complained Belle. 'Don't keep us in suspense.'

'OK. There are two ways of winning roulette – though I'll tell you now that the theory is simpler than the practice because the casinos know both of them and take steps to stop them working.'

The first strategy, said Carol, was biased wheel play.

'Nobody can make a perfect roulette wheel that'll always run true. And even if they did, wear and tear will sooner or later have an effect. All of them tend to favour a number or more often a group of numbers, though most of the time the bias is too small to notice or it's too slight to beat the house advantage. The only way of knowing to is clock up a huge number of spins and then analyse them against chance. But it can be done.'

'Have you seen anyone do it?' asked Poppy in admiration.

Carol shook her head. 'Cruises are too short for the ordinary holiday punter to collect enough data, and the pros want to operate where they can make a quick exit, not be stuck in the middle of the sea. Bias wheel players normally work as a gang so that they can cover enough casinos and enough wheels before they find one that's worth the effort. They can spend months at it.'

'Then you can't have won that way,' Veronica pointed out.

'Maybe.' Carol grinned. 'I'm sorry to tell you but I cheated. I've been spinning the wheel on my own on and off all week and keeping a record. As you've seen, our wheel is just a kids' toy; so the manufacturers haven't been fussed about fine tolerances.'

'You mean it *is* biased?'

'Yeah, in fact quite a bit – towards one number either side of seven. It gives an advantage of about two percent to the player who notices it.'

'Wonderful.'

'Hey, you wanted to learn didn't you?'

Janet said, 'Go on. You seemed to say there was another way of winning.'

A nod. 'You have to watch the wheel. Most people apply roughly the same force every time they make the spin. So the wheel turns more or less the same number of times and the ball lands in more or less the same place relative to its starting point. There's nothing exact about it, but it means that on each turn the numbers in one segment of the wheel are favoured over the others. The casinos know it happens. They teach the staff to vary their spin and switch them between tables and between right and left hand wheels – anything to break up a pattern or stop it being noticed. Gamblers fix on particular dealers who get sloppy in varying their spin. They follow them from table to table and try to catch them at the end of a shift when they're tired.'

'Bloody hell,' said Belle.

'You all used a consistent spin,' said Carol. She gave them a defiant look but seemed a little ashamed even though there was no reason to be. 'Would you like your ten Euros back?' she asked Janet.

Janet chuckled. 'Not for the world. We must all expect to pay for experience, and now I've got a story to tell my daughter.'

Janet walked home with Belle. She asked, 'Where was Joy today? I was a few minutes late arriving. Did anyone give an explanation?'

'Veronica said she phoned. She was under the weather apparently. Flu or something. Arnold probably doesn't allow her to be sick when he's about, so a couple of days in bed must count as relaxation.'

At the Maison des Moines Janet asked if Belle would like to come in for coffee.

Belle checked her watch. 'No, I need to get home to give Charlie his tea.'

Janet waved as her friend stomped off up the lane to her house, then went inside, poured herself a glass of orange juice and took it onto the veranda where she could sit and watch the swallows in the early evening glow.

She was sitting there when the front door of Belle's house opened and the village girl came out: the same one she'd seen on the night they all went dancing.

14

In blackjack the object of the game is to score twenty-one or as near as possible without exceeding the limit and while beating the dealer's hand. The Ace scores as eleven or one, usually at the player's choice. Court cards count as ten. Two cards are dealt face up to the players, and two to the dealer of which only one is face up. The second is called the 'hole card'. A straight deal of an Ace with a card counting as ten is a 'natural' or 'blackjack'. The dealer must draw another card if his score is sixteen or less, and he must hold on seventeen. A player may hold or draw on any number. The game is played against the bank. The stake is lost if the player's hand fails to beat the dealer's. If both hands are equal the result is a stand-off or 'push' and the stake is returned. The bank pays even money on all winning bets except blackjack, when it plays three to two. Many variations of the rules exist.

Janet remembered how, after her family's Christmas dinner, they used to play pontoon on the cleared table – all except Great Auntie Cissie, who was plonked in front of the fire and supplied with bottles of Mackeson stout until she fell asleep. It seemed that everyone was there. The small house, normally cold, was heated by the press of bodies: her mother and father, her brothers and sister, her cousins Mikey and Jean, and her two handsome dancing uncles, Jack and Harry, as well as Harry's wife Beryl. For some reason – perhaps a television programme that went with the memory and fixed it in time – Janet was always eight years old and had plaits. But the custom of the Christmas party was as everlasting as her childhood and never changed in essentials. Her father, who ordinarily smoked Woodbines, puffed doubtfully on his annual cheap cigar; and he and Harry and Jack, all of them beer drinkers, polished off a bottle of Johnny Walker Red Label scotch while Janet's mother and

Auntie Beryl quietly got through tumblers of Gordon's Gin with orange cordial until Beryl felt inspired to strike up a raucous rendition of *Abide with Me* and Mother followed with *The Hills are Alive with the Sound of Music*.

'Like a cat with its tail on fire,' said Janet's father. He could sing *Cwm Rhonda* in a warm, rich tenor like a Welshman meeting Judgment Day. A man with such a voice could be certain of salvation.

'You'd think they'd get better with practice, wouldn't you?' said Uncle Harry. 'But they never do.'

They gambled wickedly. The grown-ups played for sixpences and the children played for matches, though, if they won, they got to keep the sixpences. What a wonderful game! And with all the cheating that quick wits and sleight of hand would allow.

'You're swindling me!' Janet's father complained with laughter in his voice and his eyes whisky-bright and wet with tears from the smoke of his horrible cigar.

'No I'm not!' Janet lied.

'Oh, what a little fibber!' he said, and tickled her round the midriff until she was helpless and crying for him to stop.

Uncle Jack used to pull sixpences from her ear.

Alan the Hindu priest left Carol with a memory and an address in Brisbane. At the end of the cruise, she made her way there, not expecting much except bed and board for a few weeks while she figured out what to do about her pregnancy. When all was said and done, a shag on a beach in Bali didn't feel like the start of a lifelong commitment. Yet stranger things had happened. Maybe he would accept that the child was his, though it was something of a tall order for anyone who could count. Also his willingness to acknowledge his fatherhood might well depend on the baby's colour. Not something Carol was prepared to bet on.

The address turned out to be a squat. Alan wasn't there and no one had heard of him; and then again no one much cared.

They welcomed her with a lack of curiosity, pointed out her corner of a room, and shared whatever they had in the way of food, booze and dope. She paid for them the old fashioned way and none of the other women seemed to mind. Their attitude towards her varied between high-flown plans for communal rearing of the child, herbal remedies to get rid of it, and various native enchantments whose purpose was never wholly clear. Carol arranged herself a medical abortion, left the squat and returned to the boats.

Carol was never sure if she was attracted to cruise liners because she saw Life as a gamble, or whether she saw Life as a gamble because of her experience on the boats. She was conscious , even amazed that she had no taste for cards or roulette or any of the other casino games, no need for the excitement they offered, and no overwhelming desire to win money. Yet she ran her life as if it were a matter of pure chance, a wager against whatever Fate chose to throw at her. It wasn't even a way of living she particularly cared for – not in those moments when she bothered to think about it. Why did she do it, then? She supposed she must be in rebellion against her parents: against their innocent humdrum existence. But if that were the case, it was an incomprehensible rebellion because she didn't hate them or despise them or even dislike them. She loved them.

She was distraught when she got the news of her father's death. It came too late for her to attend the funeral, and in any case it was when she was living in Naples with a sadistic Italian gangster and more or less confined to purdah in his luxurious apartment. Her mother's suicide, on the other hand, left her unmoved. What did that say about her?

Carol thought most introspection was garbage. You could never really know what you were like. You could never make plans with confidence. Blokes called Dave would always let you down, but for some reason they were essential in order to keep going and not top yourself.

'You have to stare Life in the face and tell it go to hell,' she told Belle.

'Rather you than me,' said Belle in wonder. 'I like my comfort too much.'

She poured another drink and a mischievous little question popped out.

'After the . . . you know . . . did you ever have any children?'

'No,' said Carol.

She'd never had children. Indeed never become pregnant again. Gonorrhoea probably didn't help.

Joy hadn't reappeared. The story was that she was still sick. Telephone calls got only a recorded message from Arnold in a rough Brummie accent. Janet decided she'd call on her.

After a week of grey skies and heavy showers the sun came back. Janet wanted exercise and a decent walk to Campmaurice and back seemed just the ticket.

'I'll pass,' said Belle when invited. 'If I try walking that far, there'll be two of us sick. Give her my love.'

'How's Charlie?'

'Oh, you know Charlie!' said Belle with a laugh.

But Janet didn't know Charlie. She'd never seen him. Never even heard his voice. That was the point.

'Nobody's seen him,' said Carol. 'She could have murdered him and buried him in the garden for all anyone knows. Always assuming she could dig a hole. Which she couldn't, not with being so fat.'

That theme of murder again. Janet was suspected of killing David – or possibly his brother Patrick or the tramp (she was losing the plot). Joy seemed simply to have vanished. And Charlie was like a creature of fiction, who wouldn't exist if Belle didn't occasionally mention him. Janet thought that Puybrun really was starting to look like one of those ridiculous villages beloved by lady crime writers where half the population gets slaughtered on a regular basis. It was too silly for words: the sort of plotting that offended Janet's sensibilities. Rather than think of it, it was much better to walk along quiet lanes with open fields to either side, day dreaming to the muted rumble of distant tractors, larks singing, and the drone of an aeroplane lifting a glider from the local club.

Janet whistled – badly – as she walked. Uncle Harry, on the other hand, had been a fantastic whistler. It was strange how one remembered such things: Harry at Christmas, always merry and smiling and ready to dance, pursing his lips in a piercing note every time he made pontoon, or accompanying her mother in her attempt to be Julie Andrews.

Pontoon and blackjack were essentially the same game, so Janet understood; and Carol was going to teach them blackjack. Would Joy be there to learn?

The second lesson in gambling went more matter-of-factly. Curiosity had already been satisfied with a thorough nosey in Carol's upstairs flat and the results discussed.

'I can't believe she's always that tidy in putting away her "smalls",' said Belle. 'I mean, it's not *natural*. And where are all her *shoes*?'

No one was any longer embarrassed at winning (or losing) money on a game of chance.

'At the end of the day, it's only pontoon with nobs on,' said Belle.

'Not if you're playing for thousands of pounds,' Janet said.

Belle stared at her. 'We don't do that in Clitheroe. You must be thinking of London.'

After the experience of roulette, Veronica came out straight away with her question. 'Where's the house advantage? I don't see it. The players' and the dealer's hands rank equally, and the dealer has no flexibility in how he plays, while the others do. So how does the bank make money?'

'The dealer can see the players' cards,' Earthy suggested cautiously.

Veronica shook her head firmly. 'It makes no difference, does it Carol? He has to play to a fixed set of rules whatever cards they have. Am I right?'

'Yes,' said Carol. 'But there is a house advantage.' She explained, 'It's mainly in the timing of how bets are lost. The players can choose whether or not to take more cards, but they don't know what the dealer's hole card is, which makes the draw more risky. They draw *first* before the dealer shows, and if they go bust, the bank wins immediately. Afterwards it doesn't matter what the dealer has or what he draws or whether or not he goes bust, because the player has already lost. The bank's edge is normally between five and six percent – better than roulette. It depends on the exact rules, the payout on a "natural" hand, and how many decks of cards are used in the shuffle.' She grinned and added, 'You can swap the bank between you so you each get the benefit. I won't take the bank. You'll be able to give me a good hiding.'

'Hark at Diamond Lil,' said Belle. 'Hang on to your handbags, girls.'

And so they began to play.

On a flip of a card, Janet became the bank. She surprised herself by having taken to heart Carol's lessons about the etiquette of the game: the hand signals used to indicate an intention to draw or to stay pat or to double the stake. After their first session there was a new seriousness. Gambling was still fun, and Carol was firm that they must play only for small sums, but they could see that there might be a science behind it and wondered what it was in the case of blackjack.

The bank switched whenever someone was dealt a 'natural' hand. Earthy gave a loud 'Whoop!' when it was her turn.

'Have you been casting spells again?' Belle asked her in a low voice, sarcastic because she was losing. Then she took the bank and began to win. They each found their fortunes improving when they were banker, exactly as Carol predicted. As for Carol herself, she neither won nor lost. The overall winner was Veronica.

Today they changed their routine after the game. Because the weather was fine again, they decided to go to the *buvette* for an early evening meal by the lakeside. Ravi was there, drinking a beer and playing his guitar. Janet wondered aloud where his 'muse', Hatshepsut, was.

'Oh, she's in England,' said Earthy. 'Ravi was taking her to the airport when you saw them on his bike.'

Janet paid no particular attention to the answer. Belle was asking about Joy, and Veronica was repeating that she was sick and describing her symptoms, which sounded like a summer flu. They discussed the next session of lessons, which Veronica had volunteered to give. Janet caught the enthusiasm in their voices. She shared it. But what would they do, once each of them had taught her skills to the others? Revisit them in more depth? Discover they had still further skills, ones they hadn't even identified? Janet was sure The English Lady Murderers' Society would continue because it was so fulfilling: the lessons themselves, but more than that the friendships. Still, the future was unknown.

Please God, don't let us turn into a ladies' afternoon mah jong club, she told herself.

And then she realised: *Veronica is lying about Joy.*

That morning she'd walked to Campmaurice in the drowsy heat: spinning her memories of family parties and dancing uncles and games of pontoon played for matches. And when she reached Joy's house, she saw Veronica's Peugeot parked there behind the wrought-iron gates Arnold had installed when he re-named the house *Mi Palacio* because, no matter what foreign country he lived in, he wanted to recreate his ideal of a Spanish holiday.

She knocked at the door.

Veronica opened it, and Janet could have sworn she looked shocked.

'Hullo, Janet.'

'Hullo, Veronica. How is Joy?'

'Rather low – headaches – shivers – you know.'

'Has she seen a doctor?'

'I don't think it's that serious. I've been to the pharmacy in Chalabre.'

'Is there anything I can do to help? I imagine she has a cleaner. Shopping? Can I go to the *supermarché*?'

'That's kind of you, but she'll be fine.'

'May I see her?'

Veronica looked over her shoulder into the house. 'Let me ask,' she said. She closed the door and Janet found herself standing at the threshold like a Jehovah's Witness. When Veronica came back she said, 'I'm afraid Joy's asleep. I don't want to disturb her. It's best for her. You understand?'

'Of course,' Janet agreed. It made sense. Yet the scene had an oddity, reminding her of those old Italian films where the dialogue was dubbed and one had a feeling that the actors might in reality be talking about something completely different.

Veronica offered her a lift, but Janet said she preferred to walk. She was half way back to the village before Veronica's Peugeot passed her and the driver gave a cheery wave. Perhaps her suspicions were mistaken after all.

She thought of retracing her steps and returning to the house. But Joy might really be asleep, and she imagined Veronica would be furious if she found out. Then before there was time to think, there would be a row and people taking sides and the circle of friends they were working so hard to create would be broken apart. Janet didn't want that. She valued these women. Also, by comparison with men, who were noisy and easily ashamed, women were such persistent and sneaky enemies, and, what with fraud and murder, her life was complicated enough without that.

Now at the *buvette* in the balmy evening she heard Veronica, in her easy, cultured voice explaining Joy's illness while Ravi sang in a bad impersonation of Bob Dylan and Earthy watched him, mesmerised. The others were eating and Sandrine bustled back and forth with trays of food. Janet noticed she had a new tattoo.

They finished the meal and sat a while over coffee. Veronica drank a brandy and the others finished their glasses of blanquette. Poppy had brought a costume and proposed to swim; the lake was enticing with its still waters reflecting the white cliffs and sky.

'I'll see you at home,' Veronica called out to Poppy's back as she walked away, swinging her costume. Janet watched and caught the small agony in her eyes, one of those flashes even happy people have, which pass unnoticed for the most part until tragedy drags them up like dead fish from a stagnant pond. It was curious but Janet doubted it had anything to do with what concerned her.

'I'll walk with you,' she said.

Veronica turned and composed a smile. 'All right.'

They strolled in silence to the village past chalets and farm houses covered in wisteria, and small plots where plum trees grew. Doors were open and French families ate their dinners and their voices came out into the evening.

'There's something you want to ask,' Veronica said. Not exactly a question.

'Yes,' said Janet.'

Veronica nodded. 'Then ask,' she said, and waited.

'Joy is a chronic alcoholic, isn't she?'

15

Texas hold 'em is a form of poker popularised in the final of the World Series. Each player is dealt two pocket cards face down and the betting opens. Three community cards are dealt face up ('the flop') followed by a second round of betting. Players bet after two further deals of a single community card and then the showdown takes place and the highest hand wins. A player may always fold instead of betting. The aim is to make the best five card poker hand from the player's two pocket cards and the five community cards.

Veronica considered herself a risk taker not a gambler. There was a difference. Taking a calculated risk was a science: a rational assessment of likelihood and the impact if an event occurred. Gambling was all lucky rabbits' feet and systems based on delusion and a failure to understand probability theory.

While they were sitting over dinner after the blackjack game, Earthy asked with obvious admiration, 'How did you manage to manage to win so much? Was it just luck?'

Which made Poppy burst out laughing. 'Luck? Nar! Not with our V'ronica it ain't!'

Veronica glanced at her but said nothing. Carol helped out.

She said, 'It wasn't luck. I was watching. Go on, Veronica, tell them what you were doing.'

'Well, really, it wasn't very much. It's obvious that blackjack isn't simply a game of chance . . . '

'That's news to me,' Belle said. She closed her eyes and smacked her forehead with the heel of her hand. 'D'oh!'

'Oh? I thought . . . What I mean is that it isn't like roulette, where – as long as the wheel isn't biased and the croupier is doing his job – there's nothing the players can do to affect the odds.'

Janet was intrigued. 'Aren't the odds fixed in blackjack?'

'Oh no!' said Veronica. 'The five or six percent house advantage is just an average, but the *actual* odds vary with every hand that's played.'

It hadn't occurred to her that the others hadn't seen what she saw, and now that she realised, she found it slightly unsettling as though she weren't a part of the group.

She hesitated. 'How to explain? Take a deck of cards with four Aces. It means that at the start you have four chances to be dealt "blackjack" – yes? But imagine all four Aces come out in the first round. What then? Well, one thing's certain: there's absolutely no chance of anyone getting "blackjack" during the rest of the game until the shuffle. So, obviously, the odds have changed. And that's true generally. You see: once a card is played, it can't be played again – can it?'

'What she does is called card counting,' said Carol. 'It requires a terrific head for figures. I can't do it, but Veronica has the gift.'

Veronica blushed. 'I don't know about that.'

'I still don't understand,' said Earthy plaintively.

Veronica tried again: 'It comes down to the rules governing the dealer. He's forced to draw extra cards if his score is sixteen or less. It means that if he's holding twelve or more, he'll go bust if he draws a ten or a face card. Now think of my example of the Aces and imagine that the high value cards aren't random but happen to be nearer the bottom of the deck. As the game goes on, the more likely the dealer is to draw a high card and go bust.'

'You mean you know where the high cards are?' Janet asked.

'Not exactly that. But I can see how many cards have been played and the number of tens or face cards, and so I know how many are left in the deck at any point and the odds of the dealer drawing one. If the odds favour me, then I increase my bet. The principle is really quite simple.'

Simple!

There was nothing else to say. The others were awestruck. Veronica, however, was puzzled as people can be when others don't understand something they grasp intuitively. She'd spent most of her working life trading in debt and derivatives, where there was always a risk that somebody somewhere would default. Those outside the business called it gambling, but in fact the risk could be statistically modelled and priced – or so everyone had been taught before the Credit Crunch. The behaviour of people in the mass was to a large extent predictable. The true gamble came in the intimacy of individual relationships – with Poppy, for example.

Veronica felt at times that she'd staked the entirety of her existence on her lover, only to find that long periods of happiness could be forgotten in a brutal instant and she would be confronted by the stark horror of her choice: the abyss that would open if she'd made a mistake. It could happen in unforeseen ways, out of incidents so trifling that it was impossible to explain them to other people without seeming ridiculous. Veronica was organised: Poppy was careless. Veronica was calm: Poppy was volatile. The language of love was expressed silently in the simple actions of everyday life, but so often it was misunderstood.

Veronica shuddered at the memory of standing in front of Poppy in a state of suppressed fury and saying with all seriousness: 'I am *not* talking about dirty coffee cups in the sink or the disgusting knickers you dropped on the floor. Don't you *understand*, darling? I'm talking about *us* and about whether you love me.'

And Poppy, uncomprehending, angry and tearful, had whined, 'I don't get it with you. D'you *want* me to pick up the fuckin' knickers or what?' Followed by the clincher: Poppy in triumph at the top of her voice: 'And anyway it's *not* "knickers" – it's a thong!'

On the cruise ships they played Caribbean stud poker, a game in which the players bet against the house at fixed odds. It was designed for holiday punters without the skill or nerve for the real thing, but who wanted to believe they were high rollers. It bored Carol to death.

After a few hands Belle said, 'I don't know what anyone sees in this? It's not as good as pontoon. I mean: what is there to do except turn your cards over and hope you get lucky?'

The others nodded. Coming after roulette and blackjack, the game was a failure. Carol suggested they go out to get coffee and stretch their legs and she'd have something else for them when they returned.

They wandered into the square. Workmen were dressing the *halle* for a visiting band and setting out tables. They paused to stare at Poppy, who this morning seemed almost to dance in the sunlight, so transparently gay that Veronica wanted to cry from tenderness. Yesterday Poppy had come back from swimming in a wonderful mood. She gave no reason but had simply been very loving so that Veronica was overwhelmed: finding herself filled with joy. But just as unexpectedly came the dirty, unfounded suspicion that she was witnessing the first evidence of infidelity. The thought that she might be becoming jealous was hateful, yet she didn't know what to do about it. Was it possible to dissipate it with an act of will? How could one live if every second of happiness bore the shadow of something else?

Most of the women went to the bar, but Veronica heard a voice say, 'I had coffee first thing. I don't want another.'

Veronica turned. Janet was standing next to her. She had a sense the other woman was reading her mind; not literally, but Janet was so very perceptive. In contrast Veronica felt that, for all her intelligence, she was stupid where people were concerned: that somehow she couldn't *see* them. She also thought that Janet was dangerous, though she didn't know why.

She said, 'No, I don't think I could drink any more either.'

'Then we'll just stand and take in the sun, shall we?'

'Yes . . . By the way, what made you think that Joy was an alcoholic?'

'Is she? When I asked, you didn't answer.'

Veronica had remained frozen when Janet first put the question.

'What makes you think she is?'

'A small thing. There was no bar in the house; I noticed when we were there before the first walk, and I thought how odd it was. You see it seemed to me from everything people said about Arnold, and from his general taste in houses and furniture, that he was just the sort of man who would have a bar in the house. So why wasn't there one?'

Veronica gave a humourless laugh. 'That doesn't sound like much on which to found a theory.'

'No. That's why I haven't mentioned my suspicion to anyone else. I also noticed that Joy was very firm about being the driver when we went to the fete at Le Peyrat. Of course, it meant she couldn't drink.'

Veronica looked at the other woman for a moment and wondered what else was going on in her head. 'Do you play poker?'

Janet smiled. 'No. When I was a child I used to play brag with my brothers and sister and my father. We played pontoon at Christmas and brag whenever the television broke down. The old black and white televisions were always breaking down.'

'I imagine you'd be very good,' said Veronica.

'I was very bad at roulette. I still don't understand why my betting system was wrong.' Janet wasn't sure she wanted to be good at poker. It implied she was emotionless or insincere or, at worst, a liar. Was that what Veronica thought? She hoped it was just tactlessness on her part. As it happened, however, Janet had been good at brag when she was a child.

They returned to Carol's studio.

'We're going to play Texas hold 'em,' Carol said.

'Yee haw,' murmured Belle without enthusiasm.

'It's the most common form of poker played at tournaments;

but I didn't get involved with it much on the boats because there's no bank, just a dealer to keep the game honest.' She placed some sheets of paper on the table. 'I've written the odds of drawing the various hands to help you. Beyond that, it's a matter of trying to read the behaviour of other people and mask your own feelings.'

Carol looked at the others. She reminded herself that reading the behaviour of people and masking her own feelings was precisely what she was not good at. No wonder there were so many Daves. She asked herself if the great gamble of her life had been worthwhile: the decision to sacrifice commonsense for the intensity of the moment. Probably not. Then again, was it true to say that, where living in Dave World was concerned, she had exercised her free will? The fact that you could use words to express a choice didn't mean it actually existed. The alternative to her rackety life might never have been more than an illusion. After all, had it ever been possible that she could leave a Dave unshagged as long as she believed he would offer a moment of happiness? She told herself: I'm a stupid bitch and couldn't have acted differently. She began to deal.

'Eyes down for a full house,' said Belle.

Of their lessons so far, poker was the least successful. The calculation and the lying were too stark, and the result was one or two spats: not serious but enough to take the edge off their enjoyment. Belle voiced a general feeling when she said, 'I don't think I could take to gambling, especially not poker. It's just not me. I don't mean it hasn't been fun,' she added for Carol's benefit. 'But it's a bit like tatting, isn't it? Interesting enough, but something for other people to do.'

Janet stifled a laugh. 'Sorry – I just had a picture of James Bond doing tatting. Sorry.'

The others laughed too. Janet was pleased. It was strange how a situation could tip one way or another on such a small point;

but her remark set the mood and afterwards everyone thought that perhaps they had enjoyed the lesson after all.

They had played cards all day.

'Aren't we wicked?' said Belle. She glanced at her watch. 'I'd best see to Charlie.'

The others too drifted away leaving only Veronica and Janet in the square wondering whether there was more to be said about their earlier conversation.

'Can I help?' Janet asked. 'Alcoholics can be quite difficult. If there's a mess – I mean I could do some cleaning; or perhaps there are clothes that need washing or ironing?'

'That's kind of you.' Veronica looked away. Janet noticed that Léon was loitering nearby as if he couldn't bring himself to some purpose he had in mind. Veronica said, 'It's a kind offer but . . . You'll understand that Joy is feeling humiliated. I have some experience . . . I . . . as I say, I have some experience of handling people like her.'

Janet didn't answer. She felt she'd just been given a confidence, the way that people will sometimes pass a gift, avoiding touching the other person's hand out of embarrassment at the inadequacy of it; almost on the point of taking it back. She found herself moved, yet didn't know why. Veronica was evidently finished and there was nothing for either to do than mutter farewells. Then Janet was left standing in the square and her mobile was ringing.

'Hullo – Helen?'

'You don't sound glad to hear from me.'

'I'm standing around in a public square. It's not exactly the best moment for a long conversation.'

'It never is, is it? You keep your phone turned off for most of the time.'

'It hasn't been convenient. I've been playing Texas hold 'em poker all day.'

'Mother!'

162

'Oh, don't worry. I came out twenty pounds ahead.' It so happened that Janet *was* good at poker, exactly as Veronica had predicted. 'Why are you calling? Have you discovered that long-lost Uncle Patrick has taken to wearing a dress and is living here in Puybrun as a fugitive axe murderer?'

'You can be so facetious sometimes.'

Yes, I can be, Janet thought. 'I'm sorry, darling,' she said more gently, and for a minute or two they chatted about Chloë and Henry, who was still in a Black Mood and worried about his Position At The Bank.

'But to what do I owe the pleasure?' Janet asked at last. 'Have the police turned up something new about your father's business? Has Jeremy confessed to fraud?'

'Not exactly. In fact I'm not sure exactly what it is. They've been doing something – tests – something – with the organs left over from the post mortem: the ones they found in a drawer or a cupboard somewhere. Have they spoken to you?'

'Not a word.' Janet was curious. 'Have they found something?'

'I don't know. I suppose so.'

'What?'

'Was Dad seeing the doctor? Did he have a heart problem?'

Janet was astonished. 'No, of course not. Are they saying he had a problem? He said nothing to me and he certainly wasn't seeing the doctor.'

Like most men, David didn't visit the doctor from one decade to the next; he probably didn't even know his doctor's name. In fact in his case it would be close to the truth to say he had a phobia of the medical profession. It was impossible that he'd received treatment for a heart condition without making a noisy fuss and quite possibly refusing point blank to see anyone about it. So if the dead man was being treated for a heart condition . . .

'Are we back on the subject of the mythical identical twin?' Janet asked cautiously.

Helen didn't answer. While there might be some doubt about

whether he was an *identical* twin, Patrick certainly wasn't mythical, and her mother knew it.

There was nothing else to say and the conversation wound down to an unsatisfactory close leaving Janet feeling bad tempered again. One call was enough. She turned off her phone, and put it in her bag. When she looked up again she found Léon there in all his ugly attractiveness, apparently wanting to say something.

'Will you have dinner and go dancing with me tonight . . . Janet?' he asked.

'Yes, of course!' Janet snapped.

How to Identify Wild Flowers

16

Love Lies Bleeding (*Amaranthus caudatus*) has brilliant red-purple, drooping, tail-like flower spikes. It is a frequent garden escape.

Janet was appalled. What have I just agreed to? Did I understand what Léon was saying? Did I really say I'd go for a meal and dancing with him? It's ridiculous! I must be thirty years older than he is. Am I trying to spite Helen? Am I going mad?

Yet she did nothing: simply watched as the young man walked away and reminded herself that he was a dancer; it was obvious in the easy confidence of his movements.

She returned to her cottage. For a while she sat in silence, astonished at herself as if she were a stranger. Then she began slowly to shower, dress and make-up against the possibility that she might actually keep this insane date, telling herself that the preparations meant nothing because until the last moment when he was on the doorstep she could decide not to.

If I've murdered my husband, it would make sense to take a lover.

She could hear David laughing. He'd been a thorough-going atheist and thought the living owed nothing to the dead. He'd told her often enough, with a twinkle in his eye, that he didn't give a damn what she did when he was out of it: she might take lovers of any age, sex or species for all he cared, and dance on his grave.

Perhaps that was the explanation. She was sharing a joke with her dead husband. He would unquestionably have found her predicament hilarious. It hadn't occurred to her before that the continuation of a humorous conversation about death might form a part of the grieving process. Now she supposed it must. And quite likely a lot of other conversations.

She put on a red dress with a shawl collar and a full skirt that would allow her to move freely, and over it she draped an embroidered pashmina against the evening chill. When Léon arrived, in a white shirt and jeans worn over his trademark scuffed cowboy boots, she thought he looked like one of the extras in the Sicillian scenes from *The Godfather*, as if he should have a shotgun slung over his shoulder. She realised she was thinking of a movie made before he was born.

'We shall go to the Altay,' he said.

Janet hadn't eaten at the Kazakh restaurant since her first evening in Puybrun.

'Oh? Aren't they serving food in the *halle* before the band comes on?'

'The villagers eat there. They will stare at us and talk.'

'They'll stare and talk once we start dancing.'

'Yes. But when we eat, we are like everyone else. But when we dance, we shall be beautiful.'

My God – Janet thought – the things young men can say and get away with. Though, in fact, David might have said exactly the same, and she could never be certain if he was making fun because he had a disconcerting knack of joking and being deadly serious at the same time. Léon was apparently serious.

They walked the short distance to the restaurant. Léon didn't try to hold her hand, but Janet wondered if he wanted to and if she would have let him. In for a penny, in for a pound? Exactly how much was 'a pound' in present circumstances? Did he have a mad notion that at some point he was going to kiss her? Touch her breasts? Sleep with her? David was still laughing, and of no help at all.

If this is grieving, it isn't at all what I imagined. More exciting, for one thing. Funnier, too. Then suddenly she wanted to cry, but she managed to hold the tears back. I'm getting better at that, she thought.

A few campers and other strangers sat at the tables and paid no attention to an attractive older woman with, presumably, her son.

'I suppose I'll have goat pizza,' Janet murmured over the menu.

'They have goat pizza?'

'No. A joke – it's too complicated. I'm English,' she added in case that explained something.

They ordered pizzas and wine. Léon seemed to lose confidence; at all events he said very little except when Janet pressed him. He revealed he came from Lille, where he'd taught dancing for a while. The equivalent of coming from Leicester, Janet thought, which was what she'd guessed. For all his sexual swagger, he was just a boy from the provinces.

She said, 'Why did you ask me here?'

'You don't like the food?' He smiled. 'The goat?'

'I didn't mean the meal. I don't know the French word for a "date". You asked me on a date.'

'I like to dance. You are the only woman in Puybrun who know how to do the dance.'

'There are girls . . . '

'*Bof!* Disco! It has nothing in it.' He looked down at his plate, avoiding her eyes.

'Then we'll go dancing,' Janet said. She paid the bill and refused any contribution. If she was going to perform this bizarre role of a predatory older woman she was going to enjoy it by doing it properly. After all, she was old enough to have seen *The Graduate* when it first came in the cinema, and she admired Anne Bancroft.

Night was falling. They crossed the road by the bridge, taking a moment to pause at the parapet and stare into the water. Janet remembered how she and David had often done this: in Wales, spying on a dipper in a fast flowing stream; in Madeira, where a yellow wagtail bobbed cheekily. There was something companionable about standing on a bridge watching the water flow by. It was a metaphor of something, no doubt, but Janet couldn't be bothered to think what it was. Instead she felt an urge to invite Léon to play a game of Pooh Sticks, but that would be too English and even more difficult to explain than goat pizza.

The square was full of people. The trestles and benches had been drawn to the edge of the *halle* to free the floor for dancing. The band was a trio of sax, accordion and drums. Janet looked about nervously for her friends but saw only Carol, who was standing outside the P.T.T., smoking. Carol noticed her, grinned and mouthed a single word that Janet thought was 'Dave'.

The band began. A singer emerged from the bar carrying a foaming *demi*: a raddled type who might have been fifty or seventy and wore a leather biker's jacket and a T shirt. He showed no interest in the audience but on a signal to the others started singing *Que reste-t-il de nos amours?*, an old Charles Trenet number that Janet loved. Léon seemed to sense this because he immediately took hold of her gently, and they did an uncomplicated foxtrot. The singer followed with a couple more of the same vintage, then switched to something more modern.

Unsurprisingly Léon was an accomplished dancer: better by far than David, if not as mischievous. Janet imagined he was holding himself back so as not to embarrass her with any steps outside her ability, and he was probably nervous too, as one is when dancing with a stranger. What she hadn't expected was his subtlety. She'd thought he would follow the set routines with fine technique but little feeling. Instead he danced delicately, even tenderly: not pretending they were lovers, but hinting that they might be.

It was delicious.

'So what was *that* all about?' Belle asked when she came bustling to Janet's house at breakfast. 'I wish I'd have been there; I'd have paid good money. Talk of the village, eh? Who's the scarlet women, eh? Literally, if what I heard about the dress was true.'

'I suppose Carol told you.'

'She came round to my place like she does, and we got plastered, like we do. I couldn't have stopped her telling me if I'd tried. And, of course, I didn't try. So what's he like?'

'He has no conversation,' Janet said. She imagined his intelligence and education were of a very ordinary sort, and didn't know if it mattered. Normally she preferred the company of bright, witty men. David could be sparkling at times (and boring at others, admittedly). It was a question of the nature of the relationship, which in this instance was a mystery.

'Did he . . . ?'

'He kissed my hand as we said goodbye.'

He hadn't known what to do and fumbled over it.

'Your hand? Oh, well.' Belle sounded disappointed. ' And will you be seeing him again?'

'He hasn't asked to meet my parents.'

Belle nodded. 'That means he mustn't be serious.' She grinned. 'Why on earth did you go out with him – I mean apart from him being gorgeous and sexy, except for being a bit hideous?'

'I don't know.'

'I think it's pure devilment,' Belle said firmly. 'I think you've got a mischievous streak, you.'

Janet thought she might have.

Léon had said that there were many country dances, which Janet already knew. If she would like, they could go dancing every weekend for the rest of the summer. She said that would be nice. What else could she say in thanks for such an enjoyable evening?

Belle looked at her watch. 'Come on, our kid. It's time to go. Veronica's got us looking at wild flowers if you believe it.'

Veronica's father had been a vicar with a country parish in Kent. He was good natured and socially inept, and bumbled his way into his forties always hoping to marry but latterly not expecting to. Then out of the blue a woman, still in her middle thirties, had set her cap at him (if such an active expression could be used about someone as passive as Veronica's mother). Veronica was a beautiful woman and her parents too might have been considered very good-looking, except that from childhood they'd been so lacking in confidence and style that they'd been considered 'plain'. The people they might have been were apparent only in their photographs, where no one could hear her father hesitating and stumbling through one of his idiotic sermons, or her mother wilting like the flowers that always seemed to die on her. The vicar went to his Maker when he was seventy-five and Veronica was thirty. Her mother followed at the age of sixty-eight for no obvious cause. Having no purpose in life she seemed to have died out of nothing more than tact.

Leaving me as a lesbian with a lover twenty years my junior, thought Veronica. Not that she attributed either fact to her parents. She was unwilling to regard her life as a form of pathology to be analysed and excused: still less to be excused by blaming others. However she did attribute her love of wild flowers to her parents and the long walks they used to take together.

They made their first expedition locally. They did a wide circuit of the castle by well marked paths over the hill and back past the cemetery and the lane on which Belle and Janet had their houses. Had they chosen, instead of returning they might have continued along the line of wooded hills that bordered this side of the plateau until they reached Vieux Moulin. Indeed Earthy suggested they should do.

'You absolutely must see the *sentier sauvage* and the *temple des fauves*,' she said.

Janet had vaguely heard of them as a strange natural feature of the area, but nothing more. Belle was more practical.

'It's too far to walk. There and back is twelve miles at least. I've had enough of trekking.'

The objection was unanswerable. Earthy said, 'Well, never mind. We'll go there when it's my turn.' In the meantime they followed the original proposal.

They took a dry path covered in limestone dust. It rose from the highway past a small lady chapel then threaded through brush until it reached a broad, stony road used by tourist coaches on their way to the castle. Either side grew a profusion of pinks and scentless broad-leafed peas. The pinks were large-flowered, resembling carnations and so bright they seemed to fluoresce. The peas had long winged stems and straggled over the other plants, resting their blowsy blossoms like butterflies.

They skirted the castle. Janet was puzzled that she'd never bothered to visit it. The answer, of course, was that she lived here and could always pay a visit tomorrow. It was why the inhabitants of places seemed to know less about them than the tourists.

'Do they all know about Léon?' she asked Belle as they found themselves together. She nodded towards the other women.

'Of course,' said Belle. 'What did you expect? It would have been inhuman not to tell. Anyway, Veronica and Poppy are hardly likely to be jealous that you've found yourself a fella. I can't speak for Earthy. She'd probably sympathise since she seems to have her eye on Ravi – God bless her. And as for Carol . . . '

'I haven't got "a fella".'

'If you say so.'

'I *haven't*.'

'If it looks like a duck and quacks like a duck. – I'm only kidding. What do you think Léon's game is, then?'

'I don't know that he has a game.'

'Oh – so you mean it could be sex after all? Then go for it, is all I can say.'

They passed the overgrown path to the Metairie d'Oc, a small farm that served as a B & B for ramblers, and turned for the home leg. Belle was tiring.

'This is getting to be like one of Joy's Death Marches. I wonder how she's getting on. Is she over her bug?'

Janet wondered too. Veronica had still not actually admitted that Joy had a drink problem, and so there remained the possibility she was ill. No – Janet was certain.

To the left was the cemetery. It was edged with a line of

cypresses and dominated by the hill and the long flank of castle. To the right were dry fields of scrub dotted with intense blue flowers of vipers bugloss and paler meadow cranesbill. Stonecrop grew among the rocks.

'They're beautiful, aren't they?' said Belle, and added, as if it was a cause for great sadness, 'When I was a girl me and my friends used to pick them and put them in jam jars, even though we didn't know their names. But there's no point. They never keep. Nothing does, does it?'

'No,' said Janet. *Nothing keeps. Everyone knows that.* It struck her then how the trite observations of life are also the most mysterious. Her memory of David might picture him laughing over this moment and telling her in a warm, reassuring voice that he was all right and she must go on and be happy, and indeed have fun whenever possible. But the reality was that he was dead and wasn't telling her anything at all. Everything he had to say had been said while he was alive and she wasn't paying attention. Now the only consolation was that most of it was no more than amusing nonsense. David had been emphatic that he wasn't wise. And he'd been right.

As they passed Belle's house, she said she would call it a day and see to Charlie. The village girl was sitting in the small paved area at the front. She stood to open the gate. Janet hesitated whether to return to her own home but was prevailed on to take coffee at the bar.

The tables and benches of the previous evening had been cleared from the *halle* and the square was silent except for an occasional *ping* and cry from someone playing the pinball machine.

The women went into the bar and found that Joy was there, sitting primly over coffee in a high collared blouse and a beige linen skirt.

'Hullo, everyone,' she said, and treated them to an uncertain smile.

17

Wood Forgetmenot (*Mysotis Sylvatica*) is a short, softly hairy perennial with sky blue flowers found in woods and grasslands and on mountains.

At the age of thirty-five Earthy found herself alone. Sir Gawain Warlock of the Shire was doing his two year stretch, she'd given her child to adoption, and after a bout of depression she was left with a life that had lost its savour.

Her looks went. An outdoor life scrubbed her face to a rough rosy glow and a high carbohydrate diet and fibroids thickened her figure. The men who showed interest became old, or strange or downright mad, until there came a time when even the mad ones wanted her only as someone to rant at.

As a consolation she imagined herself growing wiser with the years: steeped in knowledge of the Goddess, of earth magic, of the lore of the tribe and the ways of the social security system. In this guise her single status would mark her as a Wise Woman, an object worthy of veneration. Children would sit at her feet to hear her stories, maidens beg use of her mirror to scry the faces of their lovers, and callow youths ask for love potions.

Instead of which she got twelve months probation for benefit fraud – consideration being given to a degree of mental instability caused by two miscarriages and the loss of the third child in respect of whom she'd been claiming allowances. Also it was difficult to imprison someone who sounded like the Queen.

But surely – she told herself – if there were anything to this New Age life, she *must* be becoming wiser? Yet no one sought her advice. No one called her by the beautiful name of Earth Child. She was plain Earthy, no longer the offspring of the earth but a mere clod, an agricultural implement with legs, who could be relied on to do every kind of back-breaking work among the vegetable plots; the camp skivvy and ever available baby sitter. It was hateful. And it went on for years – for decades – because she had no skills, no money, no contacts, no knowledge of the world outside a few rain-sodden acres of Wales. Because, as she finally saw, she had allowed herself to become not a Wise Woman but a half-idiot creature: Caliban, not Prospero.

She told the gist of this to Belle during one of the long walks organised by Joy. She made a mess of the story, unable to convey the tragedy of her life because even now she didn't truly see it; but Belle caught a glimmer; and curiosity and her own warm nature made her want to know more.

'So what happened?' she asked, when Earthy got to the worst part (a conviction for receiving stolen goods – two lambs and a hen – and six months inside, notwithstanding the regal voice: 'in order to send a message to the travelling community that this is something Society will not put up with'). 'How old were you? How did you get away?'

Earthy didn't want to go on – it was too distressing – but Belle pressed her. 'You need to let it all out, love. Tell your Auntie Belle. Anyway it's too exciting to stop. It's like a film: *The Great Escape.*'

'I saw that,' said Earthy, cheering up. 'In a cinema in Builth Wells. I thought Steve McQueen was very handsome.'

'Yes he was.'

'Yes . . . he was . . . ' She paused at a memory. A visit to a cinema in Builth Wells might have been a high point in her life. She went on, 'To answer your question, I was fifty-three. My parents died within three months of each other, and it seems my father was quite rich from his job as a consultant and investments and houses and things. At least I suppose he was rich – by what little I know. Certainly there was enough, even divided with my brother and sister, to buy my small cottage and provide me with something to live on if I'm careful. My brother was very kind. I hadn't expected that. He said I was his big sister and he'd always looked up to me when he was a boy – isn't that strange? He's a doctor – very clever. He found me and then helped to set me up here. I couldn't have done it on my own.'

Earthy was religious in her fashion. Her beliefs were a rat's nest of bits and pieces of garbled traditions. She made sense of her brief joys and long sufferings by supposing that a benign Providence looked over her and that behind everything, including the horrible parts, there was a Deep Purpose that she would understand if she grasped Life's Lessons. Otherwise, for her sins, she would be doomed to be reincarnated, possibly next time in a part of Wales even wetter and more depressing than the one she knew.

'I felt that God was trying to tell me something,' Earthy said.

'Oh, I'm sure he was,' Belle agreed. 'He gave you a pile of dosh and said: "There you are, love. It's time to give up communism." '

Earthy was slightly put out when Veronica volunteered to teach the others the beauties of wild flowers, but too kind to resent her. She told herself that her own speciality lay in the mysteries of herbs: their healing virtues – not the same as recognising tufted vetch or bryony, and picking them only to press their petals in an album (though in fact Veronica didn't do that). In her imagination Earthy collected her plants by night when the dew was on the grass, moonbeams broke through the forest canopy, and the magic of Selene was over them.

In fact she bought them mail order from a wholesaler in Paris along with oriental tat made in Nepalese sweatshops.

Mondays meant Mirepoix where Earthy and Carol took piles of their wares in Carol's beat-up van and flogged them in the market. Veronica said she knew an easy stroll on the further side of the river beyond the road to Carcassonne and Castelnaudary. While Earthy and Carol sold their stuff, the others could mooch and browse the stalls; then they would snack and afterwards walk off lunch with a little botanising thrown in. Joy, still subdued, offered to drive them in the Tank. The town being crowded, they parked in a lane just off the highway along the line of the river, and Veronica began her lesson by pointing out a stand of fennel growing on the verge.

Mirepoix is a *bastide* town. Mediaeval buildings surround a large square and at one end is a small, shabby cathedral with a gloomy charm. A mad woman haunts it and asks the English tourists, 'How is Her Majesty?' and they always say that she is very well, thank you.

The women made a circuit of the square, following the shadow of the arcade, then up and down the rows of stalls and to the islands of buildings around the covered area. They bought vegetables and cheeses and charcuterie, and held up flimsy cotton dresses as if to say, 'How do you fancy me in this?' and they laughed at each other. They tested perfumes. They sniffed at soaps. They put earrings to their ears and tilted their heads in mirrors. They tried on improbable hats that seemed to be made from the fluff found under beds, except that they were plum coloured or orange. They picked up old Gallimard paperbacks from second-hand bookstalls and found that they were always volume two of three and by someone they'd never heard of.

'I'm knackered,' said Belle after an hour of this. 'I need to rest my feet. Hey, there's Léon and Ravi.'

The two young men had set up a table in an out of the way corner by a van selling country sausages. Ravi, in his saffron kurta pajama, was squatting on the cobbles plucking notes from one of his unnameable instruments. Léon had stacked some pamphlets advertising the wit and wisdom of the Brotherhood of Om and surrounded them with ranks of his crude, haunting figures.

Janet hadn't seen or spoken to him since the dance, an occasion she still thought of as their 'date', a word she tested for its past associations and present absurdity. She realised she was revelling in her own foolishness. Of course this relationship was going nowhere, but it was pleasurable like one of those romantic comedies one could immerse oneself in for an hour or two, with the advantage in this case of having a speaking part.

He saw her. He called out, 'Janet!' His mouth broadened into his snaggle-toothed smile.

Janet went to him and they began talking shyly about incidental matters. Then he said, 'Next Saturday there is a fete in Belesta. Will you come with me?'

Janet said she would. It seemed perfectly natural to say so. She explained as much to Belle afterwards.

'I can see you and me are going to have to have a motherly chat, my girl,' said Belle. 'I've warned you before about wearing make-up and showing too much of your buzzooms. Boys! They're only after one thing!'

'My pension?' asked Janet.

They lunched outside under the arcade. The stallholders were closing and putting away their wares. Carol and Earthy joined them as they were finishing.

'We had to pack the van,' said Carol. 'But don't worry; we managed to grab a bite. What was it, Earthy? Falafel? Aduki bean fritters? Summat to save the planet anyway.'

Janet wasn't paying attention. She was settling the bill, and something about it jogged her memory. An anomaly? Yet the bill was obviously correct, nothing more nor less than what they'd ordered. It would come to her later, no doubt, and in any case it was probably unimportant.

Then, equally unbidden came a question. She asked, 'Earthy, have you ever heard of Llannocksyn? I can't swear to how you spell it.'

'Llannocksyn? I can't say I have. But some of these places in Wales are just a farm and a chapel.' She smiled gently. 'As I know well enough to my cost.'

'It's a garden in Cornwall,' said Belle. 'Charlie and I went there once.'

Janet nodded; but she was sure the garden in Cornwall had another name. In any case neither she – nor David, as far as she knew – had been or proposed to go to either the garden or the real or mythical place in Wales. She remembered where the word came from: a note on a scrap of paper. It looked as though David had spelled it phonetically, which suggested he'd never been there: always assuming there was a 'there' rather than an 'it' or even a person. She wondered if she were creating a mystery out of something that was innocently unfamiliar: a name associated with his business for example, in which she'd never had any interest. He might have said 'Llannocksyn' a dozen times and she hadn't noticed.

They left the town and set about their walk. On the far side of the river and the Carcassonne highway, they found a path across open fields to a low ridge and followed the crest to the margin of a wood. Veronica pointed out flowers as they walked: thyme growing in the short grass along the path and marjoram in the verges among the ladies bedstraw; sainfoin, yellow vetchling and spiny rest harrow.

Poppy knew the way. She was in a good mood and strode forward with her blonde hair teased by the breeze. Like an Angela Brazil heroine, thought Veronica, who collected children's books, especially stories of valiant schoolgirls. She was conscious that she'd deliberately made something old-fashioned out of her lover but never examined the reasons.

She walked with Joy. She asked, 'How are you feeling?'

'I'm all right,' Joy said meekly. She placed a hand on Veronica's wrist. 'I owe you so much.'

'You don't need to thank me,' Veronica said. She was uncomfortable with thanks. The truth was she didn't particularly like Joy: after all what was there to like? Her involvement in the other woman's life was for different reasons: compassion perhaps, though Veronica didn't think she was a particularly compassionate person and couldn't imagine anyone saying it of her.

She looked back down the path to check that the others were keeping up. Belle and Earthy were walking together: two jolly fat ladies, not exactly old but definitely 'getting on'. Carol was behind them, paying close attention to the flowers, thinking of painting them perhaps. Veronica could imagine that Carol had once been beautiful; could conceive of a time when she'd cut swathes through Dave World. But now she was scrawny, if anything looking older than her years – what was she, fifty? – fifty-five?

And finally there was Janet. She made no effort to disguise her age – sixty or so – but she was lovely in Veronica's estimation: so elegant, assured and full of life and fun. Veronica didn't find it in the least surprising that Léon, the French boy whose own attractions were a mystery, should apparently be so strongly drawn to her.

Veronica knew there would come a time in her own life when she would be seventy – even eighty. She wondered how age would take her. Poppy would be middle-aged and possibly still very beautiful, and her years with Veronica would have polished her so that she would be suave and self-assured. Was it possible to believe that such a woman would want to associate herself with someone who by then would be old? It took very little to expose the implausibility of the vision. Nothing at all, really: only one sentence. Could she really hear herself asking: 'Poppy, be a darling and pass me the incontinence pads.'?

Or there was another future. Poppy might have the fair looks that quickly fade, so that by forty she would be a plump woman with slack muddy skin and dry wiry hair. By any standard she wasn't especially bright, and Veronica's efforts to mould her might fail and her inner coarseness re-emerge. She used to smoke and might smoke again. In this vision of the future, Veronica was bedridden and lying in darkness, and from the next room came whispered voices, harsh laughter, the clink of glasses and the stink of cigarettes creeping under the door.

However Veronica thought about the future it confronted her with horror.

The path bordered a field where fallow deer grazed, then entered the trees (blue self-heal and white-admiral butterflies floating drunkenly in the shadows). Janet saw a large fungus. It resembled a mushroom but was a greyish green.

She asked, 'Does anyone know what that is?'

Earthy peered at it. 'It's a death cap.'

No one asked if it was edible, and the sight of it seemed to subdue them; at all events they were silent for a while. Janet spent the time picking at the memory of the restaurant bill, which she thought was a clue to something else.

They came out of the trees onto open ground and the return leg of their stroll. From here they could see Mirepoix dreaming in afternoon sunlight, the air creamy and still and the sun beating down, and in the far distance mountains streaked with snow. They passed a small spinney, where sheep had taken shelter in the shade, all piled on each other in a dark woolly heap. Used to seeing sheep in the open, Janet found this little scene deeply mysterious like a picture by Samuel Palmer. Veronica pointed out herb bennet and wood spurge, and red pyramidal orchids dotted about the open meadows, and, just once, a lizard orchid.

They sat a while. They snacked on fruit and drank water, and Belle stretched out and said they might leave her there to die – would Janet see to Charlie's dinner: microwave lasagne? Then by degrees they became aware of a faint scent of honey and vanilla hanging in the air.

'Broom,' said Veronica.

'Beautiful,' said Janet.

'Like the cosmetics department in Debenhams,' said Belle, and when everyone stared at her, she burst into laughter.

They wandered back towards the town and collected the car. On the spur of the moment they stopped at the supermarket and spent half an hour buying nothing very much. And then they drove home.

Everyone agreed that this second lesson in identifying wild flowers was a success.

'All the same, I think someone was taking the mickey when they named a plant "squinancywort",' said Belle.

Janet returned to her cottage and made herself some coffee. She noticed some of David's papers on the table – the ones she'd been sorting – and among them the credit card slip for the meal he'd paid for on the night he died.

As far she could remember from what David had said of his plans for that evening – and no one had said any different – he'd gone to a roadhouse on the A34 for the purpose of dinner and a business conversation with Jeremy Vavasour. No other name had ever been mentioned.

She picked up the slip and looked at it again. It was an unitemised sum paid for a meal. A thoroughly unremarkable piece of paper, and yet something had always seemed odd about it that Janet had never been able to put a finger on.

But now she knew.

She was certain that a third person had been present at that dinner.

18

Foxglove (*Digitalis purpurea*) is a tall, downy and unbranched perennial reaching to 1.5m. The leaves are broad and lanceolate, wrinkled and soft to the touch. The two-lipped flowers in long spikes are normally pinkish tending towards purple, though there are white variants. Foxglove may be found from June to September in woods, scrub, heath and mountain. The plant is the source of the poison digitalis, which is also the basis for a number of drugs used to treat the heart.

Despite the late hour, Janet phoned Jeremy Vavasour. He answered as the recorded message was kicking in.

She said, 'Jeremy, it's Janet Bretherton.'

'Janet?' he drawled. 'Right.'

'Are you recording this call?'

A pause. A click.

'Is that on or off?'

'Hardly matters. Between you and me and whoever else may be listening, I am up shit creek without the proverbial – despite being fucking innocent!' he added Then, 'Sorry, I just wanted to get that off my chest.'

Janet thought he was drunk. She gave him time to collect his thoughts and decide whether to be polite to her.

He asked, 'To what do I owe the thingy – the pleasure?'

'It probably sounds odd, but I want to talk about the meal you and David had, the night he died.'

'You want to know what we talked about?'

'If you feel like telling me. But for the moment I'm more interested in the meal itself.'

'What the hell for? The place was just a steak restaurant in a pub we picked because it was handy.'

The answer made sense. David hadn't been one for fine dining.

'Who proposed it?'

'The place? God knows. We'd been there before. It pretty much picked itself once David said we should meet.'

'So it was David who suggested the meeting?'

'Yes. Look, why are we talking about the restaurant? The police haven't shown the least interest in it; they just want to know what we talked about, so they can figure out who was robbing the investors blind. Which wasn't me, by the way.'

'Bear with me. What time did you get there?'

'Time? As far as I remember I arrived about 7.30. David was ten or fifteen minutes late; some story about an accident; not to him: someone else. I've no reason to suppose that wasn't true.'

The timing fitted with Janet's recollection of when David left home. 'And then?'

'What's to say? We had dinner.'

'You had a drink first – yes?'

'Christ, are we going to turn over every . . . whatever it is one turns over? Yes, we had drinks. Mine was gin and tonic – I say that because it's what I always have. David had . . . oh, some bloody soft drink or other.'

'Did you pay cash or charge to the bill?'

'Are you joking?'

'Humour me.'

'Let me think. Really, this is too trivial . . . I don't remember. We probably charged it: it's what we'd normally do.'

'OK. Now the meal.'

'That's easy. Two courses. Neither of us likes puddings.'

It occurred to Janet that Jeremy wasn't describing this particular meal but a confection of memories from all the times he and her husband had eaten together. Most likely they'd followed the same pattern on this occasion, but one couldn't be sure.

Jeremy said, 'I had a Caesar salad to start. It's a favourite of mine and it's on the menu. Can't say what David had. Is it important?'

'Probably not. And then?'

185

'Pepper steak. It was the special, though actually it was a tough piece of rump and the pepper sauce was over the top. I think David had fish. He was picky and complaining of indigestion. Given the state of affairs I'm surprised I had an appetite.'

'Drink?'

'A glass of the house red – both of us. We were driving.'

'Brandy? Cigars? Anything like that?'

'Do me a favour, darling. It was a business meeting to discuss why the firm was going tits up and who was to blame. You don't have brandy and cigars on an occasion like that. We skipped pud and went straight to coffee.'

'And then?'

'We left.'

'And that was it? Aren't you cutting things short? You obviously had a row. You're not suggesting you simply shook hands and left together, are you?'

Jeremy hesitated and his voice dropped. He sighed, 'All right, if truth be known we had the most almighty bust up with each of us calling the other a thief.' He sounded almost contrite, perhaps sorry for Janet. 'But obviously one of us was lying and it wasn't me.'

'I'll let that pass,' said Janet. 'Just tell me exactly how it ended.'

'If that's what you want. We were calling each other names, and the management was getting shirty – disturbing the customers etcetera – insist you leave – police – blah blah. I couldn't take all the barefaced lies and told David so. I was tired. It must have been only nine o'clock but I was feeling like shit with the stress and the . . . the *lies* – I have to keep on saying it. I left the coffee and stormed out leaving him to settle the bill. I thought that if David was going to put on this piece of theatre, he could pay for the fucking privilege.'

Evidently Jeremy was going to play the part of the innocent man to the last, even though he must know Janet wouldn't believe him. She supposed that to someone else it might have been a credible account; but it wouldn't wash with anyone who knew David. At the end of the day he wasn't dishonest enough or, more importantly, *clever* enough to pull off a sophisticated financial fraud. He was an accountant with a background in local government, she reminded herself, not some giant of the City.

There was no point simply arguing. She wanted to shake Jeremy: shock him into a confession by revealing that she knew a secret he was obviously determined to keep hidden.

She said, 'There's still one thing you haven't told me.'

He was weary and sounded sober: perhaps hadn't been drunk, only tired, and she'd been betrayed by her prejudices. He said, 'Really? And what would that be.'

'A name – the name of the other person at dinner. You see, I know there were three of you.'

'A third person. Right.'

'Yes.'

'A third person . . . ' Jeremy repeated. Then: 'You're out of your fucking mind.'

The women went flower spotting once more. They stayed in the area this time, walking to the point beyond Campmaurice where the plateau narrowed and ended in steep wooded slopes and limestone crags. They'd covered much the same ground on the first of Joy's walks, when they scaled the heights to the Maquis de Puybrun; but this time they wouldn't do the climb – thank God, as Belle said.

Because they would pass her door, Joy didn't join the others in the village but waited for them to arrive. She was in a state of trepidation. Veronica had told her that Janet, with her usual cleverness, had realised she had a drink problem – well, was an alcoholic to be truthful. Would she tell the others? Veronica hadn't: in fact Veronica hadn't even confirmed Janet's suspicions. But Veronica was Joy's friend, who'd stood by her when . . . who had stood by her. Janet on the other hand was no more than generally pleasant and probably felt under no particular obligation. She might keep quiet out of simple consideration of Joy's feelings, but Joy couldn't be sure. Belle, for example, if she knew, would almost certainly tell the whole world; she wouldn't be able to resist. And Belle was Janet's bosom pal, in whom she might very well have confided. Joy was terrified and humiliated. She had so few friends and admired these women so much, and she could hardly bear the thought that they might despise her.

Her alcoholism, of course, was the hold that Arnold had over her.

'You understand,' he said, 'that you'll never be *cured*. It doesn't work like that. The best alcoholics can hope for is to be "in recovery". That's what they say: *"in recovery"*. I think they also say you have to take it "one day at a time", meaning you may be sober today, but there's no guarantee you won't be drunk tomorrow. Do you follow me?'

Do you follow me? It was an expression Arnold used when he was lecturing her, as he often did about the most trivial things, as if her drinking had reduced her to the state of an idiot.

'It was me who cleaned you up, wasn't it?' he used to say, in case it was something she'd forgotten. This was after The Disaster, when she turned up in the afternoon to teach arithmetic to year six and could hardly stand because of the wine she'd taken at lunch time and the half bottle of gin that was in her bag. 'What would you do without me?' he asked complacently. 'There's no going back to teaching, is there, eh? Do you follow me? Not,' he added, his face shining at the thought of his own magnanimity, 'that you'll ever need to. I've got a tidy bit put by that'll see both of us out. All you need to do is follow my advice and you'll never be without. Do you follow me?'

And if she didn't take his 'advice'? If she showed a spark of independence, what then? He never said. Quite possibly it never occurred to him that she might do other than what he demanded. Everyone always seemed to.

'People appreciate firmness,' he used to say. 'They like to know where they stand, and they always know where they stand with me.'

Not so much 'stand' as 'kneel', thought Joy. There were times when she felt broken by the wearisome round of always agreeing with him. She wondered why he stuck with her, given that his attitude was almost always one of contempt. Perhaps it was that she was young compared with the wives of his friends. Oh, God, his friends! Seeing them together was like watching pigs rutting: so much boasting and jostling flesh and fat self-satisfaction. And in the end, what was it all for?

Arnold had 'saved' her but only so she could worship his high opinion of himself. And now – it was an agony even to think of it – he'd revealed the full extent of his appalling nature so that nothing he'd ever done or could do for her was worth anything in her eyes and if she'd died all those years before it would have been better than this.

Joy wondered if she should kill herself. The sainted Kathleen had. But as with other big decisions, daily life intervened and she had to put the thought away. The others arrived and she offered them coffee and some scones she'd made. She scanned their faces for signs that they *knew*, but could detect nothing, not even in Janet's manner, which was neither more nor less pleasant than normal. Relieved, she even felt a flash of annoyance. Wasn't it hypocritical of Janet to mask her knowledge so well? She compared her with Veronica, whose deportment was always so cool, but who seemed to have deep, unexpressed feelings. Janet on the other hand was so competent and completely self-possessed. It was rather frightening.

'Hey up, time to be going,' said Belle, putting her cup down. 'I could sit here and scoff scones all day, but I'm trying to ration myself.'

They set off and slowly followed the lanes between the fields and clumps of trees. Today they found lucerne, peach-leaved bell flowers, common spotted orchids and even bee orchids. An hour into the walk a storm came over and they had to take shelter under the eaves of a barn until it passed. Afterwards the sky was a patchwork of purple clouds and brilliant blue. Towards Quillan it was shaded with distant bars of rain. As they walked back to Puybrun they saw the sun bathing the castle in a glow of honey-coloured light.

Whatever Jeremy might say, Janet was certain there was a third person present at that final dinner. He'd unwittingly given her the proof in his account of what they'd eaten, because Janet knew to within five or ten pounds the price of a meal for two in a steakhouse. It was the anomaly she'd noticed in the credit card slip: the total was simply too much; in fact it was half as much again as it should have been if only Jeremy and David had been there. From which it followed that a third person had eaten with them. The problem was that Janet had no idea who it might be.

A number of possibilities crossed her mind. An investor perhaps, whom Jeremy felt obliged to protect – no doubt for some nefarious reason. Janet didn't know who'd put money into Vavasour & Bretherton, but if the company was in trouble with funds going missing, it was conceivable that an investor with inside knowledge would intervene and call for an explanation. Perhaps that was what provoked the crisis. The only problem with this solution was that Jeremy had been clear that David had called the meeting, which would suggest that the concerned investor had come from David's side and also that he'd stayed behind with David when the meeting broke up in a row. In that case Jeremy would have no obvious reason to protect David's contact; no reason to deny the presence of the third party; no reason not to give a name.

An alternative was that Jeremy had brought along a girlfriend: a married woman, perhaps, with whom he'd been having an affair that had to be kept from her husband. It was part of her general prejudice against David's partner, she knew, but Janet had no difficulty imagining that such a person existed. But why take such a dangerous step as to introduce a stranger into a meeting at which it was inevitable that a lot of dirty laundry was going to be washed?

The final explanation – which Janet knew should never be discounted – was 'X' : the one she was too stupid to think of; or that was hidden because some crucial facts were unknown; or that was too wildly improbable but happened all the same. The return of brother Patrick fell into this category: the million to one shot that turns out to be true. So did Santa Claus and the Tooth Fairy. Janet felt she would go mad if she gave any credence to the idea that David's twin had suddenly come home after forty years of obscurity only to involve himself in a financial scandal and his own possible murder. As an explanation it was too contrived. When she was planning David's death, Janet had never considered anything so elaborate.

Of course, if the body that was cremated was indeed Patrick, he must have been present at the dinner, and if Jeremy knew or suspected a murder, he would have cause to distance himself from the whole business, which would explain his silence.

However, if the body was Patrick's, then David was still alive.

And Janet knew that he wasn't.

She walked home with the others after leaving Joy at Camp-maurice. Joy had looked at her suspiciously. Janet guessed Veronica had mentioned their conversation. It had been difficult to know how to behave. Part of her wanted to show sympathy, but she couldn't in the presence of the others; not without suggesting something was wrong. And, too, it was difficult to feel sympathy for Joy except in an undemonstrative way, because she just wasn't a person to whom one could display the important physical side of giving comfort. When it came down to it, Joy just wasn't huggable. Quite likely that was why she drank. She was searching for a spark of warmth and contact with another human being, and trying to make herself receptive to it when she saw it. Janet was profoundly sorry for her, but she suspected Joy was a disaster area with the potential for dragging other people down with her. She was fearful for Veronica.

She and Belle discussed an evening stroll; the clouds had cleared and the sky was limpid. They made their goodbyes for the time being and Janet went into her cottage. No sooner had she got through the door than she heard the ping of an incoming message on her mobile: probably one she hadn't been able to receive earlier when they were walking. She checked and saw that it was from Jeremy.

It read: U F***G BITCH. NOW THEY THINK I POISONED DAVID!

How to Paint Watercolours

19

The defining characteristic of watercolour is its transparency, which, combined with the technique of dampening the paper, causes the colours to flow into each other in a way difficult to achieve by other means. The thinness of the paint can give a bright effect with the underlying ground shining through. The blending of colours is perfect for reproducing the appearance of dampness or mist. Transparency means that watercolours are very obviously an illusion. They hint at something beneath the surface.

'I've got some sad news,' Veronica said. 'Something of a shock: Arnold has died. We don't really know more than that.'

They'd gathered at Veronica's house, all except Joy and Carol. In Carol's case it was because, as she pointed out, she already knew how to paint in watercolours.

'Joy got the news last night and called me. She drove to Carcassonne this morning, hoping to pick up a flight. She doesn't know when she'll be back. Not before the funeral, I imagine.'

'When did he die?' asked Janet.

'That's an odd question,' said Belle. 'It must have been yesterday. They'd have called Joy straight away.'

'I suppose so. Yes, that's what would happen if he had an accident or was in hospital. But what if he died at home? He might have lain there for quite a few days before anyone – a cleaner for example – found him. I don't suppose it matters, but it's rather a horrible thought.'

Belle bridled. She said, 'Sometimes you have a prying way of thinking that isn't called for. Who cares when Arnold died, and what business is it of ours anyway?'

Janet felt like asking how Charlie was but bit her tongue. Experience had taught her that one could lose friends by remarks so casual that one forgot about them afterwards. Not that an enquiry as to the invisible Charlie would have been casual. Belle was touchy this morning and Janet wondered what was going on.

Janet wasn't having a good day either. After Jeremy's message she was torn whether to call him back or contact Inspector Gregg. It was a choice between a tense conversation likely to end in recriminations, or reminding the police of her existence while the embarrassing hundred thousand pounds in her bank account remained unexplained and there were doubts over the identification of a corpse.

Inspector Gregg took the call but seemed preoccupied. When Janet said she wanted to talk about David's death, he interrupted her. He said, 'Look, if you want to confess to murder, I'll give you another number to call. On the other hand if you want to own up to fraud, I'm all ears.'

Janet was surprised, almost affronted. 'Aren't you interested that someone may have killed my husband?'

'Not a lot. It may be a fascinating question but it's not my business.'

'Why not?'

'Because, despite the fancy title, I'm just a humble accountant who spends his days reading boring spreadsheets and company prospectuses trying to catch con men. My only interest in your husband's death is for whatever light it casts on the shenanigans of Vavasour & Bretherton. I'm sorry if that disappoints you.'

There was a silence and Janet was reminded of two people who like each other but are unaccountably having a quarrel: a feeling of mutual astonishment. Inspector Gregg relented. His voice assumed the warm attractive tone Janet had heard before. He said, 'I'm sorry, Janet – can I call you Janet? I'll take five and try to answer your questions.'

Janet took a breath. She'd expected to be interrogated rather than the other way round. She said, 'Jeremy tells me he's been accused of poisoning David. What's that about?'

'He's putting it too strong. CID asked him a few questions, that's all.'

'But why?'

'Because there's an anomaly in the post mortem. The doctor who examined the body decided Mr Bretherton died of a stroke. However the lab report on the retrieved organs indicates that the owner had taken a massive dose of digoxin – quite enough to kill him.'

'Digoxin?'

'Some sort of drug for heart conditions – apparently very dangerous if taken in excess.'

'Is that why the police were enquiring whether David had a heart condition? He didn't.'

'We know. Obviously we've looked at his medical records such as they were and it seems he was as fit as a flea.'

'Apart from the fact that he died,' said Janet, once again feeling weary with the whole business of David's death as if it was lack of consideration on his part. 'He hated going to the doctor. If he had gone . . . ' She stopped. What was the point of speculation? David had always lived in the here and now with all its limitations, and she'd got over the pretence that things might have been other than they were. Stephen Gregg seemed to assume as much. His manner, whether brusque or cheerful, made no concession to a widow's tears. Another woman might be offended.

A question came to her: 'David died of a stroke, not a heart attack – or didn't he? Does digoxin cause strokes?'

'This is one of the days I'm glad I'm an accountant,' said Gregg. 'The truth is, we don't know what he died of. The medic who did the post mortem has been suspended. Apparently he's an old man and there are complaints about what they politely call "limited efficiency". The answer to your question is that digoxin doesn't cause strokes, which leaves us with several un-satisfactory alternatives. The first is that your husband didn't die of a stroke: it may have been a misdiagnosis and he had a heart attack caused by the digoxin. The second is that he was poisoned, but coincidentally had a stroke before the digoxin kicked in. And the third is that the organs containing the digoxin belong to one person and the brain that suffered the stroke to another – except that in that case we ought to have two corpses not one.'

Or possibly one corpse and one man walking around with his heart or his brain missing. Not impossible, thought Janet, given the general behaviour of men. He might go unnoticed for years and even hold down a decent job. She didn't say so, but it was a notion that would have appealed to David's sense of humour. It certainly appealed to hers.

'DNA proves that the owner of the organs and your husband were the same person,' Gregg said. 'Presumably that also holds true of the person who had the stroke. We have no DNA directly from the body that was cremated. We have to assume that the organs came from that body – and I see no reason not to.'

Janet didn't float Helen's hypothesis about brother Patrick; there was no point looking for trouble. Instead she asked, 'And where does that leave Jeremy?'

'Let's say the evidence puts him in an equivocal position. It strongly suggests your husband was poisoned and that it was done at the dinner with Mr Vavasour. On the other hand, no one can say at this juncture that digoxin caused his death. The damned post mortem means we can't rule out a stroke.'

'So he may get away with murder?'

'It's quite possible. In fact we may not even be able to prove he gave Mr Bretherton the digoxin. So far CID haven't come by any evidence to show he ever had the stuff.'

Belle wasn't sure how far she admired Veronica's house: its sparseness, the marble floor, the blond wood and ebony of the biedermeier furniture. Still it must be easy to keep clean, she thought, hearing an echo of Alice's voice, though in fact Alice had always gone in for fussiness that was the devil to dust. For herself, Belle inclined to comfort, and Charlie wouldn't have anything else.

'The pictures are all by Poppy,' said Veronica and smiled at her partner. Poppy seemed embarrassed by them. Despite her spectacular beauty, which was brought out by Veronica's money and good taste, it was noticeable that she never pushed herself forward.

'To listen to her,' Belle had said to Janet, 'she's just some scrubber Veronica picked up. Have you noticed how she's always watching? It's as if she doesn't know how to use a knife and fork. And has she ever said a word that was memorable? She makes Joy sound as witty as Joan Rivers.' Belle didn't mean to condemn. She simply spoke as she thought.

Now Belle found herself looking at the pictures on the walls, and at the albums set out on a low table. They contained water-colours of flowers. Perhaps inspired by Veronica the girl had painted all kinds, wild and cultivated, and they were exquisite. Where on earth had the talent come from?

The pictures made Belle uncomfortable. Like the tatting, which she both loved and hated, they reminded her of Alice.

With age her mother had lost the concentration and dexterity required for lace making; but the neediness that drove her mania never went away. It simply looked for a new outlet. She began haunting junk shops and antiques fairs. At first she'd buy any old thing on the principle of 'I think it's valuable' or 'It'll come in handy someday'. While Joe was alive, he'd discreetly clear the clutter away where it could be found only if Alice looked for it. When Belle asked if he thought Alice was turning 'funny', he'd defend her and say he was pleased she had an 'interest'. Then Joe died and the house was gradually transformed.

In time the collection began to acquire a shape. Embroidery and samplers formed a part. So did hand-painted cups and saucers, prints and watercolours. The common theme was flowers. The quality of the objects scarcely mattered. They could be broken or cracked or faded or dirty, as long as there was a profusion of blooms. The front room, already a shrine to tatting, now had an additional burden and to Belle's eye began to resemble one of those Italian churches she and Charlie used to visit on holiday: a great heap of dust and ornament served by mad old women.

In the end, of course, they had to put her in a home. The house was starting to smell of pee; not all of it due to the stray cats Alice took in. To make room for her collection she'd hauled an old three piece suite into the back yard, where it mouldered in the rain and rats made a nest in it; and the bin men refused to collect the rubbish without saying why, until Belle investigated and wished she hadn't.

Sometimes Belle wondered at her own future. Would her heart give out as it had with Joe; or would she grow senile like Alice? *Please God, let me just drop dead.* When she thought over her life with her mother, she realised that for fifty years their relationship had been darkened by her sense of shame: her fear that others would see through the veneer of her parents' respectability to the obsession and madness at its heart: her fear that it was a contagion and that, when those same others looked at her, they saw not fat and jolly Belle, but Alice reincarnated in all her gaudy horror.

Nowadays Alice was safely locked up and sedated as necessary (she was rowdy and prone to singing hymns and had lately taken to swearing). Belle arranged a skip to clear the yard, and the council to kill the rats, and the RSPCA to deal with the cats. Then she entered the sanctum. Looking at the dirty, yellowing lace and everywhere the flowers painted on countless pieces of rubbish, she puzzled over the identity of the deity to whom all of this had been dedicated. It was a mystery to which she could only add again her private prayer:

'Please, God, let me just drop dead.'

They went to the lake, carrying Cotman watercolour pads and three boxes of paints to share, and a reservoir of water in a hot water bottle with a teddy bear cover that Poppy had owned in another life. Puybrun's unreliable weather had provided them with another day in which mist and cloud hung about the mountains and draped the crags, and everywhere was vaporous and watery.

They squatted on the grass near the *buvette*, facing down the length of the lake with the beach to the right and a line of trees growing along the dyke to the left, and ahead of them the ground rising to woods and the bleak face of the escarpment.

Custom at the *buvette* was quiet and Sandrine strolled over and patrolled the line of women, glancing over their shoulders as if she were an expert.

Finally she delivered herself weightily. 'So you paint,' she said to Poppy. 'Where did you learn?'

'S'just sumfink I do,' said Poppy. 'S'like an instinct, innit?'

Sandrine nodded wisely and returned to the counter, flicking a towel at the peaceable alcoholics who brooded there at this time of day.

Poppy taught the others to dampen the paper and execute a pale wash of the sky and the mountains. Then she helped each of them in turn to sketch the foreground detail. Janet couldn't help noticing the contrast between her shy manner and her confident demonstration. It occurred to her how overwhelmed Poppy must have been to be taken up by someone as assertive and sophisticated as Veronica. She wondered if love could flourish under such circumstances.

Sandrine came back. She smiled at Poppy and said, 'You are very . . . artist? Very artist. You do tattoos?'

Poppy seemed not to understand; then grinned. 'Nar, I don't do tattoos.'

Sandrine nodded. She was about to go away, when Poppy said, ''Ere, look at this!' She slipped the strap of her dress from her shoulder and let the bodice fall so that the upper curve of her left breast was exposed and the colourful tattoo of a butterfly.

Janet thought it was a coy gesture, innocent yet beguiling. Poppy was careful to hold the dress so that the minimum was shown and she didn't allow Sandrine's gaze to linger. Yet the possibilities of confusion between the three women, Poppy, Sandrine and Veronica, were immediately obvious. Sandrine seemed merely curious; she was a fan of tattoos and here was another one. Poppy was flattered to be noticed and took a simple vain pleasure in the design that contrasted with her pale breast. Veronica was impassive. Janet could make nothing of it: not with any confidence.

Veronica was thirty before she thought of herself as a lesbian. Even then it was an uncertain identification in the way children sometimes wonder if they are adopted. Her father was a vicar and with the help of Church charities she attended boarding school and had the usual crushes; but because they'd been 'usual', they meant nothing much after the event. Afterwards she was preoccupied by ambition and the pursuit of her career in banking, and these were not only a distraction, they provided her with an explanation why she didn't involve herself in the world of dating and marriage.

It wasn't that she wasn't fond of men. She liked them well enough in the unspecial way that liberal-minded people say they like foreigners; in fact she still liked them. She even had sex with a few and thought the experience enjoyable. When these relationships failed to fulfil her she merely supposed that sex, like other consumer goods, was oversold and didn't live up to its advertising. That she wasn't in the market for the product – at least not in this version – didn't occur to her. Afterwards her failure to recognise reality was an embarrassment. Later it frightened her. She found herself at a loss to read the affections of other people. And in the case of Poppy it became a consuming anxiety.

Her first affair of any significance was with a commodities trader ten years her senior. It hadn't lasted. The focus on their careers led to an emotional flatness that amounted to no more than a sexual sufficiency: a dose of something to maintain health. Then, after several intervals of more of the same, she met Diana, who had somehow managed to remain girlish and fun-loving and altogether delightful.

They didn't live together. It would have been impossible. Diana inhabited a nest of scattered underwear and wine bottles in a flat with a heady atmosphere of American cigarettes and oregano. Yet they stayed together for two years in a whirl of dates at parties and galleries and restaurants and opera and ballet; and went on holiday to Egypt and the Maldives and some bloody place in Uzbekistan she could never pronounce that had the most famous something-or-other in the entire Islamic world. And everything was as perfect as Veronica imagined things could be – which was not exactly perfect but close, very close.

And then they found themselves one night in a club in Bermondsey.

Diana admitted she'd been there once or twice before but forgotten to mention the fact. Veronica understood immediately that she'd met some fetching little girly, who didn't mean very much, and it didn't bother her. She was just annoyed that Diana had dragged her to a place she knew Veronica wouldn't like and where she would feel uncomfortable. Most probably Diana was trying to keep conflicting promises: to her lover and to little-miss-whoever-she was, and saying her prayers that she could keep both in play. There was no point in making a scene. In any case it was barely possible to think, not with the cloying atmosphere and the noise and the kids looking at her as if she were a freak, including the white faced Goth with the poppy lips and the look of death on her. To make things worse, the band was a collection of screaming poseurs, the drinks were foul con-coctions in sticky glasses, the audience were losers, and Veronica felt ill. She left Diana and went outside to get fresh air and perhaps find a taxi.

It was a November night. The river was close by and a ship's horn was sounding and across the river a lonely light shone on a skyscraper. Cars driven by ghosts hissed past. Rainwater growled in a drain and flattened pieces of litter formed a pattern of white patches on the tarmac as if laid out for hopscotch.

Veronica heard a whimpering from an alley leading to a service area behind the club. An emergency exit gave onto the alley and from an open door came a crimson glow. She followed the noise to the skips at the rear, stepping carefully round the pavement pizzas, ignoring the rubbish and the crunch of broken glass. Three girls were there: the witches in Macbeth: two of them fat and one of them haggard.

At their feet shuddering in a pile of vomit among the discarded foil and needles, was the white-faced girl. Her poppy lips were a bruised purple in the glare of an intruder light.

20

Certain pigments are regarded as 'unsafe', which means that they are fugitive, fading even to vanishing point under prolonged light, or changing colour either because of light or a chemical reaction with other pigments. Vermillion made from red sulphide of mercury is unsafe. Crimson reds are all to some degree fugitive. Cobalt yellow is only more or less permanent and gamboge is fugitive. The combination of transparency and lack of permanence is a reminder that watercolours capture no more than a fleeting effect.

Janet kept her promise to go with Léon to the fete at Bellesta. In fact, once she'd got over her embarrassment, she looked forward to it. She'd be partnered by an attractive young man (ugliness notwithstanding) who was a beautiful dancer and seemed to be drawn to her; and, if the relationship was spiced with fun, mystery and danger, so much the better.

She told herself, 'I may be a widow, but I'm capable of happiness and I intend to be happy.' She still found herself crying at odd moments, but she doubted her tears had anything to do with David, or, if they did, that they came from as conventional a feeling as grief.

A few years ago she and David had gone to a cinema showing the classic Bette Davies weepy, *Now Voyager*. They'd given no thought to the audience. Certainly they hadn't expected to find themselves the only straight couple in a crowd of five hundred inconsolable gay men. Yet they joined in the sobbing; after all it was why they were there. Sometimes she felt it was possible to look on life in the same way: to see both its humour and its poignancy as if from the outside. Films and fiction were full of shallow emotions that served only to relieve unspoken tensions before being discarded like paper tissues. She supposed that her moments of detached insight were of the same kind. After all, when she had a crying fit, she was just as likely to be laughing the next minute. She no longer cared to interrogate this aspect of her feelings too closely. The boundaries of her emotions were too fluid, the overlays too many and too complex for her to say definitely what they meant.

So they went to Bellesta. Janet drove her car. She wore a short scarlet jacket over a simply cut blouse and a black skirt that hung close to her shape but was pleated so that she could dance any step Léon surprised her with. He wore a black suit that looked slept in, a faded work shirt with a frayed collar, and his pointed boots. Around his neck was a knotted white foulard.

They danced in the light of evening, and, when it faded, went on by the glow of coloured bulbs that now and then would spark and pop and go out. Other people were good natured and admiring and cleared a space so that Léon could take Janet through elaborate figures at a breathtaking speed that elicited sighs and clapping and cries of appreciation; and as she spun around the hall she saw the faces of young women eager with desire to dance with her partner, and young men who wished they could dance with her.

I must stop this, she thought. I could grow to love it too much.

Belle, of course, was excited about the whole business.

'Have you found out what he's after, yet? He hasn't –' her voice dropped to a whisper ' – *tried anything*, has he? Oh, God, I wish you could sell tickets!'

'You could have come.'

'What, and been a wallflower? No thanks. Anyway, I thought I'd have an evening in with Charlie and catch up with *East Enders* on satellite.'

'Nothing happened.'

Léon had pecked her on the cheek in the French manner and little more unless you counted holding her hand as they walked to and from the car. And, too, as they danced the tango closely, she rested her head on his shoulder and found that his hair was clean and smelled of soap. Janet felt a wave of affection as she had for Helen when she was young and making mistakes in love.

'I think he's an uncomplicated boy. He talks a lot about Lille. I suspect he's homesick. He'd like to go back and open a little dance school of his own, find a girl and raise babies. It's rather touching.'

'What about his art? Earthy thinks his wooden figures are fantastic.'

'He's definite that they mean nothing. He hasn't a clue why people buy them; in fact he thinks his customers must be a bit stupid. Ravi put him up to it. There isn't much else to say.'

They changed subject and caught up with news of Joy's bereavement, relayed second hand from Veronica. Janet asked, 'Do they know the cause of death?'

'If they do, they're not telling. Mind you, Arnold was seventy, and people do drop off their perch a lot younger. Oh, bloody hell . . . sorry!'

'Don't worry.'

'Right, well, as I say – did you ever meet him, Arnold?'

'No.'

'Oh? Mind you, he was never about much. He was one of those big, red-faced fellas, who must have been quite a looker when he was young but had lost it. He spent most of his time up at Campmaurice, but he'd come into the village every now and again; you'd see him slopping around in a track suit and trainers. His scalp was sunburned and he had a comb-over and those thick dangly ears that men get, like a pair of old handbags.' Belle shuddered. 'Give me Charlie any day.'

'How is he, Charlie?'

'Oh, he's all right,' Belle said.

They drove to Montségur. Without Joy and the benefit of the Tank they took two cars. They found themselves in traffic behind timber lorries but the day was hot and sunny and they were dazzled by the reflection from the limestone crags, so that the slow journey had a dreamlike quality. Finally they came to the small village and the ruin of a castle on a plug of rock so high and sharp it seemed impossible anything could be built there.

In the village they searched for a patch of shade and settled in a line to paint. Poppy moved behind them, making suggestions about composition and colour and sometimes small corrections to the drawing. She was an instinctive painter, Janet thought, just as she herself was an instinctive dancer. The lack of formal training made teaching difficult. Poppy could show but couldn't explain; not that anyone minded. Earthy was overjoyed to be here at the centre of the famous Cathar mystery; and after a while Belle was content to yawn, lie back and snooze. Tourists stared from their tables in the cafés or drifted past on their way to visit the ruin, and one or two took photographs of the women and probably wondered afterwards why they'd bothered.

After an hour they tired of painting. Earthy wanted to visit the castle.

'You go on without me,' said Belle. 'There's no way I'm climbing that mountain. I'll tell you one thing about them Cathars though: they must have been a fit lot. Legs like tree trunks, eh?'

So they climbed to the castle. Earthy grew excited as they approached the pinnacle. She spoke with emotion of the tragedy that had overwhelmed the area in mediaeval times.

'The Catholic Church behaved *dreadfully* towards the Cathars,' she said. 'And the Northern French were simply *unspeakable*.'

Janet remembered that the Catholic Church and the French knights had burned and murdered their way through the south, destroying the courtly Occitan culture. Earthy, however, made the entire crusade sound like a case of bad manners.

'Puybrun was absolutely *ruined* by that simply horrible man, Simon de Montfort, and as for Béziers, what was done was frankly *unforgiveable*. I mean it wasn't as if the crusaders were southerners; it wasn't as if they actually lived here.'

Janet didn't want to ask about Béziers, in case Earthy felt obliged to tell her. She nodded to show that, whatever it was that happened, she disapproved.

'It all came to a head at this very spot.' Earthy said and waved her arms. They'd reached the peak, where the sun was so intense that ground and sky glittered white and nothing moved in the landscape except a pair of buzzards. Earthy was magisterial in flowing robes of tie-and-dye cotton, a pair of enormous working man's boots, and enough ethnic jewellery for a self-respecting shaman. A party of German teenagers halted mesmerised to listen to her.

She said, 'This was the final Cathar stronghold. The crusaders laid siege to it and finally captured it and burned two hundred and twenty poor souls for heresy. And what for? Why couldn't they just leave them alone? Of course – ' she added ' – the Cathars had a very high regard for women and allowed them to become *parfaits*, whereas the Catholic Church has always behaved *appallingly* in that regard. If the Virgin Mary could see what was being done in her name, I think she would be very *disappointed* with the Papacy.'

Of the defenders, she said, twenty-five had taken the sacrament of the *consolamentum*, in the last days, knowing that this act of devotion doomed them to be burned alive. In the longer term, thought Janet, their fate was to be the focus of treasure hunters, charlatans and popular novelists like Dan Brown. She wasn't certain how she felt in general about tragedy, suspecting that much of it was just sordid violence done from petty motives then dressed up grandly in order to look respectable. It wasn't surprising that, in the effort to extract meaning, it was often turned into something vulgar and ridiculous – and vice versa of course. Despite her shock at David's death, Janet was unable to see dying in a lay-by on the A34 as tragic, whether or not he was murdered.

They found a restaurant in the village and took lunch in a small courtyard under an awning of canes. They ate goat cheese and trout and a good ice cream accompanied by a sugary glass of sauternes. They passed round their watercolour sketches and chuckled over them except for Poppy's, which was deftly done. Veronica said, 'It's wonderful, darling,' and her eyes lit up and she kissed Poppy on the cheek. Janet, too, admired it but was more interested in Veronica's response. For a woman so intelligent and cultivated, it must be difficult to find something to praise in a young woman as limited as Poppy. Yet it was evident that Veronica adored her. And Poppy? One might just as well ask about the feelings of a cat.

They settled the bill and went for a stroll. They called at a shop that sold books, most of them nonsense about alleged secrets and fanciful conspiracies. Janet found a novel about Guillame Bélibaste, the last of the Cathars to be burnt. It was many years after the fall of Montségur, during the short revival of heresy among the peasants of Montaillou. After the Inquisition had again suppressed dissent, Bélibaste went into hiding and continued to keep the faith as best he could until he was betrayed and killed. She thought that in some respects his tale was sadder than that of the great massacre, because he must have been lonely and conscious of his inadequacy and living in fear. She didn't buy the book because she couldn't bear the thought of reading it.

They returned to Puybrun. Belle told Janet she must drop in on Charlie to see he was OK. She proposed that afterwards they go to the *buvette* for a drink and a chinwag.

Later, while Belle was ordering at the counter, Janet checked her messages. She found one from Stephen Gregg.

It said: THERE WAS A THIRD PERSON AT DINNER. WHAT DO U KNO ABOUT IT? Janet wondered how he'd found out.

Belle came to the table and Sandrine followed with the drinks. They sat for a while watching the campers bathing or playing on the beach; and Belle began to talk about the mystery of Joy and Arnold, and Veronica and Poppy, and where did Carol's money come from that allowed her to give up life in Dave World, and what was going on between Earthy and Ravi?

And between me and Léon, thought Janet. To which the answer is: God knows because I don't. And as for mysteries, what about Belle and Charlie? She'd had this sort of gossiping conversation before and it never went anywhere because there was no new information; one simply talked in circles. She didn't mention her belief, more or less confirmed, that Joy was an alcoholic; it wouldn't be fair.

'The police think that David may have been murdered,' Janet said.

'Bugger me,' said Belle, and after a moment, 'Do you fancy another drink?' She called Sandrine over and ordered for both. Then she said, 'I don't mean to be rude, but did you kill him? I promise not to tell anyone if you did.'

'Do you think I could have?'

'Not especially, but what do I know? People are always saying that so-and-so couldn't have done whatever it is they're accused of. "It's out of character," they say, even though, whatever they may believe, the evidence makes it obvious that good old whats-hisname did it. I always think it shows lack of imagination. I mean: we see ourselves as free to do anything we like; but we seem to think of other people as if they're trained dogs who can't do anything that's "out of character" – like we had a clue what their characters really are.'

'So do you think I could have murdered David?'

'Not especially. But if anyone proved you did, I could get used to the idea. Do you think I could have murdered Alice when I was younger?'

'I could get used to the idea,' Janet said.

'See what I mean? Only in this case you've got me nailed as a murderess when nobody killed her at all; she's banged up in a home, as mad as a hatter. By the way, why are you telling me all this?'

Janet thought of Guillaume Bélibaste, the last Cathar, walking through the world with his burden of secrets.

'It's by talking about things that we get our heads round them. Otherwise we're not sure we're real.' Janet stretched out her hand and Belle took it. 'Anyway, you're my friend.' She went on to tell her about the scandals surrounding the firm of Vavasour & Bretherton.

'God, it's like *Dallas*, isn't it? *Who shot JR?*'

'I still can't help thinking that nobody did.'

Janet wondered if Belle would tell the others. She assumed she would: it would be 'in character' after all. Then again, if she were to learn that Belle didn't tell the others, she could believe that too.

They finished their drinks. Janet returned to her cottage and phoned Stephen Gregg.

'I would have called earlier but I've only just picked up my mobile. I've been out all day and couldn't get a signal.'

'And what do you have to say about my message?'

'I already knew there was a third person at dinner.'

'I see. And was it you?'

'No. I was at home all evening and went to bed early, as I've already said.'

'Then how do you know about the third person?'

Janet explained how the amount of the credit card bill was inconsistent with a simple meal for two at a steakhouse. 'But I couldn't be certain, and Jeremy denied it. How did you find out?'

'The business of the poison means we've had to look again at what happened that last evening at dinner. Fortunately the restaurant still had a copy of the receipt, and there was no mistaking that three people had eaten. Unfortunately, it was too long ago for the staff to remember anything, and so we don't know who the other person was. Mr Vavasour insists that it's a fantasy whatever the bill says.'

'That's odd, isn't it? Given that he's under suspicion, you'd think Jeremy would jump at the chance to blame someone else.'

'Perhaps he's sentimental. Perhaps he's shielding you?'

'Are people really so sentimental? Well, men perhaps – David was very sentimental. But not in this case. Jeremy and I don't like each other, so you can be fairly certain I wasn't at that dinner and didn't poison David, because he would have told you.'

There was a pause. Janet wondered if her tone had been too firm and not offended enough at the implication of murder. Did Stephen Gregg have an image of what was 'in character' for her?

He chuckled. 'You know, I do enjoy our chats, Janet. I'm glad I'm just an accountant and not a proper detective, because I'm not sure I could keep the necessary professional distance. If you did kill David, please don't confess – and certainly not to me.'

'I'll remember that,' Janet said. 'By the way, how old are you?'

'Why do you want to know?'

'We've never met face to face, but we find ourselves talking like . . . ' Did she mean friends?

'I'm forty-five.'

'Ah.' *These days I prefer them to be thirty*, Janet thought. 'Thanks for that information.'

She ended the call and set about making herself a light supper, which she took onto the veranda. She looked up at the castle, trying to see it through Earthy's eyes: the crusaders storming it like rowdy teenagers throwing a party while their parents are out. Of course Earthy didn't really think that: it was just a trick of language, a relic of her respectable upbringing. Still, 'that simply horrible man', Simon de Montfort, sounded like Jeremy.

She finished the meal and went inside. Too tired to open her laptop and work, she shuffled through David's old papers and picked up the restaurant credit card slip again. On this occasion she noticed that it was timed as well as dated. It said it was issued at 10.15 p.m.

She felt that should mean something to her, but for the moment she couldn't think what. She decided it was a problem for tomorrow, and for the present she ran herself a bath.

21

The student should draw everything: just what he sees in all its
minuteness before trying to translate it into other terms. Such a
drawing should reveal the workings of the artist's mind and be
an ideograph of his creed.

Earthy announced, 'Ravi has agreed to model for a life class!'

'Would you believe it?' Belle said to Janet. 'What with that
and the price of sprouts, the world's gone mad. Hey, I wonder if
we'll get to see his you-know-what?'

Veronica explained, 'It's one of Earthy's odd notions. It has
nothing to do with painting in watercolours, but what can one
do? For some unaccountable reason she seems besotted with
Ravi and simply asked him off her own bat. I imagine he agreed
because it appealed to his vanity. At all events it was arranged
without a word to Poppy; so there was nothing to be done,
unless she was willing to hurt Earthy's feelings.'

'And she couldn't do that. It'd be like drowning a kitten,
wouldn't it?'

'Sometimes you have a vivid turn of phrase. But you're right;
one would have to be very cruel deliberately to hurt Earthy. And
Poppy isn't.'

'But you could be?' Janet asked.

'I suspect we both could,' Veronica said.

'Cruel' was a word Diana used whenever she and Veronica
quarrelled: for example over Diana's drinking and her tendency
to flirt with every attractive woman she met. All Veronica's
complaints were 'cruel' according to her lover, but Veronica
didn't know whether it was literally meant or just a handy piece
of abuse, a lazy habit of language. There was no point in pressing
for more clarity. Diana ran away from any scrutiny of their

relationship. Whatever they had between them would remain undefined. Diana could express her feelings only as clichés, and Veronica would never know what thought or emotion truly lay behind them.

Diana also said that Veronica was 'controlling'. Here she wasn't alone. At the climax of the final volcanic row at the bank – which was a mixture of professional concern over its exposure to risky derivatives and Veronica's certain knowledge that her promotion was being blocked – the CEO had thundered at her that she was 'a controlling dyke bitch!'

It was an observation that cost the bank several million and set Veronica up to take retirement at the age of forty. And in return they learned the valuable lesson that one shouldn't insult people who tape conversations.

'You should have said I was a *cunning* controlling dyke bitch,' she told the CEO once the dust had settled and he had the grace to take her to a farewell dinner (as well as the audacity to suggest her sexual orientation might be improved by the attentions of a qualified man, no names necessary).

Still the accusation rankled. Admittedly Poppy never made it, but then Poppy never accused her of any sins. The girl's response to being thwarted or told to do something she didn't want to do was disappointment, silence and a sort of dumb insolence. It was Veronica who was reduced to shouting as she tried to elicit a display of passion from her partner.

Thinking of Diana and then of Poppy, Veronica wondered if she were asking for the impossible. Was she missing something? Was she insensitive to the words and behaviour of other people? Because whatever they said and whatever they did, she could never be convinced that they loved her.

The life class was held at Léon's studio despite the fact that it had no natural light except what came through the door into the *atelier*. A rumour of the event had gone round the village and attracted a crowd, including several old ladies who brought chairs and sat themselves down in the lane under a misapprehension that Ravi was going to parade naked for the benefit of the public.

'Bring on the dancing girls,' said Belle.

Léon was loitering by the door. He put a hand on Janet's arm as she went in.

'There is another dance on Saturday,' he said. 'It is at the lake of Montbel, which is near Chalabre. You will come with me?'

'I don't know,' said Janet. 'Can we talk about it later?'

'You are doing something else?'

'Yes – no – look, this isn't the time.' People were staring and Janet already had a feeling she was the talk of the village; not that she cared. What concerned her was her complete incomprehension as to where this nonsense was going. 'I'm an elderly woman!' she told herself; then realised she must have spoken aloud.

Léon said, 'Is it not allowed me to like you?'

'Of course you can like me, but . . . ' Janet thought of something that might serve as an excuse. She said, 'My husband and I used to dance all the time and it was wonderful. When I dance with you I think of *him*, do you understand?'

'You can dance with me and think of your husband. I not mind.'

Janet decided she'd tried her best but her case was hopeless. She said, 'Good. In that case I'll come with you.'

It wasn't true that when she danced with Léon she always thought of her husband. Sometimes she did and sometimes she didn't. She loved David, but he wasn't so wonderful she had to think about him all the time. These days, when she danced the tango with Léon she thought of the young Frenchman, relished the thrill of the moment, and allowed herself to dream a little. That was the problem.

Léon said goodbye and walked away. Carol came out of her own studio and joined the others.

'You didn't think I'd miss the chance of seeing Ravi in the buff, did you?'

'Do you think he might be a secret Dave?' asked Belle.

'It's entirely possible. I was wondering what colour his hair is.'

'Who knows? He shaves his head. Oh no! You mean his . . . ? No, please! Don't start me laughing!' Belle covered her mouth.

They took seats in a row and a chair was placed in front of them for the model. Ravi came down the staircase from an upper room. He was naked except for an unbleached cotton *dhoti*. Seeing it, Belle whispered, 'I'm not sure I altogether hold with grown-up blokes wearing nappies. Do you think he powders his botty when he changes? If he needs help, I haven't lost the knack.'

He took his place on the chair. Since it was supposed to be Poppy's class, she arranged him as she thought best and he cooperated, treating the matter seriously. But he would, thought Janet, because he has a high opinion of himself. He'll want the drawings to be a success. She recognised that he was very good looking, broadly made with good muscle tone, without being beefcake. His complexion was fair; he had reddish brown fuzz on his chest and a number of freckles and moles; but by careful sunbathing he'd acquired a good even tan. All the same he left her unmoved in a way that Léon with his skinny ugliness didn't. But Léon was lithe and vivacious and had a quiet sense of humour that made all the difference.

They drew for an hour. Poppy let Carol give instruction, not that it made much difference. In the end they came up with very individual results. Poppy and Carol naturally produced good drawings using different techniques: Carol's being spare with assured control of line, while Poppy's was full of hatched light and shadow. Veronica's effort was worthy: generally recognisable for what it was though Ravi looked as if he was about to fall off the chair. Janet's was incomplete and full of erasures. Earthy appeared to have paid no attention to reality but drawn a purely iconic figure with a few extra arms thrown in and some writing –

a prayer perhaps – in Indian script. And Belle drew a stick figure with a lascivious grin and a speech bubble that said, 'Come up and see me some time, Big Girl.'

'Eats and a glass of plonk at my place,' said Carol once they were done. They crossed the lane to her studio where there were two bottles of chilled blanquette and a tray of snacks. She showed them the commissions she was working on for galleries in England: some ceramics and a multi-media piece.

She said, 'It's called *English ladies murdering the past*. There's no particular reason since it's abstract.'

Still everyone agreed it was a good title and highly appropriate, though no one could say why. It was a while since they'd thought of the origin of their group name: the observation Janet had made about their reasons for coming to Puybrun. It wasn't something they talked about. Indeed it was possible that only Janet remembered, and that was because with time she was more certain she was right.

She took Belle aside. She said, 'Léon has invited me to another dance.'

'Stop it, you'll make me jealous.'

'I've said I'll go with him but . . . What would you do if Charlie had died?'

'A big fat lump like me? Chance'd be a fine thing. Seriously? Wild horses couldn't hold me back.'

'Why not?'

'Because . . . ' Belle became quiet for a moment. Then she said, 'I've always thought that we – I mean us, you know: *people* – are like survivors from a shipwreck we know nowt about, except that we're in the water and its cold and it's dark and we're drowning. Here and there there's a lifeboat, and those of us who are lucky find one and try to pull other people out of the water or we throw them a lifebelt. But you always have to remember: the one thing you don't do is get back in the water and let the people who are drowning put their arms round you. Because if you do, you're finished and you'll both drown together. Do you understand? David's gone and you can't let him take you with him – not that I suppose he'd want you to from what you've said about him.' Belle thought for another moment before adding, 'And you don't let the live ones drown you either. You have to keep something back.'

You have to keep something back.

Janet had loved David long and hard through the decades of their marriage, and for most of that time it had been good. He was an easy going man with a warm nature and very funny and self mocking. But he also had a dark side that was unfathomable, which he didn't claim to understand; and he was, by his own admission, foolish and lacking in common sense. As with any marriage, there had been furious arguments and moments of coldness and times when Janet had wondered whether it was worth going on or whether she should dust off one of her clever plans for killing him and give serious thoughts to implementing it. Yet, in the end, of course, they had gone on: saved by her tolerance and David's sunniness, the fact that he was fun to live with; and she thought that by the standards of these things they'd been happy.

Still there was a price to pay for living with the reality of relationships, as Belle had reminded her. It had first come to her at a time of reconciliation after a piece of David's idiocy, the details of which she'd forgotten. She looked at him and saw him starkly in all his frailty and she thought to herself: I love this man from the bottom of my heart, but I shall never let him destroy me. No matter how much I give him, I must keep something for *me*. I can't let myself be at the mercy of *his* decisions or the chances that affect *his* life. I have to be able to walk away and survive. She told him so: not to ask his permission but just so he would understand how matters stood. She didn't remember his reaction but he seemed to accept what she said. He probably told a joke. He could be damned annoying like that.

Janet was troubled by a suspicion. She had difficulty deciding if it was any of her business, and wasn't sure what she should do about it, but it wouldn't go away. In the end she was driven partly by concern and partly by sheer curiosity. She needed to know if she was right.

She booted up her laptop and began an internet search of enquiry agents. She came up with a cascade of names before realising she had no means of knowing if they were in any way competent or even honest. It seemed to her that this was a dangerous proceeding and she logged off.

The following morning she phoned her solicitor. Hector was an old friend of David from university. He practised in a small way with a couple of partners from a high street shop front office, getting by with matrimonial work, conveyancing and a few no-win-no-fee personal injury claims. It hadn't occurred to her to discuss her possible legal problems with him. The idea that he might handle a complex fraud case or a murder trial – not that it would ever come to that – was laughable. He was an amiable man like David and no doubt an ornament to the local Rotarians.

'Hector? It's Janet Bretherton.'

'Janet, yes, my secretary said it was you. I haven't seen you since the funeral.'

He was at the funeral? Janet had forgotten. It had been a grotesque occasion. Because of David's connections to charities and local government, the genuine mourners had been out-numbered by a horde of anonymous men in cheap suits, who knew no one except each other. David, thinking about death at a time when it didn't seem imminent, had said he wanted *Always Look on the Bright Side of Life* to be played at the service. He hadn't foreseen that, at the reception afterwards, the result would be an impromptu cabaret of tipsy accountants doing Monty Python impressions.

'I was grateful for your support,' Janet said. 'David valued your friendship.'

'Yes, well.' She could feel Hector searching for words, matching them out of the sock drawer of the English language until he came up with, 'I'm always here for you.'

What on earth does that mean? Janet wondered. But she said it was a sentiment she treasured deeply. 'There is a little something,' she added, 'A little something you could help me with.'

'Ye–es?'

'Do you by any chance have the name of a reliable enquiry agent?'

'An enquiry agent? That's a profession there isn't much call for these days: not since the old-fashioned contested divorce was abolished. I can't remember when I last used one.'

'But they do still exist. Companies use them for checking on employees.'

'I'm sure they do. Why do you want one?'

'I'm researching something.'

Hector knew she was often researching things and that she would tell him nothing more. He promised to ask around and let her know.

'Today?'

'Yes, if possible.'

Janet gave him her e-mail address, and they ended the call with expressions of gratitude and concern. By the following morning a name and some contact details were waiting on her machine. She formulated her questions the same day and sent them.

She asked for everything that was known about a man called Graham Southcock.

It had been agreed that each of them would give three classes on their chosen subject. With the life drawing, Poppy had finished her session. That left only Earthy, from whom they didn't expect much, and whatever it was would probably be strange. She'd been muttering darkly about 'spirituality' and 'healing energies'.

'Every time I hear that word "spirituality" I want to spit,' said Belle. 'And I'll tell you something for free: there's no way she's going to get me dancing in the altogether round some ruddy tree. You've got no idea how long it takes me to get ready in the morning. Once I get my kit off, my bits'll be off and away like greyhounds out of the starting gate, and I'll be at it all day trying to put them back.'

Janet thought it most likely that Earthy would do something in keeping with her gentle nature and the most they had to fear was a few meaningless incantations and a little embarrassment as they tried to keep their faces straight. She mulled it over when, after a restless night, she went for an early walk by the lake. The beach and *buvette* were deserted and the pedalos moored, and the only signs of life were a trickle of customers to the baker and a woman in a nightdress shaking a mat at the door of a caravan.

She felt sad. At one time she thought the group would continue indefinitely, finding new things to interest them. Now she wasn't sure. She couldn't see beyond the horizon of Earthy's lessons. Perhaps they would be inventive enough to discover other skills they could teach each other. Or perhaps not, and if not, what then? She supposed they would drift apart, barely noticing that they'd done so. For a while they might organise coffee mornings but, with winter, attending meetings would become tiresome and the group would disband itself, not deliberately but gradually so that no one would be able to remember the definite moment when it stopped. And afterwards? They would bump into each other at the minimarket or buying meat at the butcher's van or . . .

For the first time Janet had a suspicion that she might return to England once her lease had expired. In any case, if she stayed in France, there would be the English house to sell and that would mean disposing of the furniture and the knickknacks and the books that she and David had accumulated over so many years; and for that reason she would have to go home. In her mind's eye she could see herself standing in her house with the artefacts of their shared life around her, enchanting her more than any of Earthy's spells and talismans. Even in memory she felt in thrall to them. If once she was in their presence she was terrified they would fasten a hold around her and she would become their adjunct, just a dusty relic of a past no one else cared about.

Janet shook herself and went for a brisk walk along the embankment and back and returned to her cottage after stopping to buy some bread and a *pain au raisin*. She made a mug of chocolate and sat outside, dunking pieces of stale baguette in her drink and watching the early swallows. She saw the door of Belle's house open and the woman herself bustling out, waving a newspaper and in a state of high excitement.

Oh God! Janet thought. What's happened to Charlie? But Belle wasn't distraught, just agitated as if by something that was appalling yet fun at the same time.

She cried out, 'Janet! You've got the see this! It's in the paper! Arnold's in the paper!'

'Arnold?' Janet was surprised – Arnold, a fat old nonentity? 'Why is he in the paper? He isn't famous and everyone forgot to tell us, is he?'

'What? Famous? Arnold? No, of course he's not famous. Well, he didn't used to be. Maybe he is now – infamous even. He's only gone and got himself murdered!'

How to Speak with the Dead

22

Digitoxin is a cardiac glycoside. It has similar structure and effects to digoxin (though the effects are longer-lasting). Unlike digoxin (which is eliminated from the body via the kidneys), it is eliminated via the liver, so could be used in patients with poor or erratic kidney function. However, it is now rarely used in current UK medical practice. – Wikipedia

Janet thought: *Grief is a place we visit.* Some of us are travellers and some are tourists; or, at least, we make that distinction in our own mind, not quite crediting that others can fully experience what to us is so vivid and unique. It had been the same when she and David saw the Taj Mahal and the pyramids. They'd considered themselves two travellers in a horde of tourists: a silly point of view, but very human. The reality, she knew, was that there was nothing in her feelings about death, the Taj Mahal or anything else that millions of others hadn't felt. However, when David died she avoided the counselling, the pamphlets and the support groups that people recommended, and so found herself now alone and wondering; not even certain if the ebb and flow of her emotions amounted to grief or not. An advantage of associating with others is to learn the etiquette of life and death. It can be useful when one doesn't want to be forever thinking consciously about things. On the other hand, if Janet had been following the conventions of grief, she probably wouldn't have gone dancing with Léon. And that wasn't something she regretted.

'I shan't remarry,' she told herself. Not out of respect for David's memory or any sense of decency, but because marriage was a phase of life and she felt that for her it was over. Men were a doubtful piece of goods at the best of times. It took years to get used to their moods, their obsessions and nasty habits, and she couldn't imagine doing it a second time, though, of course, one never knew.

In the nature of things most women will spend their latter days living in a world of other women: relying on their own sex for support and whatever there is in the way of love or friendship unless they choose to be isolated and alone. Janet had always known this dimly, but her life in Puybrun had confirmed it. The English Lady Murderers' Society hadn't come into being from a whim or by mere chance. The women had created it out of need, and what distressed Janet now was that she was frightened it would fail them – that they would fail each other – when she suspected they needed each other most.

'Poor Joy,' she said when Belle told her Arnold had been murdered. The reaction was so instinctive and immediate, it defeated even her curiosity.

'Isn't it wonderful!' Belle said; then caught herself, embarrassed for once. 'I don't mean that exactly; I'm not saying it's a good idea or I'm not sorry for Joy or anything. But it *is* summat to talk about isn't it?'

'You read it in the newspaper?'

'I'm an idiot. The paper came out last week. I bought it in Limoux on Saturday while you were gallivanting with Léon, but I got distracted and I've only just read it.' She handed the newspaper to Janet. The story was the second item on a page dominated by news of a celebrity's breast implants:

Dudley man in bloody house of horror!
'I've never seen anything like it,' says
traumatised cleaning lady
Hardened police officers sickened by violence.
Death of largest used car dealer in the West Midlands.

'He was beaten to death,' said Belle. *'with a hammer!'*
Janet closed her eyes. She saw Arnold slumped over a blood-stained IKEA desk in a study decorated with Honda trade calendars and the computer monitor showing a screen-saver of Norwegian fjords. The reality would have been bloodier of

course: Arnold's skull smashed, and spatters, bone and brain fragments everywhere.

She felt a sudden flash of her own horror. David : poisoned – his unfocused eyes rolling and his mouth in a rictus of agony from the heart attack brought on by digoxin – vomit down the front of his suit – his bowels and bladder voided (she had researched on *Wikipedia* and symptoms included nausea, vomiting, diarrhoea, confusion, visual disturbances, and cardiac arrhythmias). Janet had never asked how the body had been found, preferring to imagine David had died laughing. Helen had seen to the sordid side of things: the dry-cleaning of the suit and the valeting of the car. David was delivered to Janet so spick and span she might have imagined he'd expired from unaccustomed tidiness: almost as if someone else had died. She received a scrubbed corpse, a set of clothes, car keys, mobile phone, wallet, and a packet of indigestion tablets. It seemed he hadn't taken any papers with him to the meeting with Jeremy, which was odd when one considered the nature of the final meeting.

The image of David was a shock. How could she not have realised it before: the pain and loneliness of his death? She put the thought away. Nothing in it would help her. It was for another time.

'When . . . when was he killed?' she asked.

Belle studied her. 'Are you all right? I thought you'd given up the crying.'

'I'm fine. I was thinking about David. When was Arnold killed?'

'They're not sure within a week or so. You were right that he might have died and no one known. He was living on his own like he did every summer when he went back to England to take care of things. The cleaner came on Wednesdays, but she'd been poorly the week before, and he never went out much; he lived out of the freezer.'

Belle mentioned dates, and Janet remembered that Joy had

been incapacitated, drinking herself to oblivion as if she knew she'd just been widowed. Janet supposed Arnold wasn't much of a husband and might drive any woman to drink. But the fact was the human species would be extinct if we didn't accept the partners we were given. Ugly horrible people were still breeding, the last time she looked.

'Have they arrested anyone?'

'I don't know. I need to buy another paper to find out,' said Belle. 'The most obvious suspect is Joy, of course, except she was sick wasn't she? And if by any chance she did pop over to England to do her hubby in, there'd be a paper trail, wouldn't there? Passports, aeroplane tickets, that sort of thing; I don't suppose she's bright enough to hide her tracks. Well, we'll find out.'

'I can probably get the story on line.' Janet said; then thought a moment. 'They should be able to get a more exact date of the murder from Arnold's e-mail account. Joy said he was always on his computer. He'd have stopped answering his mail.'

'There are times when you think like a detective,' Belle said. 'I'm surprised you have any friends.'

The uncertainty about Arnold's death reminded Janet of the vagueness of events on David's last night A passing police patrol noticed his car parked in the lay-by; it was at 7.30 or so the following morning and getting light. They thought he'd died late the previous evening; the exact hour being difficult to establish because of an air frost that might have slowed the post mortem processes; and because in the absence of suspicious circumstances no one had bothered to make the necessary checks. According to Jeremy's account, David would have left the restaurant shortly after nine. The lay-by was only ten minutes away at a moderate speed, and the theory was that he'd felt unwell and pulled over in order to recover. Then, sitting in the car, he was overwhelmed by the stroke – or, as it might be, the heart attack caused by poison. He couldn't have been there more than a few minutes when it happened, because no one, least of all David, would suffer in silence for long, not with a mobile phone to hand, which presumably had been charged (Janet didn't know for certain, but it seemed likely). He might have called for help, but he didn't. So, if Jeremy was right, David should have died at about 9.30, give or take a quarter of an hour.

Yet, according to the timed credit card slip, he'd paid for dinner at 10.15.

Why was David still at the restaurant more than an hour after Jeremy had left? Had Jeremy lied about the time of his own departure, and, if so, why? It would be his second lie. The first was about the presence of a third person at dinner: something he absolutely denied but which the police could prove from the itemised bill. It made no sense except perhaps to hide someone's identity and possibly provide him or her with an alibi by confusing the times. Or had Janet fooled herself and there was a simpler explanation?

How would it be if Jeremy hadn't lied? If he'd left at nine o'clock exactly as he said? What if, when he told her that no one else was present while he and David discussed business, he'd also been telling the truth? The mysterious third party could have arrived *after* the quarrel – after Jeremy had stormed out of the steak house leaving David behind. A man? A woman? An investor? A mistress? He or she could have sat with David for an hour or more, and in that time eaten a meal.

Janet tried to imagine the situation. Quite apart from the fact that David had always been faithful, it didn't sound like a romantic assignation: when one isn't eating, watching someone else eat isn't in the least romantic. Then too, nine o'clock on a midweek evening was late to eat, unless one happened to be Spanish. It smacked of force of circumstances: perhaps a busy man working late at the office and grabbing a meal afterwards. Or a busy woman – one shouldn't be sexist about these things. It suggested a continuation of the crisis meeting about the affairs of Vavasour &

Bretherton. Was David being pressed by one of his investors, or did he suspect the other party had been involved in the fraud? Jeremy had made no secret that he fronted for other stakeholders in the firm. It was at least conceivable that David had done the same: that he represented not just himself. He might have acted for friends from his earlier career: local government officers who saw a conflict of interest if they were part-owners in a business that managed public funds. A financial collapse and investigation would be disastrous for someone in that position.

It *had* to have been a business meeting. And that brought back an earlier thought. Janet took her mobile from her bag and composed a message to Jeremy.

She asked: DID DAVID HAVE ANY PAPERS WITH HIM AT UR MEETING?

The reply was almost immediate.

OBVIOUSLY HE DID! R U STUPID OR WOT?

Janet ignored the insult. It was enough that Jeremy had confirmed that David had papers with him at dinner. Yet they hadn't been returned with the rest of his possessions. What had happened to them?

They gathered at Earthy' cottage, except Joy, who hadn't yet returned after Arnold's funeral. No one else seemed to have read the newspaper story, not even Veronica, who said she'd spoken to Joy on the phone. Belle had the tact not to mention it.

Casting an eye round the room, Janet noticed again the good rather dull English furniture that must have belonged to Earthy's parents. No doubt her brother and sister had let 'Valerie, bless her' keep it while they got on with their own successful, lives. Yet, in her quiet way, Earthy had established herself as a person and stamped an impress on her surroundings. Her parents presumably had fitted carpets; but Earthy had chosen inexpensive colourful kilims. Janet imagined their pictures had been discreet prints and family photographs: Earthy had replaced them with oil paintings of virgins and unicorns and other faery themes. Above all and uniquely Earthy was the array of figures made by Léon and given to her by Ravi. Each one had a tea light in front of it, but today the candles weren't lit and the figures seemed quiescent, waiting for their worshippers. There was a scent of burnt wax and incense.

Earthy had made an effort with her appearance. She'd abandoned her boots for sandals with leather flowers on the thongs, and her feet looked soft and pale and her nails were painted. She wore a mid-length oatmeal coloured skirt, exposing well shaped calves covered in blond down. Her blouse was pale green linen, and her jewellery a simple string of stained wooden beads. She had plaited her hair.

She wants to be taken seriously, Janet thought. Earthy had been transformed from a mad gypsy into a Methodist missionary, and it became her. The clothes no longer distracted attention from her benign, pretty features; and Janet could see that in her youth when she'd been seduced by Sir Gawain Warlock of the Shire, she must have been quite beautiful. Earthy had confessed to having had a child, and the thought called up a modern nativity scene: Earthy lying on the bunk of a caravan with the baby at her breast; Sir Gawain grinning like a fool, and the Three Wise Men in anoraks offering joints, veggie burgers and bottles of cheap cider while Welsh rain rattled on the roof.

'I thought we could begin with the lore of herbs,' Earthy said.

Belle nudged Janet and whispered, 'Get that "lore". I don't know I've ever learned any "lore" before.'

They went into the kitchen. Earthy had set out a dozen shallow dishes on the table, each of them labelled with the contents. There were more herbs in sprigs tied with wisps of straw and an album of flower pressings. On the wall was a rack of bottles containing various infusions, and more were bubbling away on the hob. Everything was in the neatest order.

Poppy picked up the album and leafed through it. She turned

to Earthy and gave one of her radiant smiles. She said, ' 'S really like great, innit? D'you grow all this stuff yourself?'

Earthy blushed. 'I don't have a garden,' she said. Few of the houses in Puybrun did. 'I do know *how* to grow them. And, of course, one can collect plants from hedgerows and fields,' she added, forgetting for the moment the wholesaler in Paris from whom she bought most of her stock.

They returned to the other room and took seats. By way of an exercise Earthy brought the herbs through one at a time for examination and did a little test if they could tell them apart by smell and appearance.

'I need a herbal remedy myself,' said Carol. 'Anybody mind if I smoke?' She lit a cigarette and picked up a sprig of mugwort. 'I know this one, mug-something-or-other. It's a weed; I've seen it growing all over the place. What use is it?'

Earthy took the dried leaves back, muttering, 'It helps with the monthlies.'

'I didn't catch that,' said Veronica.

'It's good for the Curse,' Carol said. 'Though I suppose that depends whether you want to start it or stop it.'

Earthy said, 'You can also mix it with pork fat to make an ointment for rubbing on wens.'

'That sounds a bit mediaeval,' said Belle. 'Shades of witches. Does it cure anything we'd be interested in?'

'Well, if you suffer from sciatica, it's good taken dried with wine. And you can relieve cramp by bathing with a decoction of mugwort, agrimony and camomile.'

'Whatever they are. First it's "lore" and now it's "decoction". It's like learning English all over again! Who says this stuff works?'

'Culpeper,' said Earthy, and picked up another item.

'I think I could have done without knowing about a cure for suppurating scabs and shingles,' said Belle afterwards.

'That was cow parsnip, wasn't it?' said Janet.

'All the same, I quite took to old Culpeper. You don't see much "quinsy" or "dropsy" about nowadays; so perhaps he knew a thing or two, what do you think? I read that lungwort boiled in beer is good for broken-winded old horses. There are mornings when I could definitely do with some of that.'

Earthy had a leather-bound edition of Culpeper. Her father, the doctor, had collected herbals and medical textbooks. This one was enchanting and the women pored over it; Carol and Poppy in particular admired the hand coloured plates.

Belle said, 'I suppose there's something to it – the herbs, I mean, not the rest.'

Earthy had taken her friends' enthusiasm over the book as a chance to elaborate about 'energy medicine' and offer to rebalance the *chi* of whoever might be interested and so restore bodily and spiritual harmony. She claimed to practise *reiki* and 'therapeutic touch'.

'Five minutes of that and my aura was off-colour, my meridians were giving me gyp, and I wouldn't wish my *chakras* on my enemies. In fact I need a drink,' said Belle. 'And another thing: I don't know what effect this New Age malarkey has on your health, but it does absolutely nowt for Earthy's fashion sense or interior decorating. She makes my mother look like a paragon of good taste.'

Janet didn't want to go to the *buvette*. She offered to open a bottle of wine at home.

'Let's,' said Belle. 'All this talk about medicine and illness; let's do what my Mum and my aunties used to do and swap stories about our operations. Shall I tell you about my veins?'

'Not till we've had a drink,' said Janet. 'And first things first: we should check if there's more news about Arnold.' She booted up her laptop and left Belle to Google her way through the news.

When she returned with the bottle and the glasses, she found her friend staring very solemnly at the computer screen.

'You're not going to believe this,' Belle said.

23

Necromancy is magic by conjuring the spirits of the dead. Practitioners believe the departed can give information about their deaths and the conditions of the afterlife. They are also claimed as a source of predictions, though it is not self-evident why dead people should know more about the future than living ones.

Arnold was a child molester. That was what the news story said. The house in Dudley to which he returned for two months every summer was a child trap fitted out with a playroom. The police suspected nothing from the apparently innocent toys until the anomaly of Arnold's age was remarked on and investigations revealed he was estranged from his sons and had no children by his second wife. Only then did the police take a look at his computer, which revealed his connection to an extensive paedophile network. That was it in brief.

'They're working on the theory that a parent may have discovered what was going on,' said an appalled Belle, telling Janet what she could see for herself on the screen. 'Or maybe one of the other blokes in his network got frightened and killed him as part of a cover-up.'

'I wish I didn't know,' Janet said. She felt the terrible bleakness that comes from contemplating what other people are capable of and one's powerlessness to change things. She murmured, 'Poor Joy.' She'd said the same when first learning of Arnold's death; but on that occasion the meaning was different. She recalled a trite but truthful observation: one of those pieties that get circulated by e-mail and pass for wisdom because they are pithily written. *If you could heap your troubles into a pile and see the piles belonging to others, you'd take your own pile back.* Nothing that was happening to her in connection with David's death could possibly match what Joy had gone through and would have to go through. Janet had never expected to feel ashamed of her own sorrow, but now she did.

'I knew that Arnold was horrible, but what are we going to tell the others?' asked Belle.

'Nothing.'

'They're bound to find out.'

'Let them find out in their own way,' Janet said. She didn't want to become a ghoul, chewing over the bones of another woman's suffering until the marrow was sucked out. She didn't want to see Joy; didn't want to commiserate with her, no more than she wanted others to join in her own grief.

I don't want sympathy. I want it all to have happened to someone else. She never said so, but it was the truth of the matter. It was why sympathy, no matter how intense or sincere, never satisfied her but only made her angry. There were times when she hated those who wished her well and whose only desire was to help. She wanted to shout at them: *'Just take it away from me!'*

She wanted to shout the words so fiercely that drops of her spittle would strike their faces and the shock of that intimacy would stun them to silence.

She wanted to terrify them against claiming even for a moment that they understood her or shared in her pain or that anything they could say or do would lessen it.

She wanted them to understand that their sympathy was worthless.

She wanted them to cradle her in their arms.

'Were you saying something?' said Belle. 'I didn't catch it.'

'I was thinking aloud.' Janet gave a small cough; then said, 'In my opinion we should leave the others to find out and deal with it in their own way.'

With surprising delicacy Belle said, 'Yes, that's probably for the best. We don't want to look like we're gloating over the story.' Then: 'Oh, God! I hope Earthy hasn't got anything silly planned.'

I have something silly planned, Janet remembered. *I'm supposed to be going dancing with Léon again.*

He told her to wear trousers but didn't say why. She waited for him inside the house with the shutters closed and a light on by which she tried to read. Her book was a murder mystery, always her favourite kind. She wanted to revisit Agatha Christie's *Appointment with Death* because she'd remembered that the weapon in the case was digitoxin, a drug related to the one that had killed David – or *might* have killed him because apparently one couldn't be sure But her copy was back home. According to Wikipedia digitoxin wasn't much prescribed in England nowadays, which raised the question of how one got one's hands on it. Did that fact have any significance?

'I've no idea,' she said aloud. 'Whatever Belle says, I'm not a detective.'

Even the real detective, Stephen Gregg, seemed stumped for theories as to who had killed David – apart from Janet, obviously.

She heard the sound of a car idling in the lane and thought it must have a problem with the exhaust; it was so noisy. The front door rattled. Janet put down her book and went to answer. She checked her face and hair in the mirror and smoothed down her crisp blouse and trousers. She still felt flattened by the contemplation of Joy's misery.

I don't want to do this, she thought. Not tonight. Not ever again. The joke is over. I'll tell him I'm sorry but I can't come with him. But that would be unfair because her concerns were not his, and he'd done nothing except bring some distraction and happiness into her life; and there was no escaping the fact that the experience of being treated as if she were a young and desirable woman was marvellous. She compromised. *This will be the last time.*

She opened the door. Léon was on the veranda smoking. He

looked at her and beamed. 'But you will need a scarf,' he said. 'And also a *pull*.' He mimed one.

'A pullover? Why?'

'Or a jacket to keep warm.'

The evening was balmy; the first bats were out and a solitary planet hung bright and low on the horizon. Janet looked beyond her visitor to the lane and in the failing light saw not a car but a motorbike, the same great glittering beast on which Ravi had ridden with Hatshepsut.

'Oh no,' she said. 'I am *not* going on that. I haven't been on a motorbike since . . . ' She couldn't remember. A Lambretta scooter came to mind on which she'd gone to Blackpool with a boyfriend more years ago than she cared to recall, because a pop group whose name was on the tip of her tongue was playing on one of the piers, and the girl singer had back-combed hair and wore false eyelashes. She said, 'Anyway, I don't have a helmet.'

'This is France.'

'You mean you don't have to wear a helmet?'

He shrugged.

'You'll be telling me next that they still smoke in restaurants and park on pedestrian crossings. I . . . ' Janet felt again that sense of helplessness. She couldn't escape the fact that she wanted to go dancing. It was what she and David had always done. It was bound up with some of the happiest times in her life, and if these were the terms on which she could hold onto those memories and if dancing in the arms of this young man was the way to a future that still held something for her, she would go with him.

'A pullover will mess my hair,' she said. 'I'll get a jacket and a scarf.' She went back into the house to find them.

They rode to Chalabre and on to Montbel, following the cone of the headlight. Janet nestled into Léon's back, peeking now and again over his shoulder to see the empty road and the ghosts of trees rushing towards them. It was exhilarating.

They parked by the lake at a place where boats were moored. On a patch of bare ground was a makeshift stage, and lights and power were jury-rigged from a generator that rumbled somewhere in the background. The band was already playing and it was late enough that they were churning out hip hop for teenagers while the adults dozed at their tables or drifted away.

'I don't think there'll be any dancing for us tonight,' Janet said. 'We should have come earlier. Never mind.'

Léon bought plastic cups of warm white wine. They took them to a bench and sat with their backs to the band and looked at the sky and the black pool of the lake.

'This wine is disgusting,' Janet said.

'Perhaps they make it in China like everything?' Léon suggested. 'You want that I look for food? Also disgusting?'

'No. I never did like Chinese food.'

The band switched numbers for something with a salsa rhythm. Léon held out a hand and led Janet to a place in the shadows where they could dance alone except for the squeaks and cries of lovers kissing in the darkness and the creak of rowlocks from an invisible boat somewhere on the lake. They moved clumsily, the soft ground dragging at their feet, and Janet's mood changed again. This . . . this whatever-it-was must end. It wasn't a matter of choice but of inevitability and didn't even call for a decision on her part. The dances of summer would run their season, and without them there was nothing to bind her and Léon: no books, no theatre, no ballet, no conversation, and certainly no sex. No history. No memories. No deep tenderness and compassion born out of lives shared. Nothing even to forgive. Already Janet could feel the fading magic, and with each repetition it would fade some more, so that even before the summer closed, they would find themselves looking at each other in new, stark ways, perhaps with a brutal clarity. How would she appear then in his eyes? An aging woman who dyed her hair and whose pale skin was seamed with every year she had lived and whose bosom if he ever saw it would be . . . she didn't want to think how it would seem to him. And she would see a man who was not especially handsome or intelligent; whose conversation was banal and whose interests were limited. She wished it were otherwise. Looking at him she dearly wished it were otherwise. But it was the harsh condition of existence that it took love to find the heart's fulfilment in the undistinguished people life put in our way. No one was wonderful in a cold light.

David had been wonderful because she had willed him to be so.

She had become wonderful because she had been loved.

The music stopped. Janet said, 'It's late. We should go home.'

'Are you cold? You are shivering.'

'A little.' In fact the air was still warm. 'Someone walking over your grave,' her mother would have said. It was on odd way of putting it and made Janet think briefly of the murders, real and imagined, that had brought the women to Puybrun. David dead. Arnold dead. Charlie . . . who knew?

They spoke very little on the return journey. Léon stopped outside Janet's house but didn't get off the bike. They kissed each other on the cheek.

Léon said, 'Tonight you seem sad. You will be all right, Jane?'

'I'll be fine,' Janet said and fished in her bag for her key. She paused. 'You just called me "Jane".'

'Yes?' He judged her reaction and appeared puzzled. He said, 'I do not understand your English names. "Jane" and "Janet", they are the same, no? Just different ways of pronounce?'

Was he telling the truth?

'You do not like me to call you "Jane"?'

'I prefer "Janet".'

He laughed. 'Very good. You are Janet and I shall remember. But now I go.'

He put the bike in gear and drove down the lane, turned left at the highway and vanished. Janet watched him and felt over-whelmed by a great tiredness and sadness.

She understood now what Léon expected from their friendship.

Next day she met Belle outside Earthy's house.

Belle said solemnly, 'Mum's the word about Arnold, eh? Any more news on that front? Do we know when Joy's coming back – *if* she's coming back?'

'I looked at the on-line news, but there was nothing more. Until the police can identify the children or crack the computer codes that people like Arnold use to cover their tracks, I don't suppose they'll make much progress. As for Joy, I imagine Veronica will be the first to know her plans.'

'Poor cow. Arnold was horrible enough before we discovered he was *really* horrible. The lives some people have, eh?'

They were the last to arrive. The others were sitting round the dining table. Carol looked in their direction with an expression of relief.

She said, 'I don't think I can take any more organic carrot juice and veggie nibbles. Earthy is making a mystery of the treat she's got in store for us today, aren't you?'

Earthy nodded. Her smile looked mischievous.

'How was your date with Léon?' Carol asked Janet. 'You can tell. We all know about it. Has he had his wicked way yet? If you need a stand-in, I'd be prepared to help out.'

'You're embarrassing Janet,' said Veronica. Today she was looking very attractive: her eyes bright and her skin shining. Poppy, too, looked lovely and seemed more at ease than usual. There was no explanation, and Janet was reminded of the unknown currents that move the lives of other people, and that she no more divined the truth of what was going on between those two than they understood her relationship with Léon. Not that Janet understood it either – not in its fleeting nuances. Not even though she'd discovered his motives.

Belle said, 'OK, Earthy, what is it? Spit it out.'

Earthy went into the back room and returned with a shallow cardboard box. It reminded Janet of the game box that held Carol's roulette wheel, except that this one was battered and repaired with tape. She placed it on the table and took the lid off.

'Ta ra!' said Belle, sounding a trumpet. Then, 'What the hell is it?'

They peered into the box and saw a board printed with letters and numbers and other bits and pieces.

'Well, I'm no wiser,' said Belle. She looked at Carol. 'It looks more up your street.'

'I know what it is,' drawled Poppy. ' 'S a Ouija board, innit? You can like talk to the dead and stuff.'

Janet felt chilled. She looked to Belle and Veronica. *What in God's name was Earthy thinking of?* David was dead. Arnold was dead. Had she ignored the fact or did she have some mad idea that they were going to speak? She looked at the others, wondering if anyone shared her sense of horror at the idea.

Veronica said quietly, 'You'll have to exclude me from this one. My father was a clergyman. He was very opposed to Ouija boards. I'm afraid his prejudice has rubbed off on me. Please, don't let me stop the rest of you.'

Belle said, 'Me and a few friends tried it once or twice at university. I didn't like it. It was scary and we ended up accusing each other of cheating. I'll join in if everyone else wants to but . . . '

Janet shook her head. An inner voice was screaming; 'Dangerous! Dangerous!' David had been a committed sceptic and had told her how the phenomenon worked: the planchette moving towards the letters and spelling out messages by unconscious action, something he called 'the ideomotor effect'. Like Belle she'd attended séances at university and been shaken by the results: the stories of crime and violent death, misery and hidden murder.

She thought of what she'd written on her first night in Puybrun: 'What I most regret in life is murdering my husband . . . ' Why had she written it? It was difficult to recall now from what dark corner of her mind she'd drawn those words. If her hand was given free range over the Ouija board, what would happen? Would she make a terrible confession?

Earthy looked crestfallen. It was painful to see her, and Janet realised then that the poor woman hadn't the least thought of causing distress. Quite the contrary, she almost certainly saw the afterlife as an endless field of flowers and eternal sunshine from which the dead would send nothing but bland reports of happiness. Janet was sure that, in Earthy's hands, David would manifest himself given half a chance. How could he not do? But, unless she brought it on herself, she had absolutely nothing to fear, because there was little doubt what he would say. That he was happy – obviously. That he loved her – ditto. That she should have no fear for the future, because they would be reunited in a world beyond all pain – definitely.

That he forgave her for slipping a fatal dose of digoxin into his last meal? No, probably not that except by a slip of the tongue or wrist. Janet hadn't mentioned digoxin to anyone and it was unlikely to come up accidentally.

'While we're all here, and unless there's something better to do,' said Carol, 'I'll tell you a story. You'll forgive me, won't you Earthy? Your Ouija board was a bit like my Caribbean stud poker – not one of our best ideas.'

Carol's eviction from Dave World wasn't as sudden as she first suggested. After the high summer of her good fortune, when Daves seemed to grow on trees, she entered into a brief but golden autumn: still a good-looking woman but now with an air of sophistication and experience about her.

She gave up the boats and settled for a while on the Riviera, where she worked at the casino of St. Symphorien la Plage.

'It was a nice clientele,' she said. 'Russian gangsters and Italian drug dealers. *Very* generous. In those days the Russians in particular were only used to Moscow tarts, so I was pretty posh in comparison.'

She met Mario.

'He was from Naples. Said he was old nobility, and he may have been for all I know. What he didn't tell me was that he was in the Camorra – which is a bit like the Mafia but not as good-natured. He had a flat in town and a weekend villa on Ischia and he made a living smuggling African immigrants and running brothels.'

'But you didn't know that?' said Veronica.

'Of course I bloody knew!' Carol snapped. 'But like an idiot, I thought that being a madam meant swanning around in a fancy frock and talking nice to the customers, not locking up girls so they couldn't escape and keeping them out of their heads on smack. I . . . ' She shook her head. 'No, I don't want to talk about that bit.'

Mario saw that her heart wasn't in it, but he was a sentimental man and was in a quandary whether to kill her or not. He imprisoned her in the apartment in the Viale Antonio Gramsci while he made up his mind; and, like Scheherazade, Carol kept him and his thuggish friends amused so that he didn't come to too hasty a decision.

While Mario took his time about the matter of her murder, Carol watched him every day putting money into the wall safe in their bedroom. Together with what she'd already saved, it was enough at the end of each month to set a girl up very comfortably.

Carol lived this life for a year.

'And then I left him and came here to Puybrun,' she said. 'That was when I discovered I was an artist. It only goes to show how unpredictable life can be. You'd have thought I'd have been more suited to running a brothel, wouldn't you?'

'Why are you telling us this?' asked Janet.

'I don't know.' Carol stared at the ceiling, then fumbled in her bag and asked Earthy if she might smoke. She went to the door and stood outside smoking in the sunshine, looking now at the sky and now back into the room. She said, 'Because you're my friends, I suppose. And maybe because we all want someone to know us as we really are.'

They all nodded, but Janet wondered if it was true. Perhaps as a desire it was, but she doubted anyone had the self-knowledge or the courage to really make the attempt. Earthy, however, looked merely confused.

She asked, 'I'm sorry, but does this mean we are going to try the Ouija board or not?'

'The Ouija board?' Carol repeated. Then she remembered something. She said, 'And that's another reason for letting the truth come out. I don't want that lying bastard Mario coming back from the dead to tell you it was me that blew his fucking brains out. It wasn't. It was his gangster pals. All I did was steal his money.'

24

In 2003 Charles Cullen confessed to killing 40 hospital patients with overdoses of digoxin during his sixteen-year career as a nurse at hospitals in New Jersey and Pennsylvania.

In 2008 and 2009 there were warnings and product recalls in respect of two brands of digoxin because of variability in strength or tablet size affecting the dose. The result for some patients was to raise the dosage to toxic levels.

Joy returned. Veronica went to the airport to collect her and bring her home.

'I don't get that relationship, do you?' said Belle. 'It was the same when Joy was poorly and on her own at her place. Veronica was always going up and down to Campmaurice doing little things for her. She even did her cleaning.'

'She did her cleaning?' Janet was surprised.

'So Joy said. Can you imagine Veronica with a toilet brush, scouring out the loos? You wouldn't think she'd have the right clothes. Still, she may be used to it. Poppy looks the type to leave her tights on the floor and never clean the shower. Veronica may have to traipse behind her, clearing up all the time. I'm guessing. You never really know about other people. I'm still getting over what Carol told us.'

Janet's theory about Veronica was that she was a compassionate woman, who probably didn't realise it and would have been embarrassed if she knew. Voluntary organisations thrived on the efforts of women whose feelings were disguised by their practical energy. Most likely Veronica saw Joy as a managerial task and hadn't examined her motives too closely. But I'm guessing, Janet reminded herself, echoing Belle.

To welcome Joy's return they arranged a late lunch at the *buvette*, sitting at tables in the shade of the acacias.

'I don't know how this is going to go,' Belle said. 'What are we going to say to her? "How was the paedophile's funeral?"' Carol and Earthy have said nowt, so I'm supposing they haven't heard about Arnold. Veronica has kept quiet as well – has she said anything to you? I can't believe she doesn't know. If you cleaned my toilet, I think I'd tell you if my husband was a child molester.'

The weather had returned to a fine hot spell. Close by the *buvette* was a patch of ground, little more than a paddock with a couple of huts, where a small *colonie de vacances* was set up in summer. Today the children were riding ponies or swimming in the lake. The air was full of their voices.

Belle asked, 'You don't think anything of that kind was going on at Campmaurice, do you?'

Janet shook her head. Joy hadn't been frightened to invite them all to her house. And Arnold wouldn't have needed his refuge in Dudley if Joy was complicit in his crimes even by her silence.

Carol and Earthy came together. Poppy followed on her heels and said Veronica had phoned and the flight was on time and she and Joy would be here soon. They ordered drinks from Sandrine.

'What are we going to talk about while we're waiting?' said Belle. 'Have you got any more confessions, Carol?'

'Wasn't it enough that I stole a load of money?'

'Well it wasn't really theft, was it? It was more like collecting your wages.'

'And what if I'd killed Mario?' Carol asked. 'I didn't, but what if I had?'

'I don't suppose I'd be too fussed. Some blokes could do with a good murdering, in my opinion. What do the rest of you think?'

'I couldn't kill anyone,' said Earthy.

'Nobody's asking you to. But, supposing you knew someone who had – you know – *done it*, would you keep your gob shut?'

'I don't know. It would depend.'

'See what I mean? At least you're prepared to give the idea house room *in some cases*. If circumstances were right – if you could make an argument that putting someone out of the way was a public service – I fancy most people would turn a blind eye, eh? What about you Janet? You're not as squeamish as Earthy. I bet you'd keep your mouth shut – in fact I bet you'd knock someone on the head if you thought they deserved it.'

Janet was reluctant to speak. The conversation had become dangerous in the way children's games are sometimes unintentionally dangerous.

She said, 'I think it's one of those questions you can't answer in the abstract. Some things are simply outside our experience. When they come along we have no precedents about how to act and we surprise ourselves with our own behaviour. I've heard people who've received medals for bravery talking on the radio about how astonished they were to find themselves heroes. I suspect it's often the same with people who kill other people. They're shocked to find themselves murderers. They may even have considered themselves as kind.'

'Crikey,' said Belle. 'I didn't intend it as an exam question. Change of subject? Anyone? Earthy, what are you going to teach us next? The Ouija board turned out to be a success in the end, what with Carol putting her hand up to being a villain – tut tut, how dreadful. Can we expect more scandalous revelations?'

'I thought we should try some healing,' said Earthy.

'Healing – right. Do you mean more herbs? I took whatever it was you gave me and my bowels weren't right for two days.'

'Not herbs – a ritual.'

'Magic?'

'A ritual.'

'You mean magic. I've told Janet already that I'm not capering about the woods in my birthday suit.'

Earthy shook her head and smiled gently. 'You can keep your clothes on. In fact you should wear things that you love and your favourite jewellery and make yourself up and do anything that makes you feel happy.'

Belle looked at the others. 'I see. And where are we doing it, this "ritual"?'

'I thought we would hold it at the *temple des fauves* at Vieux Moulin.'

'I've heard mention of it, though I've never been there. It doesn't mean another ruddy hike, does it?'

'It's an easy walk from the village.'

'I see,' said Belle warily. 'Well, I suppose you know best.'

Veronica arrived, bringing Joy. The women were holding hands and Joy's dejection was painful to look at. Janet thought how acute her sense of humiliation and confusion must be and how brave she was to appear in front of the others. But what were the rest of them supposed to do or say? What rules did life offer for situations like this? On reflection Veronica's unfussy practical compassion seemed wise and admirable.

'Good flight?' asked Carol.

'A little bumpy,' said Joy. 'We had to avoid thunder storms.'

'How was the funeral?'

Someone had to ask.

'Quiet.'

'Good . . . not too gruelling, I hope.'

Joy shook her head.

'I imagine it was mainly family.'

Carol made a few more comments before noticing that no one else was speaking, and then Earthy joined in, presumably thinking it would help. The exchange was unavoidable, but it was agony to watch.

To change the subject, Belle said, 'Earthy is planning on holding a healing ceremony for us all. That sounds like a good idea, doesn't it?'

'Yes,' said Joy. 'I'd like to come.' And to Earthy: 'I'm sorry I missed the other things you did. The lesson about herbs sounds interesting. And what was the other one?'

'The Ouija board,' said Earthy.

'I've heard of that.'

Janet held her breath waiting for Earthy to explain that it was a means of communicating with the dead. Having been thwarted once, she might out of misplaced kindness offer a private séance to contact dear departed Arnold.

Presumably he would tell Joy that he was happy and at peace and waiting for her in the hereafter.

Presumably he would say he loved her and that they would be bound together in bliss for all eternity.

Janet returned to her cottage. It was mid afternoon and after a meal she was feeling drowsy in the heat. She lay down and dozed a while. She was woken by her phone ringing. It was Inspector Gregg.

'Not disturbing you, I hope.'

'I was resting, but I'm fine. I haven't heard from you for a while.'

'I assure you I've been busy. But most of my work has been trying to trace monies through the banking system. Somebody has been very clever. Frankly I'm surprised your husband was up to it.'

'It was Jeremy.'

'I don't think so. No offence intended, but Mr Vavasour is a moron.'

'Well, I don't know who else it could be.'

'Really? Well, we'll see.' There was a pause and voices off. 'I wonder . . . I wonder if we could return to that final dinner, the one where you and I agree that three people were present. Mr Vavasour still denies it, by the way.'

'Oh.'

'Which is odd, don't you think? He knows he's on our radar for poisoning Mr Bretherton. It ought to suit his book if he can cast suspicion onto a third person.'

'He may be trying to shield someone.'

'That doesn't sound like Mr Vavasour, does it? You have a pretty low opinion of him, and, while I may not share it completely, I don't think he's a natural gentleman who would lie to protect a lady or a friend.'

'We can deceive ourselves by thinking people always act in character.'

'We can,' agreed Stephen Gregg. 'But mostly we don't. The odds are that Mr Vavasour is telling the truth and there was no third person there *while he was eating his meal*. But, of course, that leaves open the possibility that someone arrived after he left.'

'I don't know who that could be.'

'But the thought had occurred to you. I'm surprised you didn't share it with me.'

'I had no evidence.' Janet decided this wasn't the moment to mention the timed credit card slip.

'That's very scrupulous of you.'

The purpose of the call suddenly became clear to Janet. Stephen Gregg had more or less dismissed her as a suspect as long as he believed that David, Jeremy and the third person had all dined together, because he accepted that Jeremy disliked her and would have named her if she'd been at the meal. However this consideration didn't apply if Jeremy had left before the mystery guest arrived. In that case, there was no one to say it wasn't her. Indeed there was no one more likely to have joined David for dinner than his wife.

Yet he surely wanted information? He wouldn't have called simply to voice suspicions?

'Did your husband have any siblings?'

Janet was stunned. 'Patrick?'

'I believe that's the name. What can you tell me about him?'

'Very little. I've never met him. He was David's twin – fraternal, not identical as far as I know. I can't even tell you if he's still alive.'

'I take it then that you can't give me an address or contact details?'

'No. Last heard of, he was in Australia, and that was forty years ago. Why are you asking about him?'

'Just ticking boxes,' said Stephen Gregg. He chuckled. 'It is nice to speak to you again.'

For once it didn't seem appropriate to ask Joy to drive them in the Tank. Janet gave a lift to Belle and Carol, and it was left to Veronica and Poppy to bring Joy if she was up to it. Earthy had gone on ahead to make her magical preparations.

'I have bad feelings about this,' said Belle. 'There's no telling what that mad bugger will get up to.'

'Well, I'm out of confessions,' said Carol. 'Unless you want all the pornographic details of the fellas I've slept with. What about you two? Has anybody we know killed anybody lately?'

'It's not a joke,' said Belle. For a moment Janet was afraid she would tell Carol the full tale about Arnold. Then again, would it really matter?

The road into Vieux Moulin was narrow and bordered by pollarded plane trees and an open storm drain. There was a small parking area by the church and a bar nearby that advertised Jupiler beer. Earthy was waiting at the bar with Veronica and Poppy.

'Joy is in the ladies room,' said Earthy. 'I trust you've brought torches as I asked.'

The women waved them.

'It's bad enough that we're going walking,' said Belle. 'Why at night?'

But it wasn't yet dark and the torches were only precautionary. The sky was still bright with broken cloud after a late afternoon storm.

Joy came out of the bar.

'Hullo everyone,' she said. Janet, Belle and Carol stared. She was wearing make-up and quite a pretty cotton dress with a geometric pattern of yellows and reds. Prompted by Earthy they'd chosen clothes they liked, regardless of the occasion, but they were so used to seeing Joy in her dowdiness that she was almost unrecognisable. Joy's manner, too, was lighter than they expected, though in this respect Janet wasn't surprised. She had recollections of her own moods in the early days after David's death and of the struggle to find a way of presenting herself to others that was sincere or, indeed, made any sort of sense.

Belle broke the tension by asking, 'Is this some sort of religious service, you've planned, Earthy? I'm not in the habit of going to church and these days I find myself forgetting whether, afterwards, I'm supposed to go to a wedding breakfast or the cemetery.'

'It's just a healing ceremony,' Earthy said. 'We'll be in a mysterious and beautiful place and being there should help us.'

Belle shrugged. 'Lead on, then.' Earthy set off down the road back in the direction of the main highway and the other women followed her.

After a short distance a lane led off to the right. A signpost read *sentier sauvage*, marking the route to a wilderness at the heart of which was the *temple des fauves*, which they knew of, though no one except Earthy could say what it was, and she wouldn't beyond muttering vaguely about 'karst': apparently some sort of limestone landscape caused by the action of water.

The path rose gradually and passed a stable block and the stump of an old windmill before dividing to cross a stretch of scrub and meadow broken by stands of oak and pine. After a few minutes of this, it began a descent towards a dense pine brake. The light was fading and birds flying in to roost.

They were walking in this direction when they passed a man and a woman coming the other way. The strangers were holding hands and smiling.

Belle nudged Janet and said, 'Did you see those two? They

were wearing kaftans and had nowt on their feet; and they had to be sixty if they were a day. They've been up to summat New Agey. It's a Bad Sign.'

Janet had noticed the smiles. The smiles of strangers were often equivocal. She asked, 'Did you never have a hippy moment – when you were young?'

'Me?' said Belle, and thought. 'Well, a small one maybe. In my first term at Uni I went barefoot for a few weeks, but I was always worried about stepping in dog mess or broken glass. Then Alice found me an outsize twin set in Lewis's sale, and that was the end of the Revolution. You can't go around barefoot in a twin set and pearls – not even fake ones.' She changed the subject. 'Does anyone have a map of this place?'

They were standing on a broad forest road surfaced in crushed stone. The view looked the same in both directions.

'We've only come a mile or two at most from Vieux Moulin and I don't think we can be going much further, can we Earthy?' said Veronica. 'Even if we got lost, we could probably find our way back.'

'We're almost there,' Earthy said, and she pointed to a foot-path leading into the pines. 'Follow me,' she added with her usual enthusiasm.

Belle grumbled, but they all followed.

The path was narrow and wandered through an underbrush of box and juniper, falling away on one side into an impenetrable tangle of trees. Here and there, large flat rocks protruded from the earth like the remains of an abandoned cemetery until at last the path was pinched by a pair of limestone boulders. They filed through the gap singly and into a space with four paths radiating off between more boulders. Earthy took one to the right and they found themselves in a narrow corridor, hemmed in by the smooth rock. It exited by a flight of natural steps, but only to enter another arena with more paths leading off in all directions. Here the tree canopy was denser. Pine and beech saplings pushed through each tight space or from fissures in the rock; the surfaces were covered in moss, overhung with swags of ivy, and ferns and cranesbill grew from every crevice. There was an overpowering sense of greenness and growth; the boulders themselves seeming to emerge from the ground smooth and grey-white like enormous fungi.

'Awesome!' said Poppy.

'Beautiful!' said Carol. 'We should come here and draw.'

Belle grunted but Janet stayed silent. The maze of rock and trees was unlike anything she'd seen before – at least, nothing existing in this world. It reminded her of illustrations in books of fairy tales or some German paintings she and David had seen in Berlin: the world as it would appear to animals and earth spirits: beautiful, mysterious and full of immanent danger from the impersonal cruelty of life.

Another corridor led into another arena. The exits could no longer be called paths. They were too narrow and twisted every few feet, offering new choices. The rocks were taller than a human being and topped by ferns and saplings that bowed over to form an arcade through which they glimpsed only snatches of a purple sky. One by one the women switched on their torches, so that moving beams and reflections of light caused sections of the green and grey wall to appear and disappear and slide against each other. The women began to call out.

Janet felt a hand in hers.

'Who is it?'

' 'S me, innit,' whispered Poppy. She shone her torch on her own face, causing the shadows to fall upwards and the rest of the light to bleed away into the ghostly canopy. 'Like a bit bloody scary, eh?' But she didn't sound scared. None of the women did. Their cries were nervous but also excited, and, although they were invisible except for the bobbing torchlight, they were within a few yards of each other.

'Where's this sodding temple Earthy promised us?' someone complained.

'Is that Belle?'

'No, it's the Tooth Fairy! And she's just wrecked her shoes!'

Next a cry: 'Poppy, darling!'

'V'ronica! I'm here with . . . I was with Janet like two seconds ago.'

Another voice: 'Joy, are you all right?'

'Does anyone have a clue where we are?'

'I do!' said Earthy. 'We're at the Temple.'

They stumbled blindly into another circular arena. It was probably no more than sixty feet across though the dimensions were uncertain by torchlight and they couldn't be sure whether a shadow was an object or an invitation into more hidden space. After threading their way through the tight confines of the *sentier sauvage* it seemed enormous.

Like the other junctions in the maze, this one was walled in by huge boulders and a curtain of trees, except that the gaps between the rocks no longer looked like points of escape; instead they reminded Janet of processional aisles funnelling wanderers into this place. Three standing stones occupied the centre, and there were more low stones – perhaps ones that had fallen – either side of them. Natural? Or made by men or gods? It was impossible to say.

One of the fallen stones was covered in a cloth and laid out as an altar and it blazed with light.

'Léon's figures,' said Janet.

Earthy nodded. She stepped forward and put a match to one of the tea lights that had gone out.

The crude wooden carvings were arranged in a way Janet had seen before: in groups and hierarchies; some with a single candle before them and others with several. It implied a system of relationships, a structure, a secret theology filled with gods whose names and attributes were not known. Janet remembered that Léon had said plainly that his work had no meaning, but at this time and in this place it was impossible to believe him.

'This is a bit too pagan for me,' said Veronica.

'You haven't been asked to do anything,' said Carol, adding: ' – yet.'

But what *could* one do? Janet asked herself. Worship them? Sacrifice to them? The idea was horrible.

A breeze filtered through the maze into the temple and caused the candles to flicker so that the idols were only patchily lit and flitted in and out of darkness. The same play of light and shadow gave them expressions, and these too changed at every movement. Yet however they changed, it was impossible to read anything into them except hatred and malice.

Earthy began to sing. It was some absurd anthem of the sixties, full of nonsense, platitudes and unfulfilled hopes: the ones Earthy had believed in when she immured herself in Wales. She went at it full throat in her high pitched, ladylike voice, and accompanied herself by waving her arms and moving in a heavy-footed dance.

'Oh, for God's sake, woman – *shut it!*' said Belle. 'And stop that ruddy prancing about. You look like a demented Shetland pony.'

Earthy glanced at her and Janet caught a fleeting look of dismay and panic. She realised then that, in respect of certain matters, Earthy really was quite mad and unstoppable. The singing ended but only to be replaced by a truly frightening wail, and the slow movement of the dance became a rush as Earthy circled round the arena with her grey ropes of hair flying. The effect was to herd the women towards the altar and its terrifying figures.

Poppy began to cry. Veronica took her in her arms and began to cry too. Joy was hysterical. Carol was calm but yelling 'Fuck!' repeatedly at the top of her voice.

'Stop it you crazy bitch!' Belle snapped. And she grabbed

Earthy and gave her a resounding slap on the face. The shock was palpable. Everyone fell silent; appalled at the realisation that one of them had actually struck another. Still, it was effective. Earthy came to an abrupt halt.

She stared at Belle. Then, still staring, but not speaking directly to her, she shouted at the top of her voice: 'Help me, Lord!'

'No one is going to help you except us,' said Janet, laying a hand gently on Earthy's wrist.

But, as if in reply a new, strange, hollow voice sounded out.

It cried, 'One of you has murdered her husband!'

How to get away with Murder

25

Digoxin preparations are commonly marketed under the trade names Lanoxin, Digitek, and Lanoxicaps. It is also available as a 0.05°mg/mL oral solution and 0.25°mg/mL or 0.5°mg/mL injectable solution.

The unexpected voice booming through the shadows caused chaos. Somebody – perhaps thinking the idols were the cause – yanked on the altar cloth, and the figures and the tea lights scattered on the ground, where most of the lights went out, which only added to the gloom. More screams and crying, and Earthy singing again: a terrible dirge by Leonard Cohen made more eerie and bizarre by her upper class screeching. Even Janet, ordinarily so level headed, felt a mounting panic and sense of entrapment. How was she to escape from this place? What creature was waiting out there in the blackness of the maze? The avenging angel for a murdered husband?

The women fled. Somebody grabbed Janet's hand and Janet dragged her through the nearest exit. They skittered along the narrow alley between the stones, barking their shins and bruising their skin. There was no telling the direction. It simply led into the maze and yet more confusion with yelling and crying around them. Every side the ferns and the saplings brushed against them and fronds and branches whipped across their faces. What had taken a few minutes when they came to the Temple now seemed to take an age in the horror-dilated time and the doubling and redoubling of the path as they tried to find an exit without a compass.

And then, suddenly, they were standing breathless on the forest road between two black bands of trees with the crushed stone grey by moonlight and the sky a deep purple with stars and the moon.

'Thanks,' said Carol. Embarrassed, she let fall Janet's hand and fumbled for a cigarette. 'What a fucking shambles.'

They stood for a moment, staring with torches shining in each other's face, and in the silence each felt a terrible sense of nakedness.

Janet asked, 'Can you find your way back from here?'

'Probably. What are you going to do?'

'Wait for the others – especially Earthy. I'm worried for her. She isn't . . . stable.'

Carol nodded. Thinking Janet might have some concerns on the matter, she said, 'For what it's worth, whatever that voice said, I didn't kill Mario and in any case I wasn't married to him. I didn't kill Quentin the Chinaman neither, whether I was married to him or not.'

'I don't suppose you did.'

Carol nodded again and her own question came to mind. 'Did you murder David? You don't have to say. I don't bloody care, but you may want to get it off your chest.'

'You know, I suspect everyone thinks I'm capable of murdering my husband – even my daughter – but truthfully I didn't.'

'Whatever. The interesting question is whether anyone would think the worse of you for it. I don't fancy they would.'

'You make women sound a brutal lot.'

Carol shrugged. 'Realistic, that's all. I've lived in Dave World.' She left Janet to disagree or not.

'Can you find your way back to the village on your own or do you want to wait here with me? Oh, I've already asked. You're not too – '

'Scared? No – remember: I've slept with gangsters. But I need a drink. I'll see you at the bar.' Carol gave Janet a quick hug; then shambled off into the gloom, leaving Janet alone with nothing but the restless flapping of birds in the trees. *The perfect moment for taking up smoking,* she thought for no reason than that she supposed there must be such a moment as there was for everything else – *love and murder for example.* Instead she was left to whistle badly and shuffle from one foot to the other as she waited.

She heard voices and sobs. Veronica and Poppy emerged from the trees and halted. Poppy flashed her torch in Janet's eyes.

'Oh, 's only you, innit? 'S all right, V'ronica; 's just Janet,' Poppy said. Then, 'Wasn't that like fuckin' 'orrible? V'ronica's like well upset. Who was that pillock? Comin' on with the voice of God except he wasn't fuckin' God!'

Janet didn't answer. Veronica hadn't said a word. Poppy was supporting her, dry-eyed and calm under the circumstances. It was a reversal of roles – at least as Janet had understood them – Poppy with her arm around her partner and Veronica with her face buried into Poppy's shoulder and sobbing.

'Can I help?' Janet offered.

'Nar,' said Poppy. Then, 'Well – could you keep an eye out for Joy? I've got to get this one back to the car, but she won't leave unless she's sure Joy's taken care of. Don't ask. Fucked if I understand it.' She turned to Veronica, kissed her forehead and stroked her face. She said, 'Don't worry, darlin'. Your girly is here for you, eh? C'mon, I'll get you home.' She smiled at Janet and then the two of them followed the path taken by Carol. Watching them go, Janet felt she'd been given another small insight into the mystery of that relationship, and it was different from what she'd supposed and ultimately incomprehensible. Then she remembered a remark made by Belle when they were discussing . . . well, murder as it happened. Belle had said that, while she didn't think Janet was a murderer, if it turned out she was, Belle could get used to the idea. It was indeed extraordinary, the notions one could get used to.

Joy was the next to appear. A different path had led her out from the maze and Janet spotted her further down the forest road and called out: 'Here! Here! It's Janet,' not knowing who at first it was.

Joy jogged towards her. Janet shone her torch in the other

woman's face. Her expression was tense and unhappy, but she was calm. The hysterics that affected her during Earthy's uncanny dancing had gone.

Joy asked, 'Have you seen any of the others?'

'Carol, and Veronica and Poppy. They're OK – I mean as well as you can expect. They've gone to the village. I'm just making sure everyone is safe.'

Joy nodded. 'Earthy's quite mad, isn't she? She must have arranged that voice accusing people of murder.'

'I don't think so. She isn't so cruel.' But perhaps she was. Perhaps it was another idea Janet would have to get used to.

'Maybe it wasn't cruelty,' said Joy.

'What else?'

'Maybe she wanted justice – for a murder that's gone unpunished, for example.' Joy's expression was unreadable.

'Perhaps.'

'You don't think so?'

'I've no idea,' Janet said, but something occurred to her that might be true. 'We tend to want justice against people we don't know or don't like. We forgive our friends – I mean if we're not the victim. Earthy loves us. She wouldn't tell even if one of us had done something.' Belle had speculated that, in the matter of murder, Janet too was capable of keeping her mouth shut. Janet wondered if she was, and if it was something to be proud of.

Joy took a pack of cigarettes from her bag and lit one.

Janet said, 'I didn't know you smoked.'

Joy fumbled with a lighter. 'I don't – not often. These were Arnold's.'

'Do you want to wait with me, or join the others? They're probably at the bar.'

Joy said nothing but she began to sob between drags on the cigarette. Janet realised she was pleased to see her cry, because it was at least a reaction that made sense on an evening that in other respects was incomprehensible. For a while, before the tears, it had seemed that Joy was going to become someone else.

Joy said, 'Veronica must be really cut up.'

'Why Veronica in particular? The voice wasn't referring to her. She's probably the only one of us who couldn't have killed a husband – well, Poppy, too. Are you suggesting she was married once?'

'Veronica? No!' Joy seemed horrified. After the moment of shock as she considered the implication of the question, she burst into louder tears mingled with broken sentences as if there were something she couldn't bring herself to say. Janet took her in her arms.

'Hush now. If you're up to it, you need to get back to the village. I don't know how long I'll have to wait here.'

Joy nodded. She said nothing more but dried her tears and followed the path taken by the others. Janet was once more left alone.

After another minute or two she heard a loud: 'Janet!'

Belle came crashing out of the bushes. Her dress was in shreds and her face streaked with blood and tears. She flung herself at Janet in a panic.

'I thought I was never going to get out of there! I've never been so scared in my life. Am I mad or did I hear a voice? There was someone else in that *place* or one of us is a ruddy ventriloquist.' She looked around wildly. 'Oh God, my heart was going like I was about to die. Look at the state of me! My dress is ruined and my shoes are history. What was it all about? *What was it all about?*' Belle clutched at her friend and for a few moments they hugged each other while the shuddering of Belle's body diminished. When they pulled away Belle muttered, 'I'm a mess. I'm sorry if I've left snot on your shoulder. I don't know how you've managed to hang around here on your own with all this going on. Have you seen any of the others?'

Janet told her. 'Everyone seems to be safe. There's only Earthy left.'

'I heard someone in there, rampaging about like an elephant. If it was up to me, I'd leave her. It's all her fault.' Belle repeated her earlier question, 'What's it all about?'

'Later,' said Janet. 'I'll tell you later.'

But she wondered if she would.

Janet continued to wait alone. She became aware of images and scents that would be lost in the confusion of daytime: the ghostly white flowers of dog roses now freed from their invisible leaves; a faint perfume from the tangles of honeysuckle. The evening was cooling and she moved to keep warm and now and again cast her torch at her watch to check the time. Once in a while she shouted Earthy's name, but drew no response except a bird's alarm call. After half an hour she considered leaving. Not for a second did she think of facing again the terrors of the *temple des fauves*.

Then of a sudden she heard a noise, and someone emerged by the same path as the others. The woman stopped and shone her torch from a distance before approaching.

'I'm surprised anyone waited for me,' Earthy said softly.

'You've had a shock, just like the rest of us.'

'It's nice of you to say so. I . . . I made a bit of a fool of myself, didn't I? Truly, I meant well, but making a fool of myself is what I seem to do.'

Earthy wasn't crying and didn't look as if she had been. In fact she was uncannily calm. Janet supposed it was the detachment of someone who in any case was only loosely attached to reality.

'Why were you so long?' Janet asked. 'I can't believe you were lost. You've been here lots of times before, haven't you? And at night-time, too.'

Earthy looked back towards the maze. 'I had to quieten the spirits. The Temple is a dangerous place, and if you raise Forces, you must also restore balance. I don't expect you to understand that. I don't expect any of you to understand.'

She was talking matter-of-factly and it came to Janet that her madness was of a very particular kind and not the raving sort. You might as well call a Catholic mad for believing in the Blessed Virgin. Or an atheist for not doing. Most of Earthy's oddity came from nothing more than social ineptness and the misfortune of spending her life among hippies instead of Anglicans where her excellent if unconscious impersonation of the Queen would have made a very good impression.

Janet asked, 'Have we left anyone behind?'

'Whom do you mean?'

'You know who I mean. The owner of the voice.'

'The voice?' Earthy drawled. 'Oh, that was the god Pan – or possibly not Pan, as he goes by different names. The *temple des fauves* is dedicated to him.'

'I see. At all events, you left him there?'

'Yes. He doesn't need us,' said Earthy. She laughed. 'He has his own transport!'

They walked back to the village together, crossing the open high ground with the dome of the summer sky above them and in the distance the towering wall of the escarpment, lit grey-blue by the moon. Vieux Moulin was dark and quiet except for the bar, which spilled light from the windows, and a few lamps hung over the small patio set with tables. The others were there, eating pizzas.

'I see you were worried,' Janet said.

Belle looked at her plate and then at Janet and tried a smile. 'Your attitude changes when you're not on your own. Things start to make sense again – hullo Earthy – and there's nowt like a good pizza for putting a grin on your face. Anyway, we had to do summat until you two turned up. Fancy a slice of *marinara*? Carol has *quattro stagione*.'

'*Napoletana*,' said Carol. 'It's Poppy who ordered *quattro stagione*.'

Janet saw that Joy and Veronica weren't eating. Joy was sitting behind an untouched glass of cola and Veronica had a couple of empty brandy glasses in front of her. Janet asked, 'Are you all right to drive.'

'V'ronica's fine,' Poppy interrupted. 'I'll do the driving and Joy'll come with us. Come on, darling, tip up your keys.'

Veronica stayed silent but produced the car keys from her bag. Poppy dangled them in front of Janet like a prize. Janet sensed again a small shift of the relationship, or perhaps a clarification of what had always been there.

'Earthy isn't well enough to drive,' Janet said. Earthy opened her mouth but Janet stared her down. 'I said you're not well enough to drive. You've had a shock and don't realise it. Carol, you take her car and give Belle a lift. Earthy can come with me.' She looked to Belle, who was eating another slice of pizza. 'Are you going to be OK?'

'Why shouldn't I be?'

'I'll drop in later, before you go to bed.'

'Suit yourself.'

'Yes – right – Earthy, keys first and then let's go.' Janet took Earthy's hand and led her away to where her own car was parked under the plane trees. She looked back at the others still sitting in the pool of light on the patio. None of them was speaking. Only Poppy seemed in the least animated as she tried to sooth Veronica.

Janet searched for words to capture the mood of the scene, knowing that, whatever they were, they would also apply to her. She had participated and the words, after all, would be hers.

The word was *shame* – that was it. The women were each in her own way ashamed.

Janet drove. Earthy sat in the passenger seat. There was no traffic and little to see except road signs indicating the hamlets scattered across the plateau: Campmichel; Campandré, Le Puits;

and in the distance the castle of Puybrun silhouetted against the stars. Once only, they caught a faint note of night-scented jasmine that went as quickly as it came.

They'd driven a couple of miles when Janet said, 'We need to talk.'

'What about?' Earthy asked cautiously.

'I think you know.'

'No, I don't .'

Janet sighed. 'You had a son.'

'I *have* a son.'

'Possibly. You called him Moonstone.'

'You remember his name!' Earthy was touched, scarcely believing someone had paid close attention to something she'd said.

'Yes, I remember. You put him up for adoption after his father went to prison and you fell ill.'

'His new parents changed it – his name.'

'I imagine they did. But I don't think they called him Graham – or Ravi, for that matter.'

'*Yes they did!*' Earthy said vehemently.

'We'll see. I've hired an enquiry agent to find out.' She saw Earthy was surprised. 'It's possible to do that nowadays, especially if you aren't too scrupulous. And in some matters, I'm not,' Janet added, having surprised herself with this recent discovery. 'We can wait for the results, but in your heart you know the answer. Long-lost children don't suddenly turn up in small French villages out of sheer coincidence. That's something out of fiction.'

In life long-lost children don't turn up, no more than long-lost identical twins called Patrick – whatever anyone might think. And husbands aren't murdered with exotic poisons in lay-bys on the A34. Except that that last part may actually be true.

Earthy fell silent with the stubborn silence of a child. Janet said, 'You've been providing Ravi with money from your inheritance, haven't you?' She was forced to repeat the question.

271

'How do you know?'

'His motorcycle – it's brand new and he couldn't possibly afford it.'

'But he has to be my son! He knew all about me without my telling him!'

'Believe me, it isn't difficult. Mediums and psychics do it every day. You gave Ravi all the information he needed without ever realising it.'

Earthy snapped, 'It isn't your business who I give my money to!'

'No, it isn't,' Janet agreed. 'But, if I'm right, it ought to be possible to find the real Moonstone – at least we can try. There, don't cry.' Earthy was sobbing in her genteel way. 'If I'm wrong, you'll have the satisfaction of telling me so.'

'I don't understand why you're interested.'

Because I'm interested in people. Because I like them. Because I loved my husband.

'The others are terrified by what happened tonight. The voice accused one of us of killing her husband, and now everyone is feeling guilty and afraid – even those who haven't killed anybody. I know where the voice came from. The great god Pan has his own transport in the form of a motorbike, doesn't he?'

Earthy began to hyperventilate. She babbled, 'Ravi *couldn't* know whoever it was murdered her husband. I haven't killed anyone and the rest of you are strangers to him.'

'Oh, I think he knows,' Janet said. 'And I know exactly how. But I need you to tell me that it *was* Ravi who spoke.' She turned in her seat and fixed her eyes on her passenger. 'Tell me.' She repeated it: '*Tell me!*' She held Earthy's gaze, ignoring the road until Earthy found the tension unbearable.

Finally Earthy nodded. She didn't say 'yes'. She never would do.

They arrived at the village and Janet deposited Earthy at her cottage before returning to her own. She parked the car outside the abandoned vegetable garden that went with La Maison des Moines, and in a stray thought considered bringing it back into cultivation if she stayed in the village – if the women's group held together – *if I'm not arrested for murder*. She looked up the lane to Belle's house and saw a single light burning in a downstairs room. Her friend was still awake.

Janet went inside. She made a mug of chocolate and picked up a novel to read while she drank it and nursed her bumps and bruises. When she'd finished she looked through the window and saw the light at Belle's house was still burning. She went outside and stood a while in the lane, wondering whether to call on her or not. At the bar Belle seemed to have recovered from the events at the *temple des fauves*. But Belle was someone who'd lived with Alice's obsessions and insanity and still contrived to seem outwardly happy. Janet heard a faint wail, but it was impossible to say where it came from.

She was standing there when her mobile chimed with an incoming text message. She opened it and saw it was from Helen. It said: I NEED TO TALK TO YOU ABOUT HENRY. But Helen hadn't phoned; so evidently she didn't need to speak to her mother urgently. Janet decided it was probably best not to call back while emotions might still be riding high.

She had a premonition. She thought: *Helen is going to leave Henry*. It was the reason for this message, or it might be in a later one. Either way it would happen sooner or later. When Janet had suggested to Stephen Gregg that we can deceive ourselves by thinking people always act in character, he'd answered that we can – but mostly we don't. Janet might be deceiving herself as to Helen's likely actions – but probably she wasn't. She didn't know if she would be pleased to be proved wrong. Either outcome promised unhappiness for her daughter.

In the meantime she had to decide what to do here and now about Belle, based on nothing more than a guess as to her state of mind. She went to the door and rapped on it. After a moment she heard Belle shifting the bolt. And there she was, standing in her dressing gown with her 'bits' somewhere shapeless inside it, the skin of her face loose and sick, and tears streaming from her eyes..

She stared at Janet and it seemed for a moment as if she was unable to speak. Then she said simply, 'I haven't murdered Charlie.'

Janet took her hand and rubbed the back of it along her own cheek.

'I know,' she said.

'I love him.'

'I know. The message this evening wasn't for you. It was for someone else.'

Belle nodded. She wiped her hand across her eyes. She said, 'Would you like to come inside for a minute? We could have a nightcap. I've had a couple already and fancy getting plastered. Charlie's been ill and he's a bit restless. He doesn't sleep well at night unless he's doped up, and I don't like to.'

'I understand,' Janet said. 'You could have told me, you know. I might have helped. He has dementia, doesn't he?'

26

'You'd better come in,' said Belle. 'Sit down. If you're anything like me, you must be as sore as anything from all that running around in the dark scraping yourself on god-knows-what.'

Janet heard a wail from upstairs, the same she had heard from the lane. It didn't suggest any particular distress, only an unearthly neediness like the annoyed complaint of a cat.

Belle said, 'He's always making noises at night. It doesn't mean anything – at least, I don't think it does. I go up every now and again to check.' She flapped her arms penguin-fashion, the way people do when they have a vague idea they are supposed to take or fetch something. 'A drink?'

'I've just had some chocolate.'

Belle nodded. She went to the kitchen and came back with two glasses of blanquette. She handed one to Janet. 'Get this down you. I can't drink on my own. In Clitheroe that sort of thing gets you a name; so my Mum was always telling me.'

They took seats. Janet noticed how guilty Belle looked at the discovery of her secret. She wasn't surprised. It's difficult to rid oneself of the notion that at some level impenetrable to our understanding we live in a just universe; that the casual miseries of life have a moral significance; and that bad things happen because we are bad people. No doubt Belle would have denied believing that her sins had in some way brought about her situation, but her behaviour said otherwise. Janet was old enough to remember a time when cancer was never mentioned in polite company because to suffer from it was to be disgraced. Even now, in the news, it was reported that people died 'after a long illness'. Perish the thought that it might be Alzheimers. Janet reached over and took Belle's hand and stroked the back of it.

'Charlie's not so bad during the day,' Belle said. 'He keeps to his work room and messes with his trains. It's his moods that are difficult. One day he's happy as Larry and the next he's down in the dumps – I never know what to expect. He's tried to kill himself twice, but the next day he doesn't know why and he says he's very sorry. On the bad days I want him to die. No, that's not true. I don't *want* him to die, but I'm hoping he'll just slip away before he's ground me to bits.' Belle paused. 'How did you know?'

'No one has ever seen Charlie, but from your description of him he ought to be around and about the village, the life and soul of everything.'

'Yes, he should be,' Belle agreed. She tried out a small joke – exercising the old Belle whom everyone loved. 'Still, he doesn't have to be ill. I could have bumped him off. We are the English Lady Murderers after all.'

Janet smiled, remembering something David used to say: *When you hear the sound of hooves, think of horses, not unicorns.* She said, 'It crossed my mind, but murder is really quite rare. It was always far more likely that Charlie was poorly. Anyway, I saw the girl a few times – the one you pay to keep an eye on him when you go out of an evening. I couldn't think of any other explanation why she was at the house. Why didn't you tell us – why didn't you tell *me*? We're your friends.'

'You don't like to trouble people,' Belle said. Janet could hear the voice of Alice. It didn't matter that she'd never met her: her own mother might have said the same thing. The words represented the last bastion of self respect among the poor: a claim to self-sufficiency even through pain and hardship. Janet had no difficulty at all in understanding.

Charlie had gone quiet. Belle said, 'Those last tablets have probably kicked in. He may be good for a few hours or he may go all night. You can't tell.' She put her glass down and leaned forward to cover her face in her hands, and after a moment of this began to sob. 'I'm a selfish cow, always thinking of myself. Alice was barmy for almost as long as I can remember, and she started going senile in her sixties. I was scared out of my wits that I'd take after her. I know it sounds daft, but I used to pray that I'd keel over with a heart attack like my Dad – anything rather than be like her.' Belle was beyond sobbing. Tears flowed down her face and leaked through her fingers and she seemed inconsolable. She muttered 'Sorry' several times but couldn't hold back.

'Hush now,' said Janet. 'It's OK.' She moved her chair next to Belle's and put her arm round her, and Belle as best she could curled into her.

'Poor old Charlie, I never thought of *him*. He was getting older and slower and a bit forgetful, but I thought that was all, you know, *normal*. He started getting depressed now and again and a bit obsessive: first with his ruddy train set, and then wanting to come to France; saying that we had the money and it would cheer him up to live somewhere that was warmer and had a bit more sunshine. And me, I was so busy with Alice and thinking of myself and worried sick that I was losing it every time I couldn't remember something on a shopping list, I never picked up the signs with Charlie. And, of course, he was like all men: never going to the doctor if he could help it; so there was no one to say any different.'

'I understand,' Janet said. She might have said more – spoken of her own experiences – and some of what she said might have been true and useful at another time and place. But at this time and in this place, Belle didn't want anyone to break the uniqueness of her sorrow. *I know this*, Janet thought, *I've been here.* Then it occurred to her that she didn't know and hadn't been here, because David had obliged her by dying and had at least given her that foundation of certainty on which she could build. But this business of Charlie, how long would it go on? What plans could Belle make? How could she avoid being destroyed by the slow horror of each day? Was love enough to get her through?

Janet stayed as silent as she could because, in the last analysis, all responses to tragedy are commonplace.

Belle supplied more details of the events that had brought them to France. The prospect of the move had cheered Charlie up and provided him with a focus, and Belle had believed he was all right and that the relocation to Puybrun would be the solution to his mood swings and depressions. But, in the event, the almost immediate effect was to disorientate him. The place was unfamiliar. He knew no one. He didn't speak the language. He was frightened that the depreciation of sterling against the euro would destroy his savings and reduce them both to beggary. He retired to his workshop and his train set and the symptoms of his dementia began rapidly to grow worse.

'And so here we are,' said Belle. 'Stuck.'

Janet returned to her cottage. Next morning she called on Belle again, but this time Belle didn't invite her in. Instead they stood for a few minutes chatting on the doorstep. Belle said she was OK and that Charlie had passed a good night once he was settled and he was presently having his breakfast. She thanked Janet for coming round the previous evening. She even smiled.

Janet realised then that, because she'd seen Belle in her vulnerability, it was possible they would never be friends again: not on the old terms but instead like two criminals who have got the dirt on each other. She felt a sense of loss: a small bereavement. Then she thought: *I love her and I shan't let this go*. But it wasn't the moment to press the matter and she went back home, where she booted up her computer to check her mail and continue her researches.

There was an e-mail from the enquiry agent she'd hired. It contained a preliminary report on Graham Southcock, comprising a criminal record check. As Janet suspected might be the case, Graham alias Ravi, had a number of petty convictions for dishonesty including fraud. He'd also served a short term for assault – rather more surprising that one. The report gave his date of birth. Janet was fairly certain that it wouldn't be the birth date of the missing Moonstone. In fact by her rough reckoning, Graham Southcock was probably one or two years younger than Earthy's child and, since it was an unlikely coincidence that he too was adopted, there should be no difficulty in getting a copy of the birth certificate to prove the point.

Poor Earthy. To find a son and then lose him again.

No news from Helen. No call. No e-mail. Janet's instinct had been correct: the business with Henry that resulted in last night's message on her mobile was no more than a row that had blown over for the time being, and she'd been right not to respond. Any question of Helen's divorce was tomorrow's problem and today Janet could return to her research. She googled 'Digoxin' again.

Digoxin – the poison seemed to be at the core of the puzzle. Janet asked herself, why digoxin rather than something else? She supposed the most likely explanation was availability. In the past, the heyday of the great Victorian poisoners, arsenic had been the instrument of choice, largely because there was so much of it around in paints, weedkillers, insecticides and a host of other preparations. In contrast modern products were highly coloured and perfumed, and extracting poison from them required know-ledge and effort. That was no doubt why contemporary murderers turned to pharmaceuticals.

Even so, why digoxin rather than another medicinal drug? It was a preparation of digitalis, a constituent of foxglove. Its use was as a heart treatment, mainly for atrial fibrillation and atrial flutter (whatever they were – Janet didn't know). It was hazardous because the beneficial effects were in a narrow range, outside of which the risk of a harmful overdose was significant. The American serial killer, Cullen, had used digoxin, but he was a nurse with access to it – availability again. Who did David know, who might have access? Was Jeremy Vavasour taking digoxin for a heart condition? No – Janet remembered Stephen Gregg saying the police couldn't link David's partner to the drug. But if not him, who?

I'm not a detective. Janet had more than once reminded herself of the fact. It was silly to suppose she could solve the mystery, and yet she felt she had all the information in her hands. What factors could there be except for David's history and character, his business activities, the events at the restaurant, and the fact that digoxin was the chosen instrument of murder?

Digoxin preparations are commonly marketed under the trade names Lanoxin, Digitek, and Lanoxicaps as well as others. It is also available as a 0.05°mg/mL oral solution and 0.25°mg/mL or 0.5°mg/mL injectable solution.

Janet had pulled this passage off Wikipedia, thinking there was something in it. There was mention of an oral solution and an injectable solution, and from elsewhere she remembered that there were tablets, because some brands had been recalled due to manufacturing errors. She tried to imagine concretely how the poison might have been given and whether the victim could take it unknowingly, but in this respect the information was insufficient. She simply had to assume that the victim could easily be fooled because David apparently had been.

Then again David had been such an idiot that it wouldn't be difficult. There was probably a clue in that as well.

Someone came to the door. It was Veronica. She'd made up carefully, the way some women do when they are distressed and Janet thought that today she looked her age – forty-five, wasn't it? – and wondered what if anything that portended for her relationship with Poppy.

Not my business. Janet didn't want this conversation.

'I wasn't expecting you. Please come in. I think there's still some coffee in the pot, would you like a cup?'

Veronica shook her head at the mention of coffee. 'Can we sit outside? After what happened yesterday, I'm feeling claustro-phobic.'

'Yes, it was dreadful, wasn't it?'

'Frightening.'

Janet nodded.

They sat on the veranda. The morning was clear and sunny and the first tourists were already visible as small figures on the high *donjon* of the castle. Janet was curious why they went there; they would know neither more nor less for the experience. Veronica sat stiffly, every bit the successful woman banker as Janet imagined one, though she knew the image was probably no more than a prejudice and Veronica was simply sore from small injuries sustained escaping from the maze. Not for the first time her conversation with Belle about what was or was not 'in character' came to mind. She couldn't predict with confidence how this conversation was going to go, but she was sure that in hindsight it would make perfect sense and seem somehow inevitable.

Veronica said, 'Earthy came to see me last night.'

'Oh?'

'She wanted to apologise for the disastrous so-called "ritual". But, of course, she made a mess of the apology because she kept insisting that the great god Pan had manifested himself, which I don't suppose is likely, is it?'

'It was Ravi.'

'She told me that was your opinion. She said you bullied her into a confession.'

Janet was about to deny the bullying, but on reflection realised she had pressured Earthy unbearably; and although she'd been right, she felt ashamed.

'I want to show you something.' Janet went into the house and came back with the enquiry agent's report. She passed it to Veronica, who read it quickly with the practised eye of an executive. Her lips pursed. Janet noticed the first small lines appearing. She felt sorry for the other woman growing older, in a way she didn't feel sorry for herself. *She has to try to hold on to Poppy. I have no one.*

Veronica asked, 'Why did you commission this?'

'Ravi has been cheating Earthy out of money by pretending to be her son. I want to put a stop to him if I can.'

'If it was him at the Temple, he accused one of us of murdering her husband. That had nothing to do with Earthy. Why did he do it? Why so publicly?'

'He's very vain – very narcissistic: all that dressing up and the Indian trappings. He also wanted to frighten somebody. I imagine he has blackmail in mind.'

'I see – I can understand that.' Veronica thought it over for a while and said that, on reflection, she would have some coffee after all. When Janet came back with a cup Veronica said, 'Poppy and I have never been married; anyone can check. And, of course, Ravi wouldn't need to blackmail Earthy if she thinks he's her son. Carol? I rather doubt she ever married any of her Daves, and, if she did and bothered to kill her husband rather than simply leave him, it must have happened years ago and abroad, and there's no way Ravi could know anything of it. As for Belle , we can easily establish that Charlie is still alive – he's senile, isn't he?'

'You know?'

'No one has ever seen him. It's the most obvious explanation, isn't it?'

'Yes.' Janet knew she ought not to be surprised. Veronica was formidably clever. And, obviously, she had to be in order to plan everything.

They watched each other. There was no hostility: only a wary respect and mutual liking, though Janet had never imagined getting very close to Veronica because, except in relation to Poppy and Joy, she was very self-contained. Janet wondered what those two had in common that had attracted her? Possibly they were both birds with broken wings: it was difficult to be sure, though fascinating to speculate.

She said, 'We don't have to have this conversation.'

Veronica turned her face away to catch a breeze and closed her eyes. 'Arnold has been murdered – it's not a secret. But Joy didn't do it. It happened in England while Joy was here in Puybrun recovering from her drunken binge. There are witnesses. I was one, and you were another – '

'I never saw her,' said Janet. 'I didn't get beyond the front door.'

Veronica waved the objection away. 'The car stayed at Campmaurice and a check of the airlines and Joy's credit cards should prove that she didn't fly home or hire another car or go by train. And what could Ravi know? He was here. Arnold was killed in Dudley, wherever that is.'

Belle had said something similar: that, because of the paper trail involved in travel, it was quite impossible that Joy should have killed Arnold.

'That leaves me,' said Janet. 'Are you suggesting I killed David?'

Veronica was genuinely shocked. 'No, of course not.'

'No – you wouldn't do that,' said Janet, 'And I do appreciate the gesture.'

'It's an appalling idea. What made you think for a second that I would suspect you of murder?' Veronica looked at the castle, then up the lane at Belle's house, then over Janet's shoulder to stare at the window and her own reflection. She seemed to catch something in her eye and wiped it with the corner of a handkerchief. She said, 'I just want to know what it is that Ravi knows.'

'He knows that Joy murdered Arnold,' said Janet. 'And that you helped her. Shall we go for a walk?'

They stood on the gravel by the *buvette* and took in the lake. It was close to eleven and children and their parents were everywhere on the strip of sand and in the water.

Janet said, 'One of the reasons I like Puybrun is that it has a sort of innocence. Have you noticed that there are no topless bathers? Even girls who wouldn't think two seconds about showing their breasts elsewhere never do it here. They're on holiday, of course, so they're playing a role: the role of nice people taking a family vacation.' She looked at Veronica, 'And we're all playing a role too, aren't we? That of Englishwomen living in a French village. But we're not certain how it should be played – for instance how closely we should get to know the locals and how we should relate to each other. We've abandoned our pasts and yet we want to talk about the past to other people who know nothing about us. Why do you think we do that?'

'I suppose by re-telling it we make sense of it. And perhaps we get reassurance that the past meant something and we learned its lessons.'

'I imagine you're right,' Janet agreed. She added, 'My husband had a very low opinion of his own capacity to learn from experience. And do you suppose that Carol learned anything? Behind the jokes, she seems to have had a miserable life. The Daves sound like fun only in retrospect.'

'You can't know that,' Veronica said.

'One of her cheekbones has been broken at some time. It shows when she smiles. Of course, it may mean nothing.' Janet kicked at the gravel. 'We were going to talk about Joy. It must have been a shock to her, discovering the images on Arnold's computer. The last thing he would have expected her to do; he no doubt despised her so much that he didn't bother with much computer security – after all, as far as he was concerned she didn't know the first thing about them. Still, I don't really understand why you feel such pity for her – I mean so much more than the rest of us. Not that you have to explain.'

'I can't.'

'I didn't expect you could.'

'And Ravi?'

'Oh, that's not difficult. He saw Joy at the airport on the day she left for England. He has a girlfriend – Earthy calls her his "muse". Hatshepsut, if you believe the name. She went back to

England on the same day – quite possibly on the same flight. I saw her on Ravi's brand new motorcycle when he gave her a lift, and I asked Earthy, who told me where they were going.'

'Is that all?' Veronica laughed in a short burst of breath that was without humour.

'Well, there's also the fact that you cleaned Joy's house – which was an extraordinary thing to do. Ordinarily her cleaner would have done it, but I fancy the cleaner was cancelled so that she wouldn't know Joy had disappeared. Once she's placed at the airport, the police will check the passenger lists. Naturally they won't find her name – but they will find yours. She used your passport, didn't she? There's a general resemblance between you, and Joy has cut her hair to look like yours because she admires you. Of course nobody in the ordinary way would confuse the pair of you. The way you carry yourself, your confidence and sense of style – who could possibly mistake you for a dispirited creature like Joy? No one except staff at the airport who've never met either of you.'

'And the plane tickets?'

'Paid for with cash –at least, that's what I'd do. And a taxi to the airport – I imagine the driver could be found – also paid in cash. It sounds quaint in this day and age, doesn't it.'

'Yes it does,' Veronica agreed. She didn't seem frightened or depressed by Janet's disclosures. Rather, Janet thought, she looked relieved that someone else knew. *That's what friends are for – assuming we are still friends.* Veronica took on a business-like tone. She said, 'My name on a passenger list could be a coincidence: an entirely different person. And if the passport itself leaves any record, it could be a copy – a clone; I believe such things exist. In any case, no motive links me to Arnold's death; the police mightn't notice my name even if they came across it. The only real evidence is that of Ravi.'

'Not even that,' said Janet.

'No?'

Janet shook her head. 'There *is* no evidence from Ravi. All you have are my speculations about what he *may* have seen and what he *may* say. But none of it has to be true. It's just a theory, and I may be mistaken. I'm not a detective.' She reached into her bag and pulled out the enquiry agent's report. She offered it to Veronica. 'I don't have any use for this. I think you should show it to Earthy. And then I think both of you should have a conversation with Ravi.'

Veronica took the papers. Janet tried to read her expression but couldn't. Gratitude didn't always make for friendship: it equally made for resentment. *Have I lost another friend?*

Veronica gave her a kiss on the cheek, but it was a dry one to which it was difficult to ascribe a meaning.

They walked back from the *buvette* to the village, which was empty in the late hour of morning before the sounds of lunch came out of open doors. They separated by the *halle* to go to their respective homes. Janet saw Léon sitting on a stool outside his studio, smoking in the shade and reading a book. After the dance at Montbel they'd made no further arrangement. She wondered if he knew about Ravi's fraud on Earthy and suspected he did, though his part was no more than concealing what he knew. Good people were forever engaged in petty dishonesties. It was something David was well aware of because he made no claims to integrity or any other virtues except a good sense of humour. His sunny temperament came partly from his ability to forgive himself his failings without ever denying they existed. Janet put up with his moral slipperiness only because he was kind and fun and because he so evidently loved her.

Oh, David, why did you die?

Damn it, she was crying again! The first time for weeks, it seemed. But now it was partly from frustration: the feeling that she held all the threads in her hands but couldn't make sense of them.

Digoxin preparations are commonly marketed under the trade names Lanoxin, Digitek, and Lanoxicaps.

The answer was in those words, and she felt she was on the point of teasing out the meaning. If only . . .

She noticed that the door of her cottage was open and the plastic strips that hung in the opening to deter the flies were waving gently. Janet hadn't locked the door when she went for a walk, but she was sure she'd closed it. Why was it open now? It occurred to her that Belle might have dropped in. She called, 'Belle!' as she went inside and surveyed the kitchen and repeated it as she entered the lounge.

A man was sitting at the table apparently working on her laptop. He turned as she came in, beamed at her, and said: 'Janet! I was just reading your wonderful confession to murdering your husband.'

27

There came a time when they decided to live romantically. It seemed a silly thing to do: they had, after all, been married for thirty years and middle-aged people who live romantically stand a good chance of looking ridiculous – in fact Janet was fairly sure that at times they *did* look ridiculous.

'It's to be expected, if we're doing it right,' said David. He didn't care. You only had to listen to his conversation or watch him dance to know that he wasn't by nature a dignified man.

Janet wasn't quite sure how it came about. They hadn't sat down and discussed romance as if it were an item on the agenda of their marriage. Rather it emerged from the shifts of perspective and relationship that come with age and from the fact that most if not all the battles that have to be fought even in a happy marriage had been fought and they had come to an honourable treaty. One of its terms was a mutual recognition that they were going to live and die together and that it was as well that they should do this in love with each other.

Perhaps they'd grown wiser – though David denied it in his case.

Living romantically meant over-dressing when they went out together, because every event, no matter how small, was Cinderella's ball. It meant long, lingering kisses in public places and David whispering in her ear, 'Let's hope your husband doesn't find out.' It meant that every morning, as he went to work and she was dozing in bed, he would tell her softly and whether she was listening or not, that he loved her and that she was wonderful, and on his return hug her and kiss her and tell her he loved her yet again as if a day's separation had been unbearable. It meant dancing on all possible occasions, and best of all on balmy summer evenings in villages like Puybrun: dancing to the music of dodgy bands with dubious haircuts; dancing in a throng of elderly French couples stamping their feet in a pasadoble; dancing under the eyes of tourists in socks and sandals, and louche young men with earrings and oiled hair, and young women with pierced tongues whose children were dressed to the nines.

At the heart of living romantically was an ever present aware-ness of their tragedy: the knowledge that in each word that was spoken there was a finality because the other person might die before it was added to or retracted; that at each parting there was no certainty of return; that each kiss might be a kiss given to a condemned man or woman; that each act or gesture had to affirm their love as far as humanly possible because the journey of their life was not to be repeated and its destination was inevitable.

Love is not undying. It's because it can die that it's important.

One evening some months before, in the spring of the year, David Bretherton had gone out to have dinner with his business partner and unexpectedly died. Before he opened the front door and went to meet his fate, he and Janet had embraced each other and each had exchanged one of their lingering serious kisses, and he said, 'I love you,' and she said, 'I love you.' And neither knew it was to be the last memory of the other.

'I take it you're Stephen Gregg,' said Janet.

The stranger stood up. Helen had said he was short, which wasn't exactly true, but he was surprisingly stocky with a round face, broad nose and dark hair that inclined to curls, giving the impression that he was a Welshman with a taste for rugby. He was wearing a pale green shirt, a linen jacket, beige trousers, and tasselled loafers: John Lewis's best, thought Janet. The most ordinary of men.

'I hope I haven't given you a shock,' Stephen Gregg said in the deeply delicious voice that Janet had been so attracted to. 'I don't know what you were expecting. People tell me I'm much taller on the telephone. I'm sorry if the reality is a disappointment. I suppose, too, that I owe you an apology for barging into your house, but the door was unlocked – which I know isn't really an excuse.'

'I wasn't expecting you. Did you send an e-mail or leave a message on my mobile? I don't recall anything.'

'It was only decided yesterday at the last moment that I should come here. There are three investigations running and two police forces involved, and the powers that be didn't want to pay for sending three coppers off on a jolly. They've spent the last week arguing about who would be the best man for the job. God knows why they picked me. I keep telling them I'm just an accountant.'

He had no business being in her house and still less going through the files on her laptop (in fact how had he managed to do that? she was sure she'd switched it off.). Janet had an idea she was supposed to be affronted. Yet when she tested her emotions, she found it impossible to get annoyed; his humorous manner was so disarming.

'I'll make some tea,' Janet said. She continued the conversation from the kitchen. 'You said *three* investigations. What are they?'

'The missing millions from the affairs of Vavasour & Bretherton; your husband's death; and the murder of a Mr Arnold Albert Morrison. Strictly speaking only the first one is my baby, though there's an obvious overlap with the second.'

'And the murder of Arnold Morrison?'

'No connection that I'm aware of. That one belongs to the boys in Dudley. The coincidence of his having lived in Puybrun has simply made it convenient to share resources and save cost.'

'Earl Grey or regular tea?'

'Regular, please. Milk and no sugar.'

Janet came back in the room. 'I'll pour in a minute. Why has Arnold's murder brought you here if it happened in Dudley?'

'To interview Mrs Morrison.'

'Oh? I'd have thought you'd have interviewed her when she was in England for the funeral.'

'We did, but something has come up. Do you know her?'

'Joy? Yes, of course. All the Englishwomen in Puybrun and the hamlets know each other – in fact we have a women's group.' Janet was tempted to tell him the name; she had a suspicion Stephen Gregg would have appreciated it. But on reflection the matter in hand was too serious for her to take risks.

'Ah, then it's possible you or some of your friends may be able to help me.'

'I don't see how.' Janet went to the kitchen and returned with two cups of tea and a plate of biscuits. 'Tuck in.'

'Thank you.' The visitor took a biscuit and bit into it. The crumbs stayed on his lips. *Not the way to intimidate a witness*, thought Janet, but she had a suspicion that Stephen Gregg was a man who proceeded by guile rather than force. He said, 'The matter that's come up concerns Mrs Morrison's alibi. According to her account she was here in Puybrun during the week or so to which we've pinned Arnold Morrison's killing.'

'She was sick,' said Janet.

'So I gather. But the problem is that we have two witnesses, who in the ordinary way one would consider reliable. They place her in Dudley round about the time of the murder.'

Janet nodded. Of course. Complicated plots could always be disrupted by chance events. For example: Ravi taking Hatshepsut to the airport. Two people who happened to know Joy by sight, and who saw her in England were quite to be expected. In crime fiction the convention was to dispose of such inconvenient witnesses by staging a second murder, but in life that must rarely be practicable and probably more trouble than it was worth. Janet parked that thought as something for another day.

'All the same,' Stephen Gregg said, 'witnesses do make mistakes. Our pair saw Mrs M – or the person they claim to have been Mrs M – only briefly and they didn't stop and speak to her. On the other hand, if she was in Puybrun – '

' – there should be more reliable witnesses,' said Janet. 'Yes –

well – I may be able to help you there. You should speak with Veronica Heatherside. She visited Joy every day when she was sick and even cleaned her house.'

'And you?'

'I called at the house too,' said Janet without a pause. It occurred to her that she might have just alibied a murderess and that she didn't care. In any case, strictly speaking she hadn't said she saw Joy and it wasn't proven that Joy had killed Arnold. Still it was odd that ordinary prudence and morality seemed to have gone out of the window. Perhaps it was something to do with this place, La Maison des Moines. At their first meeting Belle had said that a previous occupant, the mysterious Hungarian Harry Haze, was implicated in a disappearance and possible murder. One more notion to get used to.

'Very good,' said Stephen Gregg. He fixed his brown eyes on Janet with no indication of the thoughts behind that look. 'Well, hopefully a conversation with Mrs Heatherside will dispose of that part of my enquiries. After all, no one really wants to bang Mrs Morrison up for murdering her hubby, do they?'

'No,' said Janet.

'No indeed. And that brings me to the subject of your own.'

'What I most regret in life is murdering my husband . . . ' said Stephen Gregg. 'That's a wonderful opening line for a novel.'

'I'm glad you like it.'

'I shan't say I'm not surprised by the subject matter. But people deal with grief in different ways, and I imagine this was yours.'

'I've often used David as a character in my books. It made him laugh. Now it seems a way of keeping close to him.'

'I see. Do you often murder him, then?'

'No. Usually I make him the killer. His manner was very open so you wouldn't naturally suspect him, and it was possible to tweak his charm so that he became one of those oleaginous villains you're glad to find out did the deed.'

'And he didn't mind?'

'I've already told you: it made him laugh . . . ' Janet stumbled at a memory.

'Yes?'

'Well . . . he hated it on one occasion because I gave him red hair and freckles. It was in revenge for something or other he'd done that I didn't like – I forget what.' She checked to see how this remark was received.

Inspector Gregg stretched his limbs. 'I haven't fully recovered from the flight and the drive here. Too much sitting around. May I have another cup of tea?'

Janet returned to the kitchen for the pot.

Her visitor said, 'I have actually read some of your books, though they appeal rather more to my wife.'

'I can see that they might. I've been trying to create a new genre. I call it "Aga Slaughter".'

'I'm afraid that means nothing to me.'

'It's sort of like Joanna Trollope but with bodies face down in the virgin olive oil. This tea has become rather stewed; I can make fresh.'

'It'll be fine. I notice that, when you write, you call yourself "Jane" rather than "Janet" Is there a reason?'

'I used to have a day job in the local authority planning department. I didn't like to confuse the two roles.'

'You mean you don't make a living out of writing?'

'Good God, no! Authors are just slaves in the cotton fields of literature. It would be a mercy to put them out of their misery.'

Stephen Gregg chuckled. 'You know, I could stay here chatting all day, but I have to get on with the business that brought me here. There's still the mystery of your husband's death.'

'Oh, I've solved that,' said Janet.

'This note was among David's papers.' She passed across the scrap she'd found with the credit card slip for the restaurant meal. On it David had written L-A-N-O-C-K-S-Y-N (sp?). 'I asked several people what it meant and the general view seemed to be that it was a place in Wales or Cornwall.'

'What's the significance of the question following the letters?'

'David probably came across the word on the telephone or perhaps the radio, and he wrote it phonetically as best he could. He made a note to check the spelling. Of course,' she added, 'it isn't obvious that L-A-N-O-C-K-S-Y-N has any connection with David's death. But that's because he misspelled it. The correct spelling is L-A-N-O-X-I-N: *Lanoxin*. It's one of the brand names under which digoxin is sold. It means that David already knew about the drug before he went out on that last evening.'

Janet was suddenly uncomfortable sitting opposite Stephen Gregg and subject to his scrutiny. She noticed how dark the room was. Unintentionally she'd fallen into the French habit of keeping the shutters closed and wondered why. She broke off to go round the room opening them to let in the daylight.

She said, 'I was saying to a friend about – oh, another matter – that murder is such a rare event. When this story about digoxin came out, I couldn't stop thinking how *unlikely* it was that anyone would bother to murder David. Of course, you didn't know him, but – how shall I put it? – he wasn't a very *murderable* person, if there is such a word.'

'More the sort of person you'd put in a book with red hair and freckles?'

'Yes!' Janet couldn't help laughing, though she felt it was dangerous in front of this man. She stopped. 'Not like Arnold Morrison, for example. It always seemed to me more probable either that the supposed discovery of digoxin was a mistake – a complete red herring – or that we were dealing with some sort of accident.'

'What sort of accident? David wasn't being treated for a heart condition. We checked.'

'He wasn't being treated *by a doctor* for a heart condition. But, you see, David was one of those men who never goes to the doctor – he had an almost morbid fear of them. These days it's the easiest thing in the world to look up your symptoms on the internet and to come up with a remedy and, if it's a drug, you can order it from some company or other that trades on-line. I don't know if David actually had a heart condition – it's not very likely in my opinion – but what matters is that he thought he had. That's the significance of the note: he was researching the subject. I don't know if he bought *Lanoxin* or another brand, but what he was doing was very dangerous because digoxin is poisonous outside a narrow range – according to Wikipedia anyway. And if he was buying the drug on-line he could have bought a brand that had been involved in a product recall: out of date tablets that had an unpredictable strength.'

'If that was the case,' said Stephen Gregg, 'he must have taken the tablets with him to the restaurant. He'd have had them on him when he died. Well, did he?'

'I think he did,' said Janet. 'But I had no suspicion: no reason to check. After his death his possessions were returned to me, as you'd expect. There was a pack of tablets with them: indigestion tablets, so I thought, because David had been complaining of heartburn. Heartburn, you see? He may well have interpreted it as a symptom of a heart condition.'

She halted there. She was suddenly struck by the image of David maintaining to the end his outward cheerfulness while inwardly frightened that he might die soon. Why hadn't he told her of his fears? Probably because he didn't want to worry her. Probably, too, because he didn't want her to tell him that he must see a doctor – a small act of cowardice and foolishness that was so in character: far more than that he would carry on in such a way that someone would want to kill him.

'I didn't look at the tablets,' she said. 'I simply threw them away.'

'You're smiling,' said Stephen Gregg, puzzled. 'Why?'

'Am I?' Janet caught a glimpse of herself in a wall mirror and saw what might be interpreted as a sorrowful smile. 'Yes, I suppose I am. I don't know how to explain. The fact is that I loved my husband, and all this tale of murder made me wonder who it was who died. David or a stranger I'd never known?' She thought of something she'd said to Belle in the early days of their friendship. 'I thought I would only ever experience one version of David's death, not realising how ambiguous life can be. Instead I've had several and had to struggle to make sense of them. And, of course, they all make sense in their own way, and only afterwards does the true explanation seem inevitable and, no matter how surprising it is, one gets used to it. The fact is that David died in the same infuriating way that he lived. But he was the man I loved and the man who loved me.'

There was a final matter. Janet had hoped Inspector Gregg might overlook it, but he didn't.

He asked, 'Who was the third person at dinner? And who paid a hundred thousand pounds into your bank account?'

'I don't know,' said Janet. 'I can only guess. Of course you can have the money back. It belongs to the firm's creditors, I imagine; certainly I don't claim it. I'm sticking to my original theory that Jeremy took someone along to the meal: a girlfriend or an investor he wants to shield. And as for the money, I can't think of anyone except Jeremy who'd want to throw suspicion onto me. Can you?'

Did he believe her? She thought not. There was a distinct twinkle in Stephen Gregg's eye. He said, 'I was rather hoping it would be David's brother Patrick. In fact, if I were putting the story together I'd make *me* the long lost brother and then we could wrap up the missing twin and the copper-wot-done-it into a single classic whodunit solution. Of course I'd have to be a murderer as well.'

Janet laughed. She did like Stephen Gregg. He had something of David's zaniness, though she fancied he was a sight more ruthless. 'No, no,' she said, 'It won't do. If Patrick is an identical twin, you look nothing like him.'

'Plastic surgery.'

'How shall I put this? You're not tall enough.'

'It's a painful business having your legs shortened.'

'I see. Did you ever find him – Patrick?'

'No – so he could still be me.'

'Apart from the face and the legs. Yes . . . well.' Janet stopped laughing. She looked at her watch. 'You must have other people to see – Joy – Veronica.'

'Quite right, too.' Inspector Gregg got to his feet, checked that he'd picked up everything he'd brought and allowed Janet to escort him to the door.

'One final word,' he said, on leaving. 'I believe you do know who the third person at dinner was. And I know, too. Whether I'll be able to prove it is another matter, but I'm a determined man and I think I will.'

'I understand,' Janet said. She looked at him blankly. He turned his back and walked the short distance up the lane to where his hire car was parked by the walled garden. He got into it and executed a turn before driving down to the highway. He waved as he passed. Janet hoped she would never see him again.

The third person at dinner was her son-in-law Henry, of course. Janet had realised it almost as soon as she knew that the mystery man or woman had arrived at the restaurant only after Jeremy had left. From that it followed that it was someone associated with David and not his partner, someone whose identity David wanted to keep secret. Someone to whom he felt an obligation.

Janet had always understood that Jeremy had fronted the company for people who preferred not to be openly connected with it. Until this business of murder it hadn't occurred to her that David would do the same, but, given his careless attention to morality, there was no obvious reason why he shouldn't. And, too, there'd been the puzzle of the brains behind the operation. Jeremy was a lightweight, valuable mainly for his posh contacts and marketing skills. And David – it was laughable that an accountant with his background should have been able to create and deal in the complex financial instruments that were the stock in trade of Vavasour & Bretherton.

Enter Henry. Young, pushy and a banker by vocation. Someone whom David would rely on and wish to protect for Helen's sake. The overseas trust that seemed to be the key to the fraud had probably been created by Henry, and David had operated it under his guidance; and only someone so close to David could have gained the access codes that would allow the transfer of the hundred thousand pounds to Janet's account after his death. Jeremy could never have enjoyed that level of confidence, and it was rather unforgiveable of Henry to abuse David's trust even further by using the money transfer in an effort to shift blame for the fraud onto Janet, though she supposed she would have to forgive him for as long as he stayed married to Helen or until Inspector Gregg nabbed him as seemed likely.

Poor David. He'd been betrayed by his son-in-law and thought he'd been betrayed by his partner. Had he realised his mistake? Evidently he'd had doubts because he called on Henry to come along for the second part of the evening's events, probably to challenge him with Jeremy's denial and confront him with some of the dubious paperwork.

The missing paperwork told Janet that she was right. Jeremy had confirmed what was obvious: that David had taken papers with him to the meeting at the restaurant. They should have been in the car when he died and Helen should have delivered them with the rest of his possessions. But she hadn't. Why not? Only Helen or Henry could have taken them, and they were of no interest at all to Helen, who probably wouldn't have understood what they meant.

Henry didn't kill David, but he bore part of the blame. David must have been deeply confused and frightened as the crisis in the firm broke about his head. On the night of his death he'd eaten a meal and had at least one furious row and quite possibly a second. It would be enough to strain anyone's nerves and digestion, and Janet imagined him feeling increasingly unwell as the evening wore on, and at some point taking his self-prescribed medication: tablets from an unreliable source at a dosage he'd guessed from whatever websites he'd visited. It was a miracle he hadn't died before.

Poor David, the scale of his mistake was breathtaking, and yet Janet had loved him. There seemed to be no other choice if she wanted to be happy. Women had to learn to love men in their foolishness. Not because they deserved it but because there appeared to be no other way of living with the beasts. In the end, for women, this knowledge – that every man would sooner or later disappoint them and that the bargain between the sexes was at its very heart unfair – was the central problem of love.

Janet asked Belle to have lunch with her at the *buvette*.

'I don't mind if I do,' Belle said. 'Charlie's having one of his good days. He's discovered a weird satellite channel that does continuous re-runs of *The Sweeney*.'

They found that Veronica was already there. Poppy was in the water laughing and shrieking like a fourteen year-old. Veronica was smiling contentedly.

Something has happened there, Janet thought. But it was impossible to understand everything and there were times when she tired of trying. It was enough that the other women looked happy. With Belle present, she couldn't ask if Inspector Gregg had called on Veronica, or if she'd spoken to Earthy and then confronted Ravi. Belle would probably be perfectly blithe at the thought that Joy had murdered Arnold, but it was possible to test friendship too much and in this instance unnecessary – for the time being at least. No doubt if they needed a further witness as to Joy's whereabouts at the date of the crime, Belle would chip in with a bogus alibi. It seemed that the English Ladies were a little lax, morally speaking, when it came to covering up murders.

Afterwards Janet returned through the place de la Halle with Belle. She looked down the lane and saw Léon at his studio. He'd just brought out a clear plastic bag that, at a distance, appeared to contain a heap of his carvings.

'I'll see you this evening,' she said to Belle. 'We needn't go out. We could maybe watch TV together.'

'That'd be nice,' Belle said. 'Let's find a really naff talent show and laugh at it.'

Janet didn't answer and for a moment they found themselves looking at each other as if they'd never got into the habit of saying goodbye and didn't know how to do it. Then Belle took Janet's face between her hands, planted a kiss on her cheek, and strode off briskly without looking back. Janet went to join Léon.

The bag did indeed hold his carvings. Janet looked into the *atelier* and saw that the tables were empty except for a couple of maquettes in modelling clay. The idols had been ejected from their altars.

Janet asked, 'What are you doing?'

'I never like them,' Léon said. 'I do them only to make money, and now I hear the story of what happen at the *temple des fauves*, which is not good. I am very sorry if I do anything that make anyone unhappy.'

'It isn't your fault,' Janet said. Then something occurred to her. 'What will you do at the end of summer? You don't own your studio, do you? It's a lease.'

Léon look a little sad but contrived a smile. 'If I have money I would not spend it here.'

'I know. You'd spend it on your dance school in Lille.'

'Yes.'

'You know I'm a writer, don't you? You called me Jane. – the name I use.'

'Ravi tell me. He read your books and see picture on cover.'

'So you thought I was rich. Well, I'm not poor, though that has nothing to do with writing. You were hoping I'd give you money to open your dance school – yes?'

'I am ashamed. I wanted to take your money, but when I know you I find you are a very special and beautiful person. And also you dance very well which is a great pleasure to me.'

'Thank you. I shall pretend to believe you. And I'm not angry with you. You're a man and can't help it.'

'I'm sorry? I do not understand.'

'No, I don't understand either. Men and women: we're like a contraption with a leg on one side and a wheel on the other, and somehow we have to move together. You must show me the business plan for your dance school, and if you don't have one, I'll help you prepare it. Once that's done, we'll see if the result looks like something I feel like investing in.'

Léon sighed and smiled. 'You are too kind to me, Janet.' There was something both cunning and sexy in that smile, and Janet remembered Belle's words: *Hang on to your handbags girls!*

Never mind, she was grown up and could afford to make small mistakes.

'I'll help you if I can,' said Janet. 'But in return you must take me dancing everywhere we can possibly go for the rest of summer.'

'And then what will you do – after the summer? Go home to England?'

Go home to England? It was possible. She had a house to sell and might have to support Helen if she divorced the horrible Henry. But then? What was to hold her in England, or in France, or indeed anywhere?

'I think I'll stay here,' Janet said. 'It's where my friends are.'

'Good. You can perhaps visit me in Lille?'

She looked into Léon's eyes and he looked into hers, and each of them felt a regret that life had imposed a thirty years age difference between them. Then again it was a difference that put a spice and charm into their relationship, and each was comfortable with it for what it was.

'You are a wonderful lady,' Léon said at last.

And Janet rather thought she might be.

Afterword

I hope this book reads like one written by a happy man who after forty years is still madly in love with his wife, because that's what it is, and Shirley enjoyed it as I read the draft to her in the bath. The idea came to me as we were holidaying in South West France at the cottage of our friends Pamela and Ian Shelton. The village in which they live – which is the model for Puybrun – is one we love, and I've used it once before as a location for my novel *Recherché*, which makes it a delight to revisit it in imagination. It was there, in 2009, that I read and enjoyed *The Jane Austen Book Club*, and I was reminded of the women's group that Shirley is a member of: women who love and support each other against the general idiocy of men like me. This book celebrates their friendship. However I would emphasise that the plot is pure fiction and none of the characters represent real people.

My thanks go to Pamela and Ian Shelton for their kindness; to Katherine Edge, Catherine Barthélemy, Anne Dunlop, Julie Berrisford and Graham Hume for giving the draft a supportive reading; and to Nathan Roberts who provided information about working on cruise ships. As always I am grateful to my agent Andrew Hewson and to the memory of the late James Hale, who I think would have wanted me to write this book.